THE DUKE'S CAVALIER

The Duke's Guard Series
Book Fifteen

C.H. Admirand

DRAGONBLADE PUBLISHING, INC.

ARE YOU SIGNED UP FOR DRAGONBLADE'S BLOG?

You'll get the latest news and information on exclusive giveaways, exclusive excerpts, coming releases, sales, free books, cover reveals and more.

Check out our complete list of authors, too!

No spam, no junk. That's a promise!

Sign Up Here

www.dragonbladepublishing.com

Dearest Reader;

Thank you for your support of a small press. At Dragonblade Publishing, we strive to bring you the highest quality Historical Romance from some of the best authors in the business. Without your support, there is no 'us', so we sincerely hope you adore these stories and find some new favorite authors along the way.

Happy Reading!

CEO, Dragonblade Publishing

Additional Dragonblade books by Author C.H. Admirand

The Ladies of the Keep Series
Liberating the Lady of Loughmoe (Book 1)
Bargaining with the Lady of Merewood (Book 2)
Rescuing the Lady of Sedgeworth (Book 3)

The Duke's Guard Series
The Duke's Sword (Book 1)
The Duke's Protector (Book 2)
The Duke's Shield (Book 3)
The Duke's Dragoon (Book 4)
The Duke's Hammer (Book 5)
The Duke's Defender (Book 6)
The Duke's Saber (Book 7)
The Duke's Enforcer (Book 8)
The Duke's Mercenary (Book 9)
The Duke's Rapier (Book 10)
The Duke's Man-at-Arms (Book 11)
The Duke's Lance (Book 12)
The Duke's Champion (Book 13)
The Duke's Sharpshooter (Book 14)
The Duke's Cavalier (Book 15)

The Lords of Vice Series
Mending the Duke's Pride (Book 1)
Avoiding the Earl's Lust (Book 2)
Tempering the Viscount's Envy (Book 3)
Redirecting the Baron's Greed (Book 4)
His Vow to Keep (Novella)
The Merry Wife of Wyndmere (Novella)
Lady Farnsworth's Second Chance at Love (Novella)

Dedication

For DJ, the other half of my heart. I'll see you tonight in my dreams.

Acknowledgments

A special thank you to my wonderful editor Arran McNicol! Thank you for your excellent advice and innate ability to get to the heart of some of my longer sentences. I'm grateful to have you as my editor.

CHAPTER ONE

D ILLON FLAHERTY STOOD a few feet away from the broken
carriage wheel. The determined lad's protective stance in
front of the door had him wondering who was inside the carriage.
It must be someone important to the lad for him to challenge
someone nearly thrice his size.

The lad's face was partially covered beneath his battered hat.
Was he running from someone? Flaherty would show the lad that
he was not a threat, but first he had to disarm him.

Pitching his voice low, Flaherty murmured, "Ye don't want to
shoot me, lad. Hand me yer weapon."

The young man did not lower the blunderbuss aimed at
Flaherty's chest. His da's oft-used caution echoed through his
head: *'Tis always wise to take your enemy's full measure and don't
make a move that could trigger an unwanted reaction!* It went against
Flaherty's grain to wait for the lad to make the first move, but he
had no desire to get shot this early in the morning.

Flaherty narrowed his gaze, and his blood ran cold. The lad's
finger was on the trigger. Likely he knew how to fire the weapon,
but did he have the courage? The breeze stilled, and in the cool
morning air, Flaherty swore he could hear the young man's
uneven breathing.

Flaherty studied him. From the cut of the lad's threadbare
brown coat, he wasn't starving. It was the younger man's pointed

chin that seemed to be at odds with the fullness of the frame tucked inside of his coat. Either the lad was spending every bit of coin he had to eat, or he was wearing some kind of padding to make himself appear larger as a deterrent to ward off unsavory types. If so, why the disguise?

The breeze stilled, and yet the lad made no move. Flaherty studied what he could see of the boy's face for a reaction that would tip him off to what he intended to do. He had a slightly pointed chin—smooth cheeks, no whiskers. His gaze dipped lower to a surprisingly full set of lips. Lower still to a slender neck with no visible…

Bloody hell!

"Show me *your* hands." The young man's voice cracked. "Palms facing me!"

The lad could not be more than five and ten summers, which could explain the lack of whiskers. But if the slender chin and the mouth of a temptress meant what Flaherty feared, the lad and whoever was inside the carriage were going to be trouble! As his mind put the odd pieces of the puzzle together, his gut screamed not to trust what he saw—but to trust in what he felt. He swallowed the string of curses and held his tongue.

Before he unmasked the lad's charade, the wail of an infant stopped him. But it was the accompanying feminine-sounding gasp coming from inside the carriage that decided Flaherty's course of action. "I'll keep me hands at me sides if it's all the same to ye." He took a step forward and froze when the blunderbuss wobbled. "Did yer da not teach ye if ye pick up a weapon, ye'd best be prepared to use it?"

The silence irritated Flaherty, but it was the morning chill and wail of the infant that spurred him to act. He advanced. The lad took a step backward, promptly fell on his arse, and the gun went off!

Flaherty dove to the side and swore a blue streak. His side burned, and his temper shot straight to boiling as he sprang to his feet. The indignity of misjudging the lad, and getting shot for his trouble by someone half his age, pushed him over the edge. The dark side of his temper took hold of him. He grabbed the blunderbuss, tugged the lad to his feet, and shook him until his hat fell off.

Flaherty growled, "Bloody hell!"

Twin gasps of shock echoed in the still, early morning air. The faint scent of lavender surrounded Flaherty as a lock of angel-blonde hair got tangled around his wrist.

The lad—nay, lass—squirmed against Flaherty's hold. "Let go of me!"

Flaherty stared into blue-gray eyes that held a hint of panic, and a healthy dose of temper. "Are ye on the run from the law?" he demanded, swiftly working to extricate his wrist.

Her eyes narrowed, but she remained silent.

God help him, her insolence and temper had him reacting instinctively. His heart thundered in his chest as parts a good distance south of that idiotic organ had him tamping down hard on his considerable control. 'Twas always the fiery lasses that snagged his attention.

Flaherty had no time for that now! He had a volatile situation on his hands. A broken carriage wheel, and someone with a very young infant—judging from the sound of its cry—inside the conveyance who needed his help. The lass dressed as a lad, wielding a weapon without any bloody idea how to use it, could hardly be holding them against their will. Could she?

From the pain making itself known with a vengeance, he wondered if it were gravel instead of lead balls embedded in his side. He'd leapt to the side in time to avoid the full force of the shot, but not the scatter shot.

Flaherty felt the telltale warmth of his life's blood near the wound but chose to ignore it. He needed to gain full control of the situation. He'd been shot before, though not with a blunderbuss. He hoped the injury was superficial. If it had nicked an artery, he'd have felt a gush of blood. The last thing he needed was to arrive at the manor and have to listen to O'Malley demanding to know how Flaherty managed to get himself shot. Garahan had a perverse sense of humor and would remark about the location of the wound. It was low enough on Flaherty's side, just above his hip, that Garahan would probably claim Flaherty had been shot in the arse!

Of his two cousins, who along with Flaherty comprised the detachment of the Duke of Wyndmere's private guard stationed at Summerfield Chase, Garahan would be more reasonable. Garahan would no doubt interrogate Flaherty, wanting to know why he let his guard down. Then he would demand to know what had distracted Flaherty from doing his job.

What mattered now was how he handled the rest of this situation. The pair obviously needed help, were likely on the run from an untenable situation. If he brought them back to Summerfield Chase, he would be the third member of the duke's guard stationed there to bring an injured woman, and quite possibly trouble, to the baron's door. Trouble he had yet to identify.

Summerfield had been more than amenable when it came time to protect and defend the women the men in his guard brought to the manor for safety. Moreover, the baron had proven his mettle a few years earlier when, despite a head injury, his love for Lady Phoebe had had him riding with the rescue party arriving in time to thwart her abduction. Flaherty hoped the baron would be as understanding this time, too. Summerfield's worry about the baroness and the babe she carried made his temperament a bit unpredictable as of late.

Flaherty knew that he had to act quickly, as the shock of being shot was wearing off. The dull pain in his side slashed through him, and he clamped his jaw down hard. Had it nicked the bone? Setting that worry aside for the moment, he concentrated on the situation unfolding in front of him. Flaherty would need his wits about him if he were to escort the women—and babe—to safety.

One look at the lass glaring at him, and the last thread of his patience snapped! He needed to find out who was inside the carriage and how old the babe was. It sounded far too young to be traveling. Damned if the need to turn the lass over his knee cut right through his need to protect and defend her.

Blood loss must be affecting his brain.

"Answer the question," he growled. "Else I'll tie ye up and lay ye facedown over me saddle and deliver ye to Summerfield Chase that way. His lordship will be wanting a word with ye. He'll no doubt send for the constable, who will be wanting an explanation as to why ye held up—or abducted—whoever is inside the carriage."

She jolted at the mention of the baron's home. Was she acquainted with Summerfield? When she remained silent, too many possibilities—none of them good—occurred to him. It set off the anger welling up inside of him. He clamped down hard on it. "Have ye no compassion? No thought to how dangerous it is to a babe so young to be out in the chill morning air? By the sound of its cry, the poor thing is less than a fortnight old!"

"How would you know?"

Ah, he thought, the lass had found her tongue at last and decided to flay him with the sharp edge of it.

"Pippa," a soft voice called from inside the coach. "Please answer the man and apologize for shooting him. We need to see to his injury, and find somewhere warm to seek shelter."

Flaherty wrapped a hand around the shooter's upper arm. He held her against him, so she could not escape, or wrest her weapon from him. Ready to demand information from the other woman, he turned toward the carriage, and the words shriveled up on his tongue. The sight of the pale-as-flour, fragile-looking woman was a worry. She was cradling a tiny bundle wrapped in a thick woolen shawl to her breast. His protective instincts screamed at him to hurry, while his mind sorted through a number of explanations as to why the two were traveling together.

That they were acquainted was obvious. The woman with the babe was not afraid of the lass. Their difference in coloring, face, and form suggested they were not related. 'Twas obvious by the way the lass was protecting the woman and child that kidnapping could be ruled out. His best guess was that they were on the run—but from what or whom? Mayhap the young mother was escaping an intolerable marriage. Then again, the question of whether or not she was married prodded him to be extra cautious. He'd best not frighten the new mother. She could have a weapon concealed on her person.

Fire seared through his flesh where he'd been wounded. Digging deep into his reserves of control, he drew in a deep breath and ignored the pain. Blast it all, there was no time to debate. 'Twas time to act! "Get back inside the carriage and out of the chill of the morning air. 'Tisn't good for yerself or yer babe. I need to have a quick word with this one here."

The young mother hesitated. "Oh, but—"

"I'll be taking the both of ye to Summerfield Chase. Ye'll be safe there and cared for by the baron and baroness's staff. There will be a fire to warm yerselves, and a hot meal to fill yer empty bellies. The cook has a bottomless teapot and an endless supply of scones and teacakes."

The wraithlike woman stiffened at the name of the baron's home. There was definitely a connection. Whether either of these females were connected to the baron, or possibly to someone who worked for the baron, he did not know, but he would find out.

Flaherty dragged the termagant he still had a hold of with him and approached the carriage. "Me name's Flaherty—Dillon Flaherty. I'm one of the Duke of Wyndmere's private guard stationed at Summerfield Chase, guarding the duke's sister Lady Phoebe and her husband, Baron Marcus Summerfield. Ye'll be safe with me. Ye have me word of honor, no harm will come to yerself or yer babe as long as ye're under me protection."

The soft expression on the woman's face hardened. She stared at the tight hold he had on the shooter and demanded, "What about Pippa?"

Flaherty was right—they were going to be trouble! "I'll be protecting all three of ye, but we need to move swiftly to get yerself and yer babe out of the chill. With the baroness and two of the guards' wives in varying stages of pregnancy living at Summerfield Chase, ye'll not lack for company."

When her expression softened, he said, "May I ask yer name, and that of yer babe, so I can introduce the three of ye to his lordship and her ladyship? They love children. The proof of that is the twins Percy and Phineas. 'Tis a long story, but the short of it is they are cousins to one of the other guards' wives and have been taken in by Summerfield."

The pair exchanged a glance, but remained stubbornly silent. He had to reassure them to get them moving. "Before ye start to worry, ye have no reason to be fearful of the baron and baroness, or anyone else living on the estate."

They shared a telling look. Flaherty sensed they were already acquainted with someone who worked for the baron. Forewarned, he was no longer concerned. He would find out soon enough.

"Go ahead, Millie," the shooter urged. "Tell him."

Flaherty chuckled, then sucked in a breath. It hurt to laugh. "Ye just did, lass."

"That's her nickname. Go ahead, tell him," the outspoken lass—*Pippa, was it?*—urged.

"Millicent Haybrook Trentchester, and this is our"—the woman's voice wavered, and she closed her eyes for a moment before opening them to continue—"my son, Roarke."

"'Tis a pleasure, Miss—"

"It's *Mrs.*," Pippa corrected him.

He turned to meet Mrs. Trentchester's troubled gaze. "Forgive me, and begging yer pardon for me question, but are ye running from Mr. Trentchester?"

"No. Captain Trentchester is dead."

The woman's pain was palpable. "I'm sorry for yer loss."

Again Pippa spoke up for her friend. "Her husband Roarke

gave his life for the Crown."

Flaherty frowned at the outspoken woman. "I can see how ye earned yer nickname. Ye keep piping up when it isn't yer turn." When she parted her full lips to speak, he raised a hand and had to bite back a groan. Pain, accompanied by telltale warmth, had his cambric shirt sticking to his waistcoat. He'd have to have his injury taken care of soon.

"We need to be moving. 'Tisn't healthy for little Roarke, nor yerselves, to be out in the damp. Here's what I need ye to do, Mrs. Trentchester. Stay tucked inside the carriage until I fetch ye." When she did as he asked, he turned to the lass. "Do ye ride?"

"Of course! I'll have you know—"

"Tell me later. For expediency's sake, and because I'm having a wee bit of trouble lifting me left arm"—he paused to glare at Pippa—"I need yer help unhitching the team. Is there more tack stored beneath the coachman's seat?"

Startled by the question, the lass paused to consider. "I did not check before we made our esc—er...before we left. There should be. Shall I look?"

"Aye." Flaherty glanced over his shoulder, relieved that the coach door was closed. Pursing his lips, he whistled softly, alerting his horse that he needed him. He was moving slower, an indication that his wound could be more serious than he'd thought. He sent up a silent prayer for his strength to hold out long enough to deliver the lasses and the babe to the safety of Summerfield Chase.

The gelding nudged him gently in the shoulder as if the animal knew he was injured. Flaherty led his horse over to where the outspoken lass was unhitching the carriage horses. He placed the weapon he'd taken from her on the coachman's seat. "We'll bring their traces with us."

The little bit of a thing spun around, lifted her chin, and glared him. Before she could fire another round of questions he didn't have the time to answer, he asked, "Was yer blunderbuss loaded with lead balls or gravel?"

She squared her shoulders and drew in a deep breath, and the top button of her coat opened, revealing a worn lawn shirt. The fabric left nothing to the imagination and hugged her curvaceous form. How had he thought her shapeless? God Almighty, but the lass was well endowed, to the point where he blinked twice before he could tear his gaze away from her bounteous breasts.

"Lead balls, not gravel, and mind your eyes, Flaherty, or I'll be forced to reload and shoot you again!"

Irritated beyond belief, he didn't curb his annoyance when he replied, "Ye're no longer armed and 'twas yer grip on yer weapon, and the impact of falling on yer bottom, that fired the blunderbuss."

Her eyes rounded in shock, and Flaherty realized too late that he should not have mentioned that particular part of her anatomy. He stared at the heavens for a moment, then sighed. "If I beg yer pardon, will ye move yer ar—self and get on that horse's back? We need to leave now!"

Her horrified gasp had him mentally kicking himself. Too late, she'd already realized he had been about to say her *arse*…but he didn't. Thank God most of his senses were still intact—he hadn't mentioned the fact that it was tantalizingly shapely. Nor would he—ever! The lass would be the death of him long before he got around to mentioning it, or the fact that her beautiful breasts had rendered him momentarily speechless.

"I'm not certain that I can trust you, but you haven't gone for my throat, even after my grandfather's blunderbuss went off."

He kept his expression neutral. "Ye'll have to take that chance if we're to get Mrs. Trentchester and her babe to the warmth and safety of Summerfield Chase."

She hesitated, then reached into her deep coat pocket, withdrew a small leather bag that jingled, and pushed it toward him. "Here. Take it as payment—it's all we have."

Flaherty bristled as the insult went deep. "I never have been, and never will be, tempted by a bag of coin. Put that back in yer pocket, or I'll change me mind and leave ye behind."

"What about Millie and her babe?"

"She's doing as I've asked, and is inside the coach while we get these horses ready to move. I'll be taking her and her babe to safety at the manor house. Now then, are ye ready to cooperate?"

Pippa jammed the pouch into her pocket and glared at him.

Without another word, he stood next to one of the horses, bent down, and laced his fingers. "Step on me hand. I'll give ye a boost." When she didn't move fast enough, he ordered her, "Mount up!"

"You cannot expect me to ride without a sidesaddle."

He straightened and had to bite back a groan. "Bloody hell, woman! What part of 'we need to leave immediately' did ye not understand?"

Her nostrils flared and her eyes narrowed. "What part of 'I cannot ride without a saddle' did *you* not understand?"

The creak of hinges had them both turning to stare at the carriage. Millie leaned out of the door and rasped, "Pippa, please let Mr. Flaherty help you mount. You may be short, but you and I both know you're fully capable of riding bareback. We used to ride without saddles through the meadow until your father and mine caught us and tried to put a stop to it a few years ago."

Pippa's shoulders slumped. "When they caught us again, they demanded we stop acting like hellions, and warned they'd never find suitable husbands for us." Tears welled in the young mother's eyes and spilled over, and her feisty protectress was immediately contrite. "Forgive me for speaking of husbands, Millie. I know how much you miss Roarke—while I, on the other hand..." As if she sensed she'd nearly revealed too much, Pippa lowered her voice and said, "I miss him too. He was the best of men."

Mille nodded, ducked back inside, and shut the door. Flaherty doubted it was any warmer inside the coach, but at least she and her babe were out of the breeze, which had picked up again. He felt another rush of blood add to the warmth beneath his shirt and wondered if it was because his heart had begun to pound when he'd noticed the lass's exceptional figure. Short of shifting both his frockcoat and waistcoat out of the way to lift up his shirt and examine the wound, he would not be able to see the extent of the damage until they arrived at the manor house. He did not need to touch the spot to see if it still bled—the warmth confirmed it.

"I need your help mounting. Please, Mr. Flaherty?"

The frustration in Pippa's tone had him setting aside the minor discomfort of his wound. He had a job to do. "Aye, lass." He bent again, ignored the shaft of pain, and laced his fingers a second time. She placed one small-booted foot in the makeshift stirrup and hoisted herself onto the horse's back, but didn't quite manage to get her leg over the animal's back.

At the sight of her well-rounded backside level with his mouth, Flaherty silently swore and gnawed his lip. Thoughts of biting the curvaceous bottom far too close to his face were difficult to ignore. *God, help me!* he thought. *'Tis been far too long since I've bedded a woman that this one should be tempting me!*

Finally, she managed to scoot far enough onto the horse's back to seat herself. Her worried expression had him forcing a neutral look on his face. "Are you in terrible pain?"

He'd never admit to the lass the thoughts, or the desire, running riot through him. "I'll live." He handed her the other horse's reins. "Can ye manage both animals?"

Pippa inclined her head, as if she were royalty and he her servant. He wasn't, but he'd save reminding her of that fact until after they were safely within the walls of Summerfield Chase.

"Of course I can manage. I grew up in my father's stables, until I was four and ten, and he forbade me to spend my days there."

Her reply got under his skin, like a sliver of wood. Flaherty turned toward the carriage, but before he could speak, Millie was standing in the doorway with her babe bundled close against her, her woolen shawl covering the infant's head. He rushed over to help her step down. "Have a care, Mrs. Trentchester."

"Millie."

"Aye, Millie." Her hand was cold to the touch. Steadying her next to his horse, he said, "Hold still a moment." He slipped out of his coat, wincing when he had to move his injured side. Thankfully the blood had yet to soak through the heavy wool of his waistcoat. "I'm going to tuck me coat around yerself and yer babe."

She stilled and let him pull the frockcoat snugly around her.

"Now then, don't be worrying that me horse cannot carry the three of us. This fine gelding is strong as an ox, and has an even temperament. He's a good lad." Flaherty scratched behind the animal's ear. "Aren't ye?"

The horse's whinny had Millie smiling and Pippa laughing softly. Bracing himself, he gently lifted and settled Millie and her babe on his horse and mounted behind them. "I need to pull ye into me arms and on me lap to keep a draft from blowing around ye while we ride. 'Tis just over half a mile from here."

"I'm grateful, Mr. Flaherty—"

"Just Flaherty." He shifted her until she rested against his uninjured side, then wrapped his arm around her so she was snuggled against him. "Close yer eyes and try to rest."

Flaherty looked over his shoulder and was pleased to see the lass was behind him, leading the other carriage horse. "Ready?"

"Yes, Mr.—"

"Just Flaherty."

"I'm ready, Flaherty."

PIPPA COULD NOT believe the irritating man had managed to get a reaction she never expected out of her. Judging by the way he shifted ever so slightly the closer they got to their destination, he was in pain. Remorse slithered up from her uneasy belly. She hadn't meant to keep her finger on the trigger. When he stepped toward her, his expression thunderous, the need to put distance between them had had her stepping backward and stumbling.

Knowing it would probably prick the man's pride to the point where he was suffering, she moved her mount closer to his. Pitching her voice low, she asked, "How much farther?"

He frowned, but answered, "See that copse of fir trees up ahead?"

"I do."

"Watch for a road just beyond it, on the left. That will lead us to the baron's home." He mumbled a curse and straightened in the saddle.

"Do you need to stop?"

"Nay, 'twould disturb yer friend, and she and her babe are sleeping."

When Pippa saw the road ahead, she fell back so Flaherty could ride in front of her to lead the way.

"Brace yerself, lass," he called over his shoulder as a manor house came into view. "I'll be needing to signal O'Malley and Garahan that we need their help."

"What kind of—"

The loud, short, sharp whistle had Millie jolting, and her babe crying.

"Now you've done it." Pippa heard an answering shrill whistle and the pounding of hoofbeats racing toward them.

"Flaherty!" A blond giant of a man, dressed in black like Flaherty, rode toward them.

"Where's the trouble?" The second man on horseback had dark hair and was equal in size to the fair-haired man. He too was dressed in black.

A quick glance at Flaherty had her realizing all three men were not only dressed alike, but were built alike—broad through the chest and shoulders, and tall as trees! She swallowed her unease to ask, "Are these the men you spoke of?"

Flaherty grunted, and Pippa realized he had to have been

hiding how much pain he was in. She blurted out, "He's been shot!"

The woman in Flaherty's arms stirred, and her son let out another wail of distress. "Pippa? Are we safe yet?"

The blond giant leapt off his horse and approached Flaherty's horse slowly. "Aye, ye're safe now. I'll carry ye inside."

Pippa noticed the man's eyes widen in surprise, and wondered if it was at how slight Millie was, or that her babe was only a few days old. She needed to warn him. "Please be gentle with Millie and little Roarke. He is only three days old."

"God in Heaven!" the blond man said.

"Sure and he watched over these three, O'Malley," Flaherty rumbled. "Their carriage is half a mile from here. 'Twill be easy to spot when we send someone to fetch it. 'Tis the black one with the broken wheel."

"What about the sharpshooters who got a piece of ye?" the dark-haired man asked.

Flaherty glared at Pippa. "'Twas just one, Garahan, and not much of a sharpshooter."

"I did not mean to shoot you," she reminded him, watching Garahan dismount.

Flaherty growled. "I'm not so certain of that, lass."

Both men stopped to stare at her, and Garahan asked, "Why in the bloody hell did ye shoot Flaherty?"

"'Twas an accident," their auburn-haired savior admitted. "O'Malley, take Mrs. Trentchester and her babe inside. Garahan can help the lass dismount."

"I'll be hearing the whole of yer tale once we have them inside," O'Malley murmured. He strode toward the back of the building with Millie and her babe in his arms. Someone must have either heard the whistles or seen O'Malley approaching, because the door swung open and hands were ushering them inside.

Worry speared through Pippa. "Will Millie and Roarke be safe?"

Garahan grunted. "Do ye care?"

"Of course I care!" she huffed.

"Well then, why did ye shoot me cousin when he was obviously trying to help ye?"

"Cousin?"

"Aye, Flaherty's cousin to meself and O'Malley. Well?" Garahan demanded.

She shrank back from the growl in his voice until Flaherty muttered, "Leave off, Ryan. I'll tell ye all about how she landed on her ar—er…bottom to perfect her aim, after ye help her off the bloody carriage horse."

Garahan narrowed his gaze and finally grunted. "Fine." Without much effort on the man's part, she was off the horse and on her feet a moment later. Garahan turned his back on her and studied Flaherty. "Which side is it?"

"Left."

He braced his shoulder beneath Flaherty's good arm and warned, "Take a deep breath and hold it."

"How is that going to help?"

"For feck's sake," Garahan swore, "just do it, Dillon!"

Flaherty had to be in pain. Pippa's eyes stung with unshed tears, and she had to steel herself not to cry. The last thing she needed was the men thinking she was not only a horrible person for shooting Flaherty, but a weak one for giving in to tears.

She noticed Garahan kept his arm around Flaherty's back and started walking toward the manor house, only to stop when two men came running from the stables.

"These two fine animals without saddles are carriage horses," Flaherty told them. "They'll appreciate a good rub-down and a cupful of oats and water after ye've cooled them down."

"Right away, Flaherty. And an apple for your gelding?"

"Aye. Thank ye." He finally looked at Pippa, and for a fraction of a moment, she saw the true depth of his pain.

"I am so sorry. I never mean to shoot you."

"Faith, I believe ye, lass. As me cousins will be certain to tell ye, the ladies are all after the same thing." He slowly smiled at her. "And 'tisn't to shoot me."

Garahan snickered. "Let's get that wound looked at."

Standing there, she wondered whether or not she would be welcomed into the house once the truth was out. Because accident or not, she had shot one of the duke's men!

◇◆◇◆◇◆◇

CHAPTER TWO

T HE COMMOTION WAS not unexpected, but still, Pippa hung back out of the way while O'Malley carried Millie and her babe down the long hallway leading to the kitchen. She only waited a heartbeat before following behind him, asking, "Will there be a fainting couch or settee where Millie can lie down?"

Pippa tried to hide her worry for her dear friend, but couldn't. So many things could go wrong after Millie had to leave right after birthing her son for fear of being held against her will, while her babe was taken from her. The midwife had warned of the possibility of Millie hemorrhaging if she were not allowed sufficient time to recover.

O'Malley frowned at her, but did not have a chance to answer. An older woman in a black bombazine gown, a watch pinned to her breast, and a chatelaine with keys suspended from her waist motioned her forward. "I'm Mrs. Chauncey, the baron's housekeeper." She nodded to the woman who rushed toward them, wearing a dark-blue gown with a crisp white apron over it. "Mrs. Green is the baron's cook. We will take good care of your friend."

Pippa knew she looked a sight, but neither woman seemed to notice. Taking it as a sign that they would indeed help Millie and her babe, she replied, "My friend is Mrs. Millicent Haybrook Trentchester. I'm Miss Phillipa Stanhope."

"It is a pleasure to meet you, Mrs. Chauncey," Millie said. "And you, Mrs. Green."

O'Malley didn't seem to be bothered that he was in the middle of a four-way conversation between two of the baron's staff, Millie, and Pippa. When the introductions had been made, he asked, "Where shall I take Mrs. Trentchester?"

"There's a fire in the small sitting room," the housekeeper replied. "I believe her ladyship is resting there."

"Oh, but I do not want to be a bother," Millie insisted. "Isn't there a small room where I can rest for a little while?"

Fear for her friend and her infant son tightened Pippa's throat, but she forced it aside to say, "Millie and her newborn son Roarke need to warm up. It's all my fault—I didn't see the rock or the rut in the road. And then I couldn't fix our broken carriage wheel."

The housekeeper and the cook nodded. Neither one questioned that she had been driving the carriage, nor the fact that she was dressed like a coachman. "Not to worry, dear," Mrs. Chauncey said. "Come with us. You can wash your face and hands. Then we'll see to it you have something warm to eat and a nice pot of tea, and you'll sit in front of the fire."

"Oh, but I can't leave Millie!"

"If you wouldn't mind setting me down, Mr. O'Malley, I'm quite certain that I'd be comfortable on one of the wooden chairs along the wall while I wait for Pippa," Millie said.

His voice was surprisingly gentle when he replied, "I'd only have to be picking yerself and yer babe back up. Ye're in no condition to be walking anywhere right now."

Millie fell silent, and Pippa sensed her friend was becoming anxious. She washed quickly, using a round of herb-scented soap and the warm water in the alcove where a pitcher and bowl were kept for just that purpose. "I'll hurry, Millie. I need you and Roarke to be comfortable."

The baron's housekeeper handed Pippa the linen drying cloth. "Have you two been friends long?"

Pippa nodded, but it was Millie who answered, "Since before we could walk and talk."

Mrs. Green poured hot water into the teapot and nodded. "Friends made early are oft times friends for life."

Pippa smiled at Millie. "I would do anything for Millie and her babe."

"I'm so sorry that you have had to… We would not have had to leave if—"

Pippa shook her head. "Flaherty said we'd be safe here."

Mrs. Green pursed her lips, glancing from Millie to Pippa and back. "It would seem there is quite a tale to tell about how you two came to be traveling on your own so soon after Mrs. Trentchester gave birth."

"Not now," the housekeeper said. "Time enough before for that over a bracing cup of tea—with a goodly portion of cream and sugar in it for the new mother."

A dark-haired, beautiful woman wearing an exquisite silk gown rushed in through the opposite archway. "I heard the men signaling to one another, Mrs. Chauncey. What has happened—" She paused, noticing the woman in O'Malley's arms. "Oh my! Who have you brought us, O'Malley?"

Pippa knew at once this was the baroness. Relief tempered with worry had her belly churning. "Mr. Flaherty stopped to help us," she explained.

Millie added, "He insisted on bringing us here. I hope we will not be an imposition. We have a bit of coin, if there is an inn nearby—"

"Flaherty found you?" the lovely woman interrupted, then tilted her head to one side and studied Millie and Pippa. "You will of course need to stay with us until we know the whole of your situation, and why Flaherty felt it best to bring you to the safety of our home."

Before Pippa could wonder why the baroness mentioned the word *safety*, the woman continued, "O'Malley, please carry our guest into the small sitting room. I was just enjoying the warmth of the fire, reading a book, when I heard the men whistling that there was trouble."

At the sound of a tiny wail, the baroness stopped and placed a hand on O'Malley's forearm. "Is that a babe?"

Before he could answer, Pippa said, "Mrs. Trentchester's newborn son."

"And you are?"

The awkwardness of their situation hit Pippa then. She looked like a ragamuffin compared to the beautiful woman, dressed befitting her elevated station in a gown the loveliest shade of deep sapphire. While it did not hide her pregnancy, it was quite fashionable. Pippa wished she had had something to change into, but there had not been time, and there was nothing she could do about it now. Her tongue rarely got tied, but the woman's poise and grace, despite the fact that she was round with child, had Pippa feeling completely unnerved—she was the only woman dressed in a coachman's garb!

The baroness said, "Forgive me. I have completely forgotten my manners in my rush to see you and your friend made comfortable. You both have obviously suffered quite a shock. Welcome to Summerfield Chase! My name is Phoebe Lippincott Summerfield. My husband Marcus is Baron Summerfield."

Finding her voice, Pippa replied, "Phillipa Stanhope, though Mrs. Trentchester and I call one another by our childhood names."

The baroness's smile was warm and put Pippa at ease. "Let me guess, you're called Pippa?"

"That's right," Pippa replied.

"I don't believe you shared Mrs. Trentchester's first name."

They followed O'Malley into the small sitting room. The warmth enveloped Pippa as soon as she walked across the threshold. "Millicent—Millie for short."

O'Malley gently lowered Millie and her babe onto the settee, while the housekeeper rushed in behind them with a heavy quilt to wrap around Pippa's friend. O'Malley bowed and murmured,

"Caro, me wife, and Prudence, Garahan's wife, are in the nursery with the twins. I'm sure ye'll be meeting them shortly, Mrs. Trentchester. You're safe here."

"Thank you, Mr. O'Malley."

He inclined his head and turned to the baroness. "Is there anything else that I can do for ye, yer ladyship?" He turned to Pippa, adding, "I'd like to see how Flaherty is faring."

Pippa felt the full force of his unspoken censure, but did not speak up. She deserved it.

From the way the baroness looked from O'Malley to her and back again, Pippa knew she would have to explain what happened again.

As if Baroness Summerfield sensed something of import had occurred, she replied, "Of course. Has Marcus been informed of the situation?"

"I'm certain he has been by now," O'Malley answered.

"Please let me know if there is anything I can do for Flaherty."

"Aye, yer ladyship." With a bow, the guard retreated.

The baroness turned toward Pippa and waved a hand toward the empty chair next to the settee. "I am quite certain you'll be more comfortable if your remain close to your friend."

Though she would, Pippa said, "I'm afraid I'm wearing a bit more of the road we traveled to sit on anything other than a wooden seat that could easily be cleaned."

Lady Phoebe sighed and waved Pippa toward the bellpull in the corner of the sitting room. "Very well. As it is more of a chore to get up once I sit down, would you mind ringing the bellpull for me? I'll ask one of the footmen to bring in one of the wooden chairs from the kitchen for you. Will you sit then?"

"Of course, your ladyship." When she'd done as the baroness asked, Pippa walked over to stand beside the settee where Millie was seated. A few moments later, the request for the chair was given and a footman rushed off to fetch one.

Once the young man returned and placed the sturdy wooden

seat next to the settee, the baroness asked, "Now then, why does O'Malley need to check on Flaherty? Has he suffered an injury?"

Pippa rushed to reply, "It was an accident! He towered over me, and his frown was so fierce—" She fell silent, unable to force the words past the tightness in her throat. Guilt for retreating in the face of Flaherty's anger twisted around the sorrow sweeping up from her toes. She should have held her ground to defend and protect Millie! Though she'd vowed to use the blunderbuss on Trentchester if he dared to try to abscond with Millie's babe, she had never shot anyone before.

Her emotions tangled into a huge knot in her belly until it ached. She wrapped an arm around her stomach to ease the pain, but it didn't help—she had actually shot the man who was trying to help them.

Millie whispered, "Pippa, tell the baroness what happened, otherwise you'll keep it inside of you until your stomach rebels."

"Oh my," the baroness remarked. "I know what that feels like, having battled nausea upon rising for the first few months."

She motioned to the housekeeper, and Mrs. Chauncey walked over to the folding screen, reached behind it, and produced a chamber pot. "We keep one in every room."

Pippa glanced at Millie, who sighed. "I was in the carriage and did not see what occurred, though I did hear the report of the blunderbuss—"

Dark brows narrowed over crystalline blue eyes as Lady Phoebe glared at Pippa. "Please tell me that you did not *shoot* Flaherty!"

Pippa bolted to her feet, fighting to hold on to her composure. Twisting her hands together, she walked over to stand in front of the baroness. She did not need to see the woman's expression to know that she was angry. Pippa bowed her head and quickly confessed, "We have been traveling since the middle of the night, to… Well, that's not important at the moment." She glanced at Millie, who nodded, encouraging her. "We were making good time, until I hit a rut in the road and the carriage wheel broke."

"And where does Flaherty fit into all of this?" the baroness asked.

"I was trying to see if the wheel could be repaired, when Flaherty rode up. He startled me. I reached for the blunderbuss, turned, and aimed it at him." A tear escaped as Pippa rasped, "I had to protect Millie and Roarke. He could have been sent by..." She trailed off, afraid to say too much at once.

"I understand the need to protect someone you love—I have done so more than once myself," the baroness murmured. "Now then, tell me what happened next?"

Pippa nodded. "Flaherty started firing questions at me. I think he saw through my disguise." The baroness raised an eyebrow, but didn't speak, merely motioned for Pippa to continue. "When I did not answer quickly enough, he started walking toward me... I backed away from him and lost my footing."

The baroness sighed. "Forgive me for jumping to conclusions, and letting my worst fears take hold of me. I am normally able keep a level head, unless it involves my husband, my brothers, or the men in my brother's guard—they are like family to me."

Pippa was about to continue, but Millie interrupted, "I heard the report of the gun. If Pippa said she stepped wrong, you can believe that she did. She is normally an excellent shot, we both are, having accompanied our fathers' hunting parties many times over the years."

Wiping her eyes with the backs of her hands, Pippa cleared her throat and found her voice. "I did not realize my hand was still on the trigger when I landed on my bottom." When the baroness did not immediately speak, Pippa rushed to add, "You have to believe that I did not mean to shoot him."

The baroness's tone was cool when she asked, "If you had meant to shoot him, what would you have aimed for?"

Pippa replied without thinking, "The middle of his chest."

Lady Phoebe inclined her head. "Exactly what my darling

older brothers instructed when they taught me to shoot." When Pippa did not move, the baroness sighed again. "Do sit down—our tea will be here in a few moments."

As if on cue, the cook swept into the room, followed by two footmen carrying the accoutrements for tea. Millie's soft gasp had Pippa smiling and the baroness asking, "Is something amiss?"

"Millie has a weakness for scones," Pippa replied. At that moment little Roarke whimpered, before letting out a wail.

The baroness smiled. "I have heard that cry before when my niece and nephew were brand-new babes. He's hungry."

Millie nodded and glanced around the room. "I'm afraid I am still getting used to feeding Roarke." She hesitated, shifting her gaze toward the folding screen.

Pippa had a feeling her friend was uncomfortable, feeling exposed in their surroundings. A quick survey of the room revealed an alcove with two wing-backed chairs facing one another. "I believe Millie needs a bit of privacy. Do you feel strong enough to stand?"

"Yes," Millie replied. "I think Flaherty, Garahan, and O'Malley wanted Roarke and I out of the chill as quickly as possible. Otherwise I would have walked."

"They are very solicitous of myself and their wives—well, except for Flaherty, as he is not married. I am not surprised O'Malley carried you inside," the baroness remarked before turning to ask one of the footmen to move the screen to cordon off the wing-backed chairs from view. The two men retreated after setting out the tea and moving the screen. "Now then, do you need my help?" she asked.

"I think we can manage, thank you, your ladyship," Pippa answered. Once she had her friend settled in one of the uphol-stered chairs, Pippa placed the shawl over Millie's shoulder, adding a layer of warmth for her babe, and the extra privacy she knew her friend needed.

Millie reached for Pippa's hand. "Thank you."

Love for her friend twined with worry that Millie's brother-in-law was hot on their heels. Had he discovered their direction? How many hours did they have before the man came after them? She squeezed Millie's hand and smiled when she heard the snuffling sound Roarke made whenever he latched on to his mother's breast. "Shall I bring your tea to you now?"

Millie released Pippa's hand. "After he's finished. Thank you. I don't know what would have happened to us if not for your quick thinking when the vicar's niece came to warn that my brother-in-law was searching the village for us."

"He will not touch one hair on Roarke's head, nor yours," Pippa vowed. "You have my word on it." The tension on her friend's face relaxed, as Pippa hoped it would. "Call me if you need me."

"I will."

When Pippa resumed her seat, she lowered her voice to tell the baroness, "I have no experience with babes or new mothers, but I do know that Millie seems more at ease when she has privacy to feed her babe. Thank you for thinking of the screen, your ladyship."

"My sister-in-law was the same way, when she first delivered her babes. I teased my brother that I was certain Persephone carried twins when he made an offhand comment about how large her belly was—without thinking how emotional Persephone would be."

Pippa covered her mouth, but not before her laughter escaped. "Forgive me. It is not a laughing matter. Millie became more sensitive, her emotions volatile, while she was expecting."

When Mrs. Chauncey asked if she should pour, Lady Phoebe declined. "I can manage, thank you."

Once the housekeeper left, the baroness poured two cups of tea. In the quiet the women heard Millie softly whispering to her babe as his snuffling and suckling got louder. The faraway look in Lady Phoebe's eyes as she placed a hand on her belly had Pippa wondering if she had placed herself—and Millie—beyond the pale by helping her escape from what they both believed was an intolerable situation. Millie needed the protection of a strong man—not that she would admit it, because the heartache of losing her beloved husband was still too fresh. Though the last thing Millie needed was a brute of a man snatching her babe from her! Pippa vowed not to let that happen.

Pippa knew she would be considered a pariah if word got out that she'd disguised herself as a coachman and dragged Millie and her babe to parts unknown immediately after the birth. She was certain that Trentchester would twist the truth around to suit him. The blackguard would definitely leave out how Pippa had helped thwart his bid to take his brother's son to raise as his own. Trentchester was a bully who equated money with power. He was not of the aristocracy, instead using his money to take whatever he wanted. It was no secret that he had three mistresses, one wife, and not a single heir. Personally, Pippa thought it was God's way of punishing the man for trying to get himself an heir to his fortune—even one born on the wrong side of the blanket—despite the embarrassment it would have caused his poor mouse of a wife.

Once her father returned home and heard the tale of what happened, Pippa doubted he would ever find a gentleman willing to come up to scratch and offer for her hand. After the string of men Papa had received offers from—which she had refused, for one reason or another—he had threatened to marry her off to two of his elderly, widowed contemporaries. She shuddered at the thought of being wed to the cadaverous Lord Hinchman or the overweight Lord Ives.

"Are you chilled?"

Pippa blinked and shoved those thoughts to the back of her mind. "Er…no. I was woolgathering."

"Unpleasant thoughts, then," the baroness said. "I have had to learn how to conquer mine." When Pippa waited for Lady Phoebe to continue, the baroness shook her head. "It is a long story for another time."

The sound of a gurgling belch had Pippa and Lady Phoebe

laughing and a flustered Millie saying, "He cannot help it—"

"Please do not apologize," the baroness said. "I am used to hearing that particular sound. If one's babe does not burp, the alternative is quite distressing for the babe and the mother."

"I'll be right there, Millie. Don't get up!" Pippa rose to go to her friend. When she stepped around the painted screen, she reminded Millie, "You are always so tired after you feed little Roarke. Lean on me."

When Millie was settled once again on the settee with her babe sleeping in her arms, the baroness asked, "Did I hear correctly, that your babe is only a few days old?"

"Yes, your ladyship." Millie glanced at Pippa, who shook her head.

As if she sensed there was quite a bit more to the tale of how Pippa, Millie, and her babe had arrived at Summerfield Chase, the baroness said, "I won't press you for the details until and unless there is a chance that someone has caused you to flee from your home. If that is the case, we must alert the men at once with a description. They need to be on the lookout, or else they will not know who or what to expect in the way of an unwanted visitor or possible attack."

With Millie on the verge of tears, Pippa answered, "It's Millie's brother-in-law."

"Grant Trentchester," Millie added. "He has made his fortune in shipping, and thinks himself equal to those who bear a title."

Pippa snarled, "His character is reprehensible—there is not one honorable bone in Trentchester's body! He would never have threatened his brother's pregnant wife otherwise!"

Millie bit her bottom lip.

"Has he threatened you?" the baroness asked softly.

Millie nodded. "Yes."

"Physically or emotionally?"

Incensed that her dearest friend had been under threat by her dead husband's brother, Pippa bit out, "He threatened to take Millie's babe—no matter if it was a boy or girl!"

The baroness's face darkened. "Did he assault you?"

Millie's mouth moved, but couldn't form the words. Her lips were trembling.

Pippa saw Millie's discomfort and replied, "He said he needed to speak privately to Millie, who agreed. I was in the other room and heard Millie cry out. If I had known how black his heart was, I would never have left her alone with him."

The baroness hesitated, then asked, "Will you tell me what happened?"

Millie grimaced. "He grabbed me by the hair and dragged me across the room."

"How long ago was this?"

"A fortnight ago," Millie whispered.

"Unconscionable!" Lady Phoebe cried out.

The sound of heavy footsteps approaching had the trio of women staring at the door. The loud knock was followed by a gruff voice. "Phoebe? Is Mrs. Trentchester feeding her babe, or may I come in?"

"Marcus! Yes, she is finished, thank you for asking. Please come in—we need you."

The door opened, and Pippa was momentarily distracted by the tall, broad-shouldered man who strode into the room, pulled the baroness into his embrace, and kissed her tenderly. "I'm here. How can I help?" Lady Phoebe leaned against her husband, who turned toward Pippa and Millie. "Please introduce me to our guests."

"We're interlopers," Pippa mumbled.

"Nonsense," the baroness said. "Marcus, meet Mrs. Millicent Trentchester…er, Millie to her friends…and her babe Roarke. He's but a few days old."

"I did not realize he was sleeping," the baron said. "I'll lower my voice."

"Forgive me for mortally wounding Flaherty. It was an accident!" Pippa blurted.

"And her very good friend and sometime coachman, Miss

Phillipa—Pippa—Stanhope." Before the baron could speak, the baroness added, "Truly, it was an accident, Marcus. She stepped wrong and fell—"

"I have already had the tale from Flaherty himself. By the way," he replied, turning to look at Pippa, "Flaherty was concerned that the women and babe he rescued were warm enough and had been fed. He seemed to think it had been early this morning when last you ate. Is that true?"

"Yes, your lordship," Pippa replied.

"We did not want to be a bother," Millie said. "Tea and scones will be more than enough—"

"Stuff and nonsense," the baron grumbled. "I have seen the way my wife's appetite—and that of O'Malley's wife, and Garahan's wife—has increased dramatically. All three women are eating for two, and as a new mother, I understand you need extra nourishment as well. I have been well tutored in the matter from my sister-in-law, the duchess—and the wives of the other men in the duke's guard via the letters that arrive weekly. It is quite a bit of correspondence. I shall send for a proper meal for you ladies. I expect the three of you to have finished eating every last scone and drained that teapot by the time I return with a meal that will give you the strength you'll need."

When no one moved, the baron added, "Is that understood?"

"Yes, Marcus," Lady Phoebe said, brushing a kiss to his cheek before stepping out of his embrace. "Now do stop ordering us around."

Pippa noticed the way the baron stared at his wife for a moment before shaking his head. "Do you have any other orders for me?"

The baroness laughed softly. "Only that you find out what that delicious, savory scent wafting from the kitchen is, and when it will be ready to eat!"

The baron lifted his wife's hand to his lips, then turned it over and lavishly kissed the palm of her hand. "Your wish is my command, Phoebe my love."

CHAPTER THREE

Sweat beaded on his forehead and dripped from his temples. The agony was beyond what Flaherty remembered from the last time he'd been shot.

Garahan grunted and reminded him, "The last time ye had to suffer the inconvenience of being shot was a few years ago. Do ye not remember ye needed to have the entry and exit wounds cauterized?"

Flaherty bit the inside of his cheek to keep from groaning. "Now that ye mention it, the scent of seared flesh was nauseating." He was having trouble concentrating on not making a sound as the lead balls were dug out of his side. The heat of the blade that widened the wounds did not hurt as much as the physician fishing around with the tip of it to find the blasted shot that had peppered his side—thank God the weapon was moving at the time, and he'd only received a few of the lead balls, not the entire load of shot!

A strip of folded leather appeared in his line of vision. Flaherty blinked and met Garahan's worried gaze. "Bite down on it while Dr. Higgins removes the last of the balls from your side."

Flaherty took the offering, placed it in the left side of his mouth—the same side he'd been shot—and clamped down hard. The pain of the heated blade poking, prodding, and slicing had him barely hanging on to consciousness.

All at once it ceased, and there was a deep basin in front of his face. He spat out the thin, flattened bit of leather and emptied the contents of his stomach.

Garahan handed him a small cup. "Swish this in yer mouth and spit it out."

Weak, but thankfully conscious, Flaherty did as he was told.

The cup appeared in front of his face a second time. "Twice more, then I'll let ye have yer flask."

Relief speared through Flaherty when he'd spat the last of the noxious taste of bile from his mouth. He took the proffered damp cloth, wiping his face and the back of his neck. "Where's me flask?"

Garahan grinned as he handed it to him. "Nothing like *uisce beatha* to remind a man he's still alive."

Flaherty took a swig. The welcoming warmth eased the ache in his jaw and soothed his abused throat. He took another, wiped the back of his hand over his mouth, and sighed. "Whiskey truly is the water of life."

"You haven't lost too much blood, Flaherty," Dr. Higgins remarked. "I'm of a mind to close the wounds with boiled threads, though in the past I have cauterized wounds." Intense, dark eyes beneath white brows were fixed on Flaherty's.

Garahan nodded to the flask in Flaherty's hand, and Flaherty drank from it. "Searing them closed is faster."

"Aye," the doctor agreed. "It is, though you did just mention the process nauseated you. You still have to sit still while I cleanse the wounds thoroughly. Do you think you can hold down the healthy portion of whiskey you just drank?"

Though Flaherty thought the words may have been said in jest, the physician's expression gave no indication that he'd mean it to be humorous. "I won't be wasting a drop of the Irish."

Dr. Higgins nodded and began the arduous process of cleaning out the wounds. Flaherty held his breath for part of it. When the physician paused, Flaherty asked, "How much longer?"

"Nearly finished." He met Flaherty's gaze and said, "One

more deep breath should do it."

Garahan chuckled. "Faith, it reminds me of when O'Malley used his body as a shield to protect the baron from those sharpshooters who were lying in wait on the other side of the stables."

Flaherty added, "O'Ghill was here that day to cart O'Malley's arse into the house. Do ye remember how O'Malley thanked him a short while later?"

Before Garahan could reply, Dr. Higgins chuckled as he tied off the last knot.

"Ah," Flaherty said. "Ye're thinking of what happened to O'Ghill when he tried to keep O'Malley from cracking his head on the floor when he spiked a fever."

The physician was trying not to smile. "I didn't hear that O'Ghill complained about his injury."

Flaherty added, "He did not. Though nothing is harder than the back of a man's skull—"

"—bashing into a man's nose," Garahan finished with a grin for the doctor. "Ye've managed to distract himself with a tale worth repeating, Dr. Higgins, while ye stitched him up. Thank ye."

The physician accepted the thanks and then turned to Mrs. Green. "That ought to do it. Thank you for anticipating what I'd need to take care of Flaherty."

Flaherty tried to ignore the bloody bowl of water and the needle that had been used to pierce his torn flesh and pull it back together. His head felt light, but he wasn't about to admit it to anyone. He'd already disgraced himself by emptying the contents of his stomach. Keeping his thoughts to himself for the moment, he wondered how the women he'd rescued—and little Roarke—fared.

The baron's cook sighed. "I never expected to gain as much experience as I have since the baron married and arrived with not only his lovely bride, Lady Phoebe, but three of the Duke of Wyndmere's private guard."

Garahan flashed a grin at her. "Ye're a wonderful woman to keep us in scones and not bat an eyelash assisting when one of us is wounded in the line of duty."

Flaherty agreed. "We'll do our best not to get shot too often." He noticed his assurance had eased the lines of strain on the kindly cook's forehead. He thanked the physician and waited while his side was bandaged, trying not to flinch as Dr. Higgins wrapped a long strip of linen around his middle. Once the bandage was secured, and the ends tied off, the physician stood and walked over to the pitcher and bowl to wash his hands.

Flaherty heard the rumble of voices as his cousin and the physician were speaking, but ignored it in favor of taking stock of his injury. He admitted to himself that it although cauterizing a wound from a lead ball was quicker, the pain of his flesh being seared was about the same as being pierced over and over as his wounds were repaired. The worst of it was the digging out of the blasted lead balls.

Accepting that his side pained him considerably—and would until it healed enough for the threads to be removed—Flaherty said a silent prayer of thanks that he had not been hit square in his gut at close range. He doubted he would have survived the extraction, and the infection that would likely have followed. It was still possible that he'd end up with wound fever.

"Will ye be listening to Dr. Higgins's advice, then, Dillon?" Garahan asked.

"I will, as long as I can eat me fill. I'm famished."

"An invalid's diet is what ye'll be needing." The tone of Garahan's voice had Flaherty meeting the intensity in his cousin's dark-brown eyes. "Not one of us ever ignored a physician's advice when more than a few cracked or broken ribs were involved, and ye know it."

Flaherty looked at Dr. Higgins, who gave a brief nod. He knew then he'd be existing on weak broth and calves' foot jelly for the next while. "How many days will I have to suffer from hunger?"

"One thing at a time, Flaherty," the physician advised. "I'll return tomorrow afternoon to assess your wounds."

"Aye, Dr. Higgins. I'll try me best not to complain, but I'm hungry." The sound of low voices out in the hallway had him cocking his head to the side to listen. Garahan looked over his shoulder and gave a slight shake of his head. Soft footfalls moving away from the room had Flaherty's temper simmering. "Am I confined to quarters, or am I to be allowed to return to me duties?"

The physician was slipping into his coat, but paused for a moment. "I have to say, Flaherty, that I have only had one or two other patients who had been shot ever ask me that."

"Meself and O'Malley?" Flaherty asked.

Garahan chuckled. "As I have been lucky enough not to suffer the indignity—"

"Yet," Flaherty reminded him.

"Aye," Garahan agreed. "Yet."

They listened while Dr. Higgins reminded Flaherty what he could and could not do for the next few days. Flaherty was still grumbling beneath his breath when O'Malley stood in the doorway. "Well now, how many stitches was it, or do I still hold the record?"

Flaherty was grateful for the interruption. "I wasn't counting."

"Well then, 'tis done, and ye don't look half dead, Flaherty." O'Malley paused. "There's another matter I'm hoping ye'll be up to attending to. Miss Stanhope—"

Embarrassment coupled with humiliation had Flaherty's temper simmering at the mention of the woman's name. "A hundred years 'twill be too soon to have to deal with that woman. I'll be leaving that to the two of ye to sort out." At their silence, Flaherty emphasized, "I'll not be speaking to the lass again, but I will be happy to speak to Mrs. Trentchester. *She* didn't shoot me!"

When his cousins shared a knowing glance, Flaherty looked

away, ignoring them. A movement near the open door caught his eye. *Bloody hell!* Miss Stanhope's expression was a combination of horror and shame. He knew the lass was only aiming at him to protect her friend, but then he'd startled her, and she'd stepped wrong. The blunderbuss went off on impact with the ground— she had not intended it to.

Her blue-gray eyes welled with tears. It added to the guilt swirling inside of him. The first one fell—and it unmanned him. When he drew in a breath to speak, she disappeared from sight, and he knew *he'd* be the one apologizing.

Bloody hell! To take his mind off one more problem added to his day, he needed to gain back the strength that had been drained by the physician's diligent search for lead balls and the deep cleansing that followed. "Is it too soon to ask for a bit of broth and bread?"

$$\Diamond$$

CHAPTER FOUR

PIPPA'S HEART BEGAN to pound as she remembered the look of utter disdain in Flaherty's clear blue eyes. How could she make him understand she had not intended to fire the weapon? Surely he knew it had been an accident—though mayhap he did not. His anger washed over her like a summer thunderstorm. She had never been on the receiving end of such a look, never imagined a glance could communicate such feelings, stir up such emotions! God help her, Pippa knew that glance would haunt her unless she could somehow make him see reason and change his mind. The darkness in his gaze deepened until she knew without a doubt that Flaherty blamed her, but more... He would never forgive her. He *loathed* her!

She fought back tears of anguish as she hurriedly made her way back to the sitting room, her mind plagued by images of the man's grim expression. The grievous injuries he'd sustained *were* all her fault. Standing outside the room, she had heard bits and pieces of what the physician was doing and, Lord help her, what happened immediately after he'd finished. The echo of Flaherty vomiting after his silence the entire time the doctor extracted the lead balls embedded in the poor man's side was a sound she'd not soon forget.

She replayed the moment when she'd let fear take hold of her: her breathing became choppy, and her chest ached from lack of air, but she remembered wanting to shout at the time, *"My grandfather's blunderbuss is aimed at your stomach. I'm not afraid of you!"*—but she hadn't. She had been terrified that the auburn-haired giant of a man was somehow connected to the man chasing after them. Facing this man garbed in black from head to toe, his expression deadly, she'd had but one thought—protect Millie and her babe! Then he'd stepped toward her, his mouth in a grim line, no emotion on his face. Abject fear had taken hold of her. She'd stumbled backward, fallen, and a heartbeat later, the gun went off.

Why could he not understand that she did not know him, and was not about to trust him? She had witnessed the months of veiled threats Millie had received on the heels of the missive informing her that Captain Roarke Trentchester was dead. No other details—not where he'd died, or how it had happened. With both Millie's and Pippa's fathers in London attending a session in the House of Lords, Pippa had had her hands full trying to assure her friend that her blackguard of a brother-in-law had no power over Millie. The hardhearted reprobate had no right to threaten to take Millie's babe the moment it was born—nor should he have expected that she would simply hand her babe over because Roarke's elder brother ordered her to.

Trentchester must be mad!

Pippa wanted to contact their fathers the moment the threats began, but Millie had talked her out of it. She should not have listened to Millie's pleas, but at the time, capitulating had been the only choice she had. Her dearest friend for as long as she could recall had pleaded with her in between casting up her accounts—due to her pregnancy—and bouts of weeping, as she grieved deeply for the loss of her husband. Millie's fears had taken root inside of Pippa and mingled with her own! When pressed, Pippa had felt she had no choice but to acquiesce and agree to remain silent on the matter... Until that last threat had been delivered in person.

Pippa had never felt such a degree of revulsion toward another person until the moment Trentchester barged into Millie and Roarke's cottage.

She trembled as the memory assaulted her. Such evil threats levied against a woman so close to term were unconscionable, and had undermined Millie's confidence that she would be protected as long as she stayed with Pippa. In the beginning stages of labor, wild with fear and grief, Millie had believed that the monster would be waiting outside of the cottage, listening…waiting for his chance to snatch her babe the moment she gave birth!

Their fathers *would* have banded together to protect Millie. If Parliament had not been in session, they would have been home in the Lake District. But both gentlemen were actively campaigning for those brave soldiers and sailors who had been injured and retired on half pay, and the widows—like Millie—of those who had gallantly served in His Majesty's forces and given the ultimate sacrifice.

Pippa wiped her eyes with the backs of her hands, wishing she'd remembered to grab one of her father's handkerchiefs when she disguised herself for the journey to the Borderlands. Before Lords Haybrook and Stanhope had left for London, Millie had pleaded with her father to meet with the head of War Office to find out details of her husband's death—no matter how grim. Finally, he—and Pippa's father—had relented. Lord Haybrook was acquainted with Earl Bathurst, the Secretary of State for War and the Colonies, who was head of the War Office. Pippa's father counted Viscount Palmerston, the Secretary at War, who was in charge of running the War Office, as a good friend. Both had promised to uncover the circumstances surrounding Roarke's death, while collecting information pertinent to their campaign for better conditions for those who had been discharged, and were on the verge of poverty.

Initially Pippa had urged her father to the point where he demanded to know what the devil was going on. Her reply echoed in her aching head: *"If I had not given my word, Papa, know that I would confide in you."* She knew her father would understand and expect no less from his daughter. *His* word was his bond.

Their fathers had had more than one conversation about the lack of information surrounding Captain Trentchester's death, and combined with the fact that nothing had been forthcoming— no rumors from soldiers who had been on the peninsula where Trentchester was purported to have been—that finally swayed the men. Pippa had her suspicions as to why they were being kept in the dark. Though she had not confided in her father, the unanswered questions had led her and Millie to the conclusion that Roarke had been involved in a highly dangerous mission for the Crown. They suspected—though it had never been confirmed by Millie's husband—that Roarke was spying for the British.

Pippa's heart ached with the worry that poor Millie would never know the truth of what happened. The only consolation, and it was indeed a small one, was that perhaps her husband would be posthumously recognized for his meritorious service.

"Are you all right, Miss Stanhope?"

Pippa spun around with her hand to her heart. She'd been so lost in thought, she hadn't realized she was standing in the middle of the hallway. From the expression on the footman's face, he must have called her name more than once. The large trays in his hands must need to be returned to the pantry next to the room Flaherty was in.

"Er… Yes. I am, thank you." Looking about her, toward the door she and Millie and her babe had entered through, she decided it was best not to expound on her thoughts or feelings to yet another veritable stranger. "Forgive me for blocking the way. I must return to the baroness and my friend."

The young man's expression only changed for a brief moment, but Pippa could not decide if it was concern for her, distrust—or something else. Had rumors been flying around the manor house that quickly? Dear Lord, did members of the baron and baroness's staff believe that she had willfully pointed a rifle at Flaherty and shot him?

Her belly ached, and her head throbbed in time with her swift footsteps, as she rushed back to the sitting room. Her concentration must be on Milie and her babe—and finding out if Millie's mum's friend, Old Ned, was still the stable master here at Summerfield Chase. One of them should have asked Flaherty about it as soon as they heard the name of the estate. But neither one felt safe enough to do so—yet. Later, much later, Pippa could clarify the connection and take the blame for not telling Flaherty about it. She had far more to worry about right now than what others thought or said about her.

As she passed the kitchen, she returned Mrs. Green's greeting and walked through the connecting door to the main part of the house. When she noted there were four footmen lingering in the marbled hallway between the entryway and the sitting room, she realized that the baron was not taking any chances with his pregnant wife's safety. An uneasy feeling settled into her bones as Pippa wondered if the baron believed their story, of if he believed she had deliberately fired upon his guard.

She silently prayed, *Lord, please grant me the strength to protect Millie and Roarke!*

Nodding to the footmen as she hurried past each man, she was relieved no one tried to stop her. In fact, each man, in turn, inclined his head. Their deference gave her hope.

Pippa was about to reach for the door when one of the two men standing guard on either side of it moved to open it for her. "Allow me, Miss Stanhope." She tried for a smile, but was not quite certain she managed it, and thanked him before darting into the room.

The expression on Millie's face, and that of the baroness's, had her stopping in the middle of the room. "What's wrong? What's happened?"

"Millie was just asking about our stable master, Old Ned."

"Did she?" Pippa feigned disinterest.

"It does cause a bit of concern that neither one of you mentioned that bit of information to Flaherty, though I suppose I understand why you have yet to confide in him. It is interesting that Old Ned once worked for Millie's grandfather. Our stable master has quite a memory. I am certain he would remember Millie's mum."

Pippa met Millie's gaze, relieved to see her friend's eyes were not cloudy with worry.

Lady Phoebe paused to shift on her seat, and Pippa wondered if the weight of the baroness's babe was uncomfortable. She'd seen Millie move in a similar way as her pregnancy progressed.

"I was curious as to how she knew of him," the baroness continued. "It is my understanding that he has been master of the stables here at Summerfield Chase for decades."

Pippa walked back over to the settee where Millie was sitting, cradling her babe in her arms. "Would you like me to hold Roarke for you? I listened to everything the midwife advised and will be very careful to support his head."

Mille smiled and let her gaze drop to the collar of Pippa's rough coat. "Mayhap if you weren't still wearing the coachman's disguise…"

Lady Phoebe narrowed her eyes. "I knew there was far more to your situation than a broken carriage wheel. Why don't you start at the beginning?"

The knock on the sitting room door put a halt to their conversation as Lady Phoebe answered the summons, and Mrs. Chauncey and two servants entered with an enormous tray of food, and another containing a fresh pot of tea and its accoutrements. Pippa nearly salivated at the sight of the scones, clotted cream, and raspberry jam.

"The bread and stew smell wonderful," the baroness proclaimed. "I'm starving."

Summerfield stood in the open doorway smiling at his wife. "Time to feed our son…again, my love."

"Our daughter," Lady Phoebe corrected him.

Her husband chuckled, a wicked gleam in his deep blue eyes. "Mayhap both!"

The baroness's gasp had Summerfield snorting with laughter.

"You are a rogue!" she scolded him before pausing to lift her hand for him to kiss. "Luckily for you, I happen to like rogues."

"And you adore me," he added.

Lady Phoebe smiled.

Pippa strove to hide her reaction to the repartee and tender glances the couple exchanged. She had been envious of Millie and Roarke's obvious affection for one another. Would she ever experience a love like that—for just a brief moment in time? Pippa had often wondered when—or if—she would meet a man who felt that way about her. But then came the news of Roarke's death. The utter despair her friend suffered had Pippa wondering if she would ever be strong enough to give her heart to someone, only to have to grieve their loss a few years later.

Lost in thought, she let her mind wander until she felt a light touch on her forearm. Pippa glanced up and met the worried expression in the housekeeper's gaze. "Forgive me, Mrs. Chauncey. I was woolgathering."

"What you need is a bowl of Mrs. Green's savory stew and still-warm bread," the kindly servant suggested.

"Once you've finished," the baroness said, "then it's off to soak in a hot tub for the both of you."

"Oh, but we had to leave the small trunk with our belongings with the carriage because…" Pippa's voice trailed off. She did not want to bring up the subject that would lead to discussing Flaherty. She shivered, remembering his reaction.

"Between Caro, Prudence, and myself," the baroness said, "I am quite certain we will be able to find something to fit the both of you."

"Oh, but we couldn't—" Millie protested, only to fall silent at the pointed look from Lady Phoebe.

Summerfield chuckled. "You've just discovered that it is not wise to gainsay my wife. As the youngest in her family, Phoebe was cossetted by two of her older brothers when we married. She is used to getting her own way."

The baroness's soft gasp had Pippa watching the interchange between the couple with interest. It was clear theirs was a love match, though sprinkled with just enough differences of opinion to make things interesting. It made her like the couple even more. "Millie was spoiled terribly by her father, while I—" Pippa began, only to stop at the sound of her friend's loud snort. She frowned at Millie. "What?"

Millie rolled her eyes, and turned to watch one of the footmen move the mahogany table from beneath the garden window, while the other laid out their meal. When she turned back, she had schooled her features. "Your four older brothers taught you how to ride and shoot as well as they did before you were ten years old."

Pippa lifted her chin. "And your point is?"

"The same as your point, Pippa. The baroness was as fortunate as the both of us were to have grown up in a loving home. My poor Roarke did not have that luxury. His older brother..." Mille closed her mouth and gave a slight shake of her head.

"I'm sorry for dredging up unhappy memories, Millie," Pippa rasped. "I should have thought before I spoke—please forgive me."

"Everything's ready to eat, your ladyship," the housekeeper announced.

"Thank you, Mrs. Chauncey. It looks delicious." Lady Phoebe turned to her husband. "Are you joining us, Marcus?"

He walked over to help his wife to her feet, then slipped a hand beneath her elbow to steady her. "I'm afraid I cannot. A pressing matter has arisen, and I need to have a word with the men to prepare."

Lady Phoebe narrowed her eyes. "For?"

Summerfield chuckled, pressed a kiss to her cheek and helped her to sit at the table. "We shall discuss it later. Enjoy your pre-luncheon meal."

"Isn't this luncheon?" Pippa asked.

"We have altered our normal meal schedule to add in the

small meals her ladyship needs during the day," the housekeeper answered. "Mrs. Green is a wonder with tempting even the most sensitive of stomachs."

Summerfield agreed before telling his wife, "I won't be long, Phoebe. You will not argue, and I expect you to graciously accept my escort when I return." The baroness's snort of laughter had Summerfield reminding her, "Dr. Higgins's orders, my love. You will rest—for your sake as well as our babe's."

Her audible sigh swirled through the room. "I will rest, Marcus. Now go away and do whatever is so pressing that you cannot spare the time to confide in me."

Instead of bowing and striding toward the door, the baron moved closer to where his wife sat. He placed a hand to her shoulder, bent, and pressed a kiss to the top of her head. "Where is your reticule?"

Lady Phoebe burst into delighted laughter. "Upstairs in our bedchamber."

The baron's expression softened. "And are your ribbon-wrapped hatpins and paperweight inside of it?"

"You are incorrigible, Marcus. You know very well that they are. Now, kiss me and be off with you!"

Summerfield was smiling when he lavishly kissed his wife, bowed, and strode from the room.

With a hand to her heart, the baroness sighed. "Marcus can be so *irritating*."

Pippa coughed to cover her snort of laughter. Horrified that the baroness might think ill of her, she was about to apologize, but then Millie started to laugh—hesitant at first, then a wonderfully full belly laugh.

Lady Phoebe's lips twitched as she tried to contain her smile. "I do not know how I tolerate that man."

"Fortitude," Millie replied as she met Pippa's gaze. "Wouldn't you agree, Pippa?"

"I suppose it is," Pippa replied, then asked the baroness, "May I ask you a question, your ladyship?"

"Of course, as long as you do not mind that I may choose not to answer."

Pippa understood perfectly, and had felt that way on more than one occasion herself. "Why would you have hatpins wrapped in ribbons and a paperweight in your reticule?"

"It was the ransom note."

"Ransom?" Millie and Pippa said simultaneously.

The baroness finished chewing, blotted her lips, and leaned toward the pair. "I could not very well confide about the note to one of the footmen, or my brother's men ordered to guard me, now could I?"

Millie shook her head, while Pippa stared at the baroness. Hatpins were terribly sharp and could be used as a weapon if one were in close proximity to one's attacker. A paperweight hidden in one's hand when one struck out at someone would add to the impact. "Did you have the coin demanded?"

Lady Phoebe shook her head and sipped from her teacup. "I did not."

Without missing a beat, Pippa said, "You were so wise to find weapons within reach. Time must have been of the essence."

"It was."

"Did you find him?" Millie wanted to know.

By the time the women had finished their meal, they marveled at Lady Phoebe's strength, determination, and courage. Millie's had faltered, but she had been grieving for her husband and worried she would lose their babe. But now that little Roarke had arrived, she was getting her gumption back—if not her strength. Pippa was determined that Millie would get the rest she needed to regain her strength after their arduous recent journey.

Baroness Summerfield rose and motioned for the others to follow her over to the grouping of chairs by the settee. When they were seated, she said, "I have confided in you, and now it is your turn. Tell me who has threatened you to the point where you would risk your babe's health and your own by running away so soon after giving birth without an escort?"

Millie hesitated, and Pippa urged, "You need to tell her lady-ship. You know your dastard of a brother-in-law won't give up. Trouble could be heading here even as we speak."

Pippa waited for her friend to confide their situation. Millie sighed and told the baroness, "I would never want you or anyone in your household to be harmed because of my actions. But what I am about to tell you must be kept in the strictest confidence. I'm terrified of what the repercussions may be."

"You have my word," Lady Phoebe assured her.

Millie told of her husband leaving to join his regiment, fol-lowed by Millie discovering she was pregnant. When she paused, Pippa picked up the thread of the story, with the devastating missive received a few months later containing news of Roarke's death.

"After we received that missive was the first time my brother-in-law *insisted* Roarke would want him to raise our babe."

Pippa was quick to add, "When Millie refused, the veiled threats started, but when she ignored them, they quickly became outright threats."

"That is when Pippa began to plan our escape," Millie ex-plained. "There was no other way to avoid my brother-in-law unless we disappeared."

When she launched into the particulars of how they'd avoid-ed Trentchester, the baroness's expression changed from interested to incensed. She rose from her seat, walked over to the corner of the room, and tugged on the bellpull. A few moments later, there was a heavy knock on the door. When bidden to enter, the footman stepped over the threshold. "Please send someone to fetch my dark-blue reticule," Lady Phoebe said. "I left it on the bedside table."

The footman bowed. "At once, your ladyship."

She returned to her seat and glanced from Millie to Pippa. "Now then, where is your blunderbuss?"

"Flaherty grabbed it from me," Pippa replied. "Everything happened so fast after that, I'm afraid I do not remember what happened to it. He could have tossed it in the carriage. Why?"

"Do you have any smaller weapons?" The baroness seemed intent on discovering if they were armed. Was Lady Phoebe afraid that Millie and Pippa were a threat?

"Your ladyship," Millie began, "we mean you no harm."

"Of course you don't," Lady Phoebe retorted. "I should have just asked a more pertinent question. What weapons are you proficient with? My very good friend Aurelia is a crack shot with a dueling pistol. Our friend Calliope's aim has vastly improved with one, now that she's been able to resume her lessons."

"With a pistol?" Pippa inquired.

"And a rifle," the baroness replied. "A few of the O'Malleys' cousins went to America. On one of their last visits to London, they brought a Kentucky long rifle back as a gift for Patrick—he is the eldest of the Cork O'Malleys and head of my brother's private guard."

"I see," Millie remarked.

"Rory was the first of the Flahertys to get his hands on the weapon," the baroness continued. "He is the duke's sharpshooter."

Pippa marveled at the way the baroness spoke with affection about Rory. "How many Flahertys are there?"

"There are four Flaherty brothers," Lady Phoebe replied. "Rory is stationed at Wyndmere Hall in the Lake District—and was very recently married. My brother's estate is lovely. I grew up there, but we were constantly on the move between the Lake District, London, and Sussex. We hardly ever went to Penwith Tower in Cornwall."

Pippa noted the way the baroness stiffened as she spoke of being on the move, and noted the way her voice lost all inflection. "It must have been a trial moving such a great distance between locations. Days of travel and staying in coaching inns."

Lady Phoebe agreed.

Millie cooed to the babe in her arms, who was waking up and making his presence known. "Do you have homes in all of those places?"

"My brother does. Ever since the night Jared and Persephone held a ball in my honor—and that the madman burst into our family's London town house—he and my sister-in-law have been living exclusively in the Lake District."

Pippa shook her head. "Apparently Millie is not the only one who has encountered a man with malintent toward her."

"I am quite sure what happened to me, and my family, would shock you. To tell the truth, I do not speak of it often. But...if it will aid you in any way on the journey that led you here, I shall bring myself to speak of it."

The babe began to fuss. "I need to change Roarke—is there anywhere I can do that?" Tears welled in Millie's eyes.

"What is it?" Pippa asked.

Lady Phoebe rose from her seat. "I believe I know what is wrong, and what you need, Millie. Please do forgive me for not suggesting it before now. Allow me to show you to the nursery. It is quite large and consists of a number of rooms, including the schoolroom where the twins have their inside lessons. We realized early on that they needed outside lessons as well—they are quite boisterous. Marcus and I want to have a separate room for our babe when he or she arrives. Then there is the nursery sitting room. We have been gathering supplies for our babe and the others who will be using our nursery."

Millie blinked back her tears. "I'm afraid I don't have anything for my son."

Guilt filled Pippa. It was because of her reaction to Flaherty that Millie was without the trunk she had hurriedly packed with blankets, clothes, and clouts for her babe. The midwife had warned that newborn babes may need as many as a half a dozen clouts a day—or more! Who knew a babe would soil that many in one day? "It is because of me! If I had not—"

"If I have learned anything in the last few years, it is that it does no one any good to bemoan what one does not have control over," Lady Phoebe interrupted. "While the Irishmen in my brother's private guard are equally intimidating upon meeting them—did I mention that there are sixteen of them?—the Flaherty brothers are the most intense."

"If they are so protective, and skilled with weapons," Pippa asked, "why are *you* asking about weapons, your ladyship?"

"There are times when we women must be prepared to protect ourselves. We discovered that when Wyndmere Hall was attacked by the same madman who injured my brother Edward and held me at knifepoint..." Lady Phoebe trailed off, and Pippa felt responsible for the worried look in the baroness's eyes.

"I am so sorry for reminding you of what had to have been a frightening experience."

"It's always there in the back of my mind," Lady Phoebe replied. "I have worked quite hard to quell the noxious feeling that used to overwhelm me whenever the memory resurfaced." She drew in a steadying breath. "Now then, let us proceed to the nursery. I'm certain that Prudence and Caro should be available to keep you company. They have become dear friends in the short time they have been living at Summerfield Chase."

"Didn't you mention someone had twins?" Millie asked.

The baroness inclined her head. "It is an unusual circumstance, but Marcus and I have offered to care for Prudence's twin cousins, who are scamps," she said with a smile. "They can usually be found in the stables this time of day."

Pippa needed to find some way to atone for injuring Flaherty, while at the same time ensuring that Millie and her babe were well protected. The sudden realization that she could use herself as bait filled her. She could entice Trentchester to follow after her, while leaving Millie and Roarke behind, safe, protected, and well cared for here at Summerfield Chase. If the opportunity presented itself, she would take it!

"As we have had to shelter women before," the baroness continued, "Mrs. Green and Mrs. Chauncey developed a routine and will have begun the task of heating water for your baths not long after you arrived." Turning to Pippa, Lady Phoebe suggested, "Why don't you enjoy a nice, hot bath while Millie is feeding Roarke?"

"If you are certain it's not a bother, I would appreciate it, because I will not be able to help Millie take care of Roarke until I scrub the dust from our journey. I landed on my, er…posterior earlier."

A young woman was rushing toward them as they approached the entryway.

"Ah, Beth, I'd like to introduce you to our guests. Beth is far more than my lady's maid," the baroness told them. "She is my right hand, and at times my left as well. Mrs. Millicent Trentchester, and her babe Roarke, and their stalwart protector, Miss Phillipa Stanhope."

"It's a pleasure to meet you, ladies. Have they met Prudence and Caro yet?"

"We're hoping to do that now." Roarke let out a wail, and the baroness soothed him, "Soon, little one. We're headed to the nursery, Beth, so that Millie can change Roarke while Pippa enjoys a long soak in one of our copper slipper tubs."

"If it is too much trouble, I can certainly make do with a pitcher of warm water, sliver of soap, and a bowl," Pippa interjected.

"Nonsense," Lady Phoebe said, leading the women up the main staircase. "You will no doubt start to feel aches in places you did not realize had connected with the ground as the day goes by. Soak now and enjoy it."

Walking down the hallway, the baroness continued, "We will need to discuss our plans for how we will protect ourselves—without my husband or the duke's men finding out. They are insistent that we all follow their edicts as far as our safety is concerned. And they do not hesitate to tell me, and the other women under their protection, what to do."

She paused to open a door halfway down the hall. "This is your room, Miss Stanhope—"

"Pippa."

The baroness smiled. "The tub is waiting for you in the dressing room on the other side of that door, Pippa. Take your time."

Pippa glanced into the room and was immediately drawn to the soft hues of green and cream. "It looks lovely, your ladyship, but—"

"We'll discuss whatever is weighing heavy on your mind *after* your bath. But first, I thought you'd like to see the nursery so you won't worry about Mrs. Trentchester's comfort."

"Please call me Millie," Pippa's friend said.

"Of course, Millie."

"Thank you for your understanding and kindness to us, your ladyship, after we barged into your life," Pippa said. She swallowed against the lump in her throat and continued, "After I injured one of your guard."

"Flaherty has a strong constitution—all of the men do," Lady Phoebe said as they passed by several rooms. "They are all hardheaded. Mark my words, he will be demanding to return to his duties by morning, although Dr. Higgins will have warned him to ease into things a fortnight from now…or at the very least a sennight." She let her maid open the door. "Thank you, Beth. Isn't this a lovely room? We have set it up in anticipation of our babe."

Pippa was surprised to see four cradles and four rocking chairs. She was about to question the baroness, but Millie asked first: "How many babes are you carrying?"

The baroness laughed. "It would be my luck to have twins, after I teased my brother mercilessly about the possibility that my sister-in-law was carrying *their* twins."

"I see," Millie said. "It appears that you are preparing for future children."

"And for O'Malley's and Garahan's wives when they deliver a few months after me. They spend time with Percy and Phineas, the twins who are currently living with us, and it would make their lives, and mine, so much easier if their babes were tucked in our nursery. Besides, it is so lovely to have women my age to converse with. Then there is the possibility that we will have overnight guests. Jared and Persephone have their twins who are walking and talking and into everything. My brother Edward and his wife Aurelia have a son who is holding on to things, about to test his legs. Then there is Calliope and William, whose son was born around the same time as Edward and Aurelia's."

Pippa knew she had to say what was on her mind. "I imagine it would be lovely to have family and friends stay as your guests. Millie and I are not truly guests."

Lady Phoebe shook her head. "We are always ready to receive guests—whether by invitation or necessity. Please do not give it another thought." She turned back to Millie. "Let me show you where we keep the supply of clouts." The baroness walked over to one of the chests of drawers, opening the top drawer. "My sister-in-law changed Richard and Abigail in their cradle. I thought to do the same." Lady Phoebe studied Millie with a critical eye. "You're quite pale. Beth, why don't you stay with Millie while Pippa enjoys a good, long soak?"

Pippa could not help but worry about Millie, now that the baroness had pointed out how pale her friend looked.

As if she could read Pippa's mind, Lady Phoebe continued, "While you're gone, Millie will make herself comfortable in one of the rocking chairs. Persephone has a pair in her nursery. When I discovered I was expecting, I asked Marcus to procure a few for me."

"It sounds as if you speak from experience," Millie said.

"I helped take care of Richard and Abigail right after they were born," Lady Phoebe replied. "Persephone was exhausted, and I was happy to step in and rock, change, and soothe my niece and nephew."

"I am so very glad that Flaherty brought us to you," Millie rasped. "Somehow 'thank you' does not seem to be enough."

"It is absolutely enough. Now, please do sit down. You must realize that you need as much rest as possible, to recover from your lying in. Surely your midwife warned you about overdoing things and the serious issues, possibly life-threatening, that can arise. Would you want to take a chance that someone else would be raising your son?"

Millie frowned. "I would not. It is the reason we are even here. Do you think I have done irreparable damage to Roarke?" She did not wait for anyone to respond before adding, "But we had no choice—"

The baroness placed her arm around Millie's back and led her to one of the rocking chairs. "Sit."

Millie obliged.

Lady Phoebe studied her for a moment before asking, "Would you be willing to meet with Dr. Higgins? All things considered, I would feel better if he spoke with you—though if you'd rather, we could ask one of the midwives instead."

"Thank you, your ladyship. I expected to feel tired, but am more concerned about my son. Could Dr. Higgins examine him, too?"

"Of course. He may still be on the estate—one of the tenant farmer's sons fell out of a tree early this morning. I shall ask Timmons to have Dr. Higgins stop here on his way back to the village."

"Thank you, your ladyship. It would ease my mind," Millie admitted.

The baroness smiled and turned to Pippa. "Before the physician arrives, there are a few things I'd like to speak to you about. Mind if I keep you company while you bathe?"

From the tone of the baroness's voice, Pippa had a feeling the woman had questions she did not want Millie to overhear. "I would like that. Thank you, your ladyship." She reminded Millie that she would just be a few doors down the hall, squeezed her friend's hand, and followed Lady Phoebe out of the room.

Once they were alone, Lady Phoebe's expression changed to one of determination. "I need to know everything you can tell me about Millie's brother-in-law."

Pippa nodded. "He is a braggart and a bully."

"I suspected as much, but it sounds as if he is also a blackguard. No man should ever browbeat, let alone threaten, a woman, especially one who is expecting. I have yet to meet the man, and I dislike him intensely!"

"You will feel even more dislike for him when I tell you more of what he has put my dear friend through."

The baroness entered the guest room and walked over to the bellpull in the corner. "One of the upstairs maids should be along in a moment to help you into the tub. I'm not supposed to be lifting anything—or anyone."

Pippa could not help but relax the more she was in the baroness's company. A short while later, she undressed and sank into the comfort of the copper slipper tub. Pippa sighed as the heather-scented hot water eased some of the aches and pains that had started to appear.

An hour later, she was dressed in a fresh chemise and gown the color of a ripe peach, accompanying the baroness to the nursery.

They arrived just before the physician was announced and introduced. "I was planning to stop back to check on Flaherty after I tended to the Masterson boy. The men in the duke's guard do not seem to understand the concept of 'rest and recuperate.' Now then, Mrs. Trentchester, why don't I examine your son first?"

Millie's relief was palpable. "Thank you, Dr. Higgins, but he's asleep."

The doctor nodded. "As is to be expected with a newborn. It will afford me the chance to hear how his lungs are working when he cries."

By the time the physician was finished examining Roarke, Millie was swaying on her feet. Dr. Higgins said, "You need to be in bed—immediately! Did your midwife speak to you about complications if you overexerted yourself after giving birth?"

Pippa put her arm around her friend. "I was there, Dr. Higgins. She did, but we had no choice but to leave immediately for the safety of Millie and her babe."

"Flaherty mentioned safety was the issue for your journey. I would suggest the same diet and rest I have already recommended to his lordship and yourself, Lady Phoebe, after you give birth." The doctor paused to nod at the baroness, then turned back to continue with his instructions. "I cannot stress how important rest is for a new mother. It may take a fortnight, possibly longer, to regain your strength, Mrs. Trentchester. And that means no lifting and staying off your feet as much as possible. Is that clear?"

"How will I take care of my son?" Millie asked.

"I will help," Pippa offered.

"As will Caro, Prudence, and I," the baroness added. "Now then, is it too soon for Millie to soak in a hot tub?"

"Yes. Sponge baths until you are up and about and we are certain the danger of hemorrhaging is past. I shall be checking in on you—with your permission, Mrs. Trentchester."

"Yes, of course, thank you, but about your fee—"

"Leave that to me to discuss," the baroness interrupted. "You are to rest and do exactly as Dr. Higgins prescribed."

"I will, thank you, doctor. Thank you, your ladyship."

"Pippa will accompany you to your room."

"Is it far from the nursery?" Millie asked.

"I will have one of the footmen carry a cradle to your room and set it up right next to your bed." Lady Phoebe gave the bellpull a tug. "I'll have Beth gather everything you need for your babe and bring it to your room shortly."

Millie's eyes welled with tears, and Pippa wished the bully who'd put her very good friend in this position were here right now—she'd kick him in the backside!

"I cannot thank you enough, Lady Phoebe," Millie said.

"Nonsense—it is a pleasure to offer whatever we have to you. We have in the past, and will continue to do so for anyone in need. I am so happy to be able to help you, Millie. You are so fortunate in your friendship with Pippa. Now then, Beth will be along in a few moments, as will the cradle. Go get settled in."

A short while later, Millie was tucked into bed with Roarke sound asleep in the cradle beside her. Pippa listened to the soothing sound of Millie's quiet breaths, and the babe's snuffling and sighing as he slept.

She needed to come up with a plan to divert Trentchester, should he be bold enough to show his face here at Summerfield Chase. Given his previous treatment of Millie, the heinous threats, Pippa had no doubt he would.

She kept vigil over Millie and her babe, vowing to do whatever she had to in order to keep them safe, healthy, and happy. While she watched, she prayed Millie would not succumb to a fever, or what Pippa feared most—hemorrhage.

The one thing Pippa prayed and wished for with all her heart was to bring Millie's husband back from the dead. But that, she could not do.

CHAPTER FIVE

TRENTCHESTER SHOVED TO his feet, leaned over the walnut desk, and growled, "Where in the bloody hell is she?"

"I… I don't know, sir."

Incredulous, Trentchester reared back. "Any woman who has just given birth could not possibly have had the strength to get out of bed, let alone vanish! She must be hidden in her home—the cottage my brother put her up in has no more than a few rooms. Go back and do a thorough search!"

"But sir—"

Trentchester scowled at the man cowering in front of him. How did he expect the man to steal a babe, when it was painfully obvious that he did not have the backbone for that task, let alone to force his way into his dead brother's home?

"Find Millicent! Do not come back until you have her and her babe!"

From the way the wretch stared at him, Trentchester knew he'd made a mistake hiring him. The man needed money, but did not have the heart for the task he'd been given.

"Well? Don't just stand there. Go!"

The man spun around, stubbed his toe on the chair on the other side of the desk, and stumbled out of Trentchester's study.

Incensed, Trentchester grabbed the closest object and hurled it at the fireplace. Glass shattered. Too late, he realized, it still had brandy in it. The scent permeated the air, adding to his fury. It was a waste of excellent—smuggled—French brandy. "Millicent's babe has Trentchester blood… I *will* have a son and heir!"

He raked a hand through his hair, drew in a breath, and won the battle to gain control of anger. He could not believe his sister-in-law had tried to hide from him. When he learned that she had birthed a son, he knew his plans would finally come to fruition. To that end, it was essential that he retain a calm demeanor. No one must suspect what he was about to do.

Walking to the corner of the room, he yanked on the bellpull. "Yes, sir?"

Trentchester stared at the footman without speaking. When the younger man did not show any sign of unease, he realized he should have thought to use one of his servants for this unorthodox task. "You're new here."

Squaring his shoulders, the footman replied, "I was hired a fortnight ago."

Deciding the indirect approach would be best, Trentchester began to question the man, pleased to discover that, prior to being hired as footman, he'd been a laborer. From the look of him, he could hold his own in a fight, and without a doubt subdue a recalcitrant woman. Which suited Trentchester's needs. The time for direct action—and a bit of force—was required.

"And are you happy with your position here?"

"I am, sir."

He almost asked the man's name, then realized it did not matter. After the man performed the duty required of him—to steal his nephew—Trentchester would see that the footman disappeared…permanently. Then there would be no one to question that the boy was his son, except his sister-in-law.

Bloody hell, he would have to amend the task to include Millicent's abduction—and that blasted, interfering Miss Stanhope! Once the two of them were in his clutches, he would see to it the Stanhope woman disappeared permanently, then he would use the infant to bend Millicent to his will. He needed a wife capable of bearing his children. First he'd have to plan an accident to befall his wife.

Trentchester nearly laughed—there was actually no need to worry about his own wife, as he did not plan to marry his dead brother's wife...yet Millicent would merely be the vessel that would carry his *true* son once he impregnated her. Mayhap he would tolerate his wife for a bit longer until the babe he planted in Millicent was born. The idea appealed and had him realizing that if he disposed of his wife permanently, he *could* marry Millicent. A fertile wife was preferrable.

"Will that be all, sir?"

Trentchester stared at his servant, but the man did not move, did not quail beneath the hard stare leveled at him. "I have a task outside of your normal duties. You shall be paid handsomely...but you must perform it without hesitation, without question."

The footman did not bat an eyelash. "What do you need me to do?"

⬥

CHAPTER SIX

FLAHERTY WALKED TO the stables, listening to Garahan blather on about the newest additions to Summerfield Chase. For the first week after his injury, he was not allowed to do much at all. Thankfully, for last fortnight, he'd been given tasks…though they were fit for a clerk.

When he was not busy with those duties, he oversaw the twins' visits to the stables until Dr. Higgins was satisfied with his recovery. The lads had been given the daily task of feeding the baron's horses treats. Even the baron's stallion watched for the arrival of Percy and Phineas. But neither of the tasks that Flaherty had been given were fit for a man known for being the duke's cavalier—a man trained in arms and horsemanship! Flaherty was proficient in all manner of weapons, as well as hand-to-hand combat, thanks to his bare-knuckle skills.

Every Irishman worth his salt was an excellent horseman. Given the extra tasks, he had not been able to spend much time speaking with either of the women he'd rescued. Though he had made certain to inquire as to how they fared on a daily basis. He was pleased to hear Millie and her babe were improving daily and Pippa was making herself useful lending a hand wherever needed.

His wounds were healing, but unfortunately, the one to his pride was still raw. It did not help that his cousins felt obliged to ask how the lass had got the jump on him—at least three times a day! How in the bloody hell was he supposed to move on and forget the incident if Garahan and O'Malley reminded him of it at every turn? When they were not deviling him about the lead balls removed from his hide, they were demanding to know when in the bloody hell he planned to apologize to the lass and put her out of her misery!

Her misery? He was the one who been shot and then suffered through the extraction of the lead balls and subsequent stitches.

Flaherty set those thoughts aside, as they only served to rile him. His mind drifted toward Millie and her babe. They had certainly become the talk of the manor house. Flaherty sensed that knowing her babe was safe had helped Millie recover from the journey after his birth, and the birth itself. Having her here had brought Flaherty a newfound appreciation for what a woman suffered during—and after—childbirth.

These last three weeks, Millie had been following the physician's orders, staying in bed and then gradually being allowed to rise for a few hours at a time, joining the women in the sitting room and nursery. The rest and care had added much-needed color to her cheeks and a smile to her face. Much was made of little Roarke's lusty cries to be fed. How quickly the babe had taken to not only the baroness, but Caro and Prudence as well.

He smiled thinking of the twin hooligans' reaction to the babe. Upon meeting him, Percy and Phineas had immediately started talking to the babe. They seemed dejected when the babe didn't respond. They listened to Millie's explanation that her son heard sounds and would come to recognize their voices. Hearing that little Roarke would learn from watching and listening impressed the two little boys.

His smile faded as his thoughts returned to Caro, Prudence, and the baroness. Those three women were going to be the death of Flaherty. Their pointed stares had turned to glares the longer he went without actually speaking to the lass. It was as if they blamed *him* for holding a grudge—and not Pippa for tripping and accidentally shooting him!

How could he hope to forget how the curvaceous lass with the blue-gray eyes and angel-blonde hair had tried to kill him, if he was constantly being reminded of what happened by his cousins?

"Are ye not listening?" Garahan demanded.

"What?" When his cousin glared at him, Flaherty shrugged. "'Tis no wonder that Millie and her babe are thriving here. The credit goes to not only her ladyship, but also to yer Prudence and O'Malley's Caro. It does me heart good to know that they are safe, and getting enough to eat to regain their strength. Though once ye start talking about the lass, I stopped listening."

"She's been trying to speak to ye, and constantly asks after yer health and recovery."

Flaherty tried to ignore yet one more layer of guilt heaped upon his head. "I'm late for me shift."

"Ye aren't supposed to be on duty until Dr. Higgins releases ye."

"Me replacement sprained his ankle chasing after his recalcitrant cow. There is no possible way for him to guard the perimeter. Ye know well that a large part of our duties is to dismount and chase after intruders on foot if need be. I'm on me way to report in for duty. O'Malley will no doubt be asking another of the men we've trained to add to our numbers when— and if—trouble comes calling. Until and unless he finds someone to take me place, ye know where to find me."

"Ye're a horse's arse, Dillon!"

"Better that than a horse's cock, like yerself." Flaherty dodged the fist aimed at his chin, and felt the glancing blow to his jaw. "Well now, seems ye're out of practice. Is O'Malley too busy to go a few rounds with ye?"

"Shut yer gob!" Garahan growled. "Himself has enough to do, given that he and his lordship have been putting their heads together to come up with a plan to add another layer of protection around Summerfield Chase. Shifting men around to cover yer duties has put a strain on things. He's looking to hire on a half a dozen new footmen."

"What he needs is a few more fighting men," Flaherty replied.

"Aye, hopefully none with a short fuse like yers," Garahan grumbled.

Blast it all, Garahan knew how to get a rise out of him. Flaherty could not afford to lose his temper, but he was holding on to it by a thread! He knew could get his cousin's attention with a solid right cross, but then Garahan would be obliged to deliver an uppercut. Undoubtedly that would lead to a satisfying few rounds of bare-knuckle fighting, which neither had the time for. God help him, he missed sparring with his cousins… Garahan in particular.

Needing to defuse his cousin's ire, Flaherty asked, "Have ye had a look at any of the men he's taking on?"

Garahan scrubbed a hand over his face. "Ye're like a thorn in a man's hide!"

"Have I been one in yer arse, Ryan?"

Garahan snorted. "That ye have been, ye bugger. And to answer yer question, I have taken the measure of a few of the men. There's one in particular that looks like a possibility to either add to our guard…or keep a close eye on. That's without knowing the man's qualifications, temperament, and whether or not he would be willing to put himself in the line of fire to protect the baron and baroness, me wife, and O'Malley's."

"And don't be forgetting Millie and her babe."

Garahan waited a beat, then added, "And Pippa."

Flaherty pointedly avoided uttering her name. "Aye, her as well."

"Ye may be recovering from yer wounds, but have ye given a thought to easing the lass's suffering? She blames herself."

"She was the one holding the blunderbuss," Flaherty reminded him.

"When did ye become such a heartless blackguard?"

Flaherty gaped at his cousin. "Heartless? Blackguard?"

"Ye heard me. Only a man without a heart would let the lass

wallow in guilt. Mrs. Green mentioned that she barely eats."

The layers of guilt Garahan just piled on top of the ones Flaherty had been carrying were close to suffocating him. "When was the last time she ate a full meal?"

"Do ye care?"

Flaherty reached for Garahan's throat, but his cousin was quick on his feet and moved out of range. "'Tisn't just the lead balls that Dr. Higgins dug out, nor the threads he used to close the wounds that pain me."

Garahan eyed him and sighed. "'Tis yer fecking pride. I'd be feeling it meself, were I in yer boots."

"Then ye understand why—"

"Ye'll want to stop there, boy-o. I may understand the nick to yer pride, but Pippa is suffering. That ye'd let that brave lass go without the sustenance she needs is unconscionable!"

Bile sloshed in Flaherty's gut. He ignored the queasy feeling and demanded, "Why did ye not tell me the lass wasn't eating? She's a little bit of a thing and needs to eat just like the rest of us."

Garahan held Flaherty's gaze for a moment before asking, "What do ye plan to do about it?"

"Nothing until me shift is over."

"And then...?"

"I mean to see that she eats. Food has been offered without strings. She'll eat, or I'll know the reason why!"

Flaherty opened the door to the stables and stepped into the semidarkness. It was just past dawn, and the sun had yet to reach the windows to illuminate the interior. Old Ned looked over his shoulder at him and slipped the bridle on the gelding without speaking.

The stable master had never been anything but genial since Flaherty arrived at Summerfield Chase. The man communicated on a different level with the baron's horses, and every one of them thrived under his care. Something must have happened that Flaherty was unaware of. "Is something wrong with one of the horses? Can I help?"

His question went unanswered as the man kept his back turned.

Surprised that the stable master did not reply, Flaherty sensed that something was seriously wrong. "'Tisn't St. George, is it? The stallion is like family to his lordship."

Old Ned paused and shook his head. "You have no idea what you have done, do you?"

"I have never mistreated any one of the fine horses in his lordship's stables, or anywhere else for that matter."

The stable master started to walk away again, but Flaherty followed and reached out to put a hand on the man's shoulder. "Tell me what I've done wrong, and I swear I'll fix it."

Rheumy eyes locked on Flaherty. "You mean that, don't you?"

"I always say what I mean."

"That's what Miss Stanhope is afraid of."

Flaherty's gut roiled. "Garahan just mentioned that she's not eating, and I—"

"You are the reason she's heaped guilt on top of the worry that she will not be able to keep that man from stealing Millie's babe."

"What man? What do you know about Millie and her babe?"

"I knew Millie's mum, and what a fine lady she was, having worked for Millie's grandfather."

"I had no idea. Is that why when they ran and they headed here—the Borderlands?"

Old Ned sighed. "Aye. With Parliament in session, she had no one else beside Miss Pippa. That poor woman is carrying the weight of the world on her shoulders while trying her best to protect Millie and her babe."

Flaherty fought to contain the spark that would set fire to his temper. "'Tis why I brought them here, to safety."

"Are all Irishmen as thickheaded as you?" the stable master demanded.

Flaherty snorted. "'Tisn't that we Irish are thickheaded at all.

We just need ample proof before we make up our minds."

Instead of the reaction Flaherty expected, the older man gave a fierce frown. "How much more proof do you need that Miss Pippa did not mean to injure you? If you had tripped and fallen, your weapon would have gone off, same as hers."

"Ah, but I wouldn't have fallen backward because I never retreat!"

"Isn't that what you've been doing by refusing to speak to Miss Pippa? The least you can do is listen to what she has to say, and open your black heart and forgive her!"

That was the second time in less than a quarter of an hour that Flaherty had been accused of having a black heart.

With that, the stable master turned his back on Flaherty— again—and led the gelding out to the enclosure.

Shocked at the way Old Ned had spoken to him, Flaherty realized that he should have been listening to Garahan all along. His cousin had been adamant that Flaherty speak to the lass. His pride had been battered yet again, what he could not discern was why. He had done nothing wrong! 'Twas past time he made amends, spoke to the lass, and eased her guilt enough that she would eat.

God help him—his ma was right. His stiff-necked pride would be his downfall!

PIPPA WAS SMILING as she descended the servants' staircase. She'd enjoyed spending time in the nursery's schoolroom getting to know the twins. Percy and Phineas were inquisitive, energetic little boys, who repeated everything they heard with relish. Some conversations were beyond their comprehension, but they still repeated them verbatim. She shook her head, remembering something Percy had overheard one of the stable lads say and repeated. Some things were best left unsaid, but she appreciated knowing that they trusted her as someone they could repeat everything they overhead to, without fear of her chastising them for eavesdropping.

Her thoughts still on the entertaining pair, she stepped into the kitchen, and hit a wall of muscle. A deep grunt was followed by a strong arm wrapping around her. She needed to thank whichever guard she'd run into, but was afraid by the silence that followed the sound that it was Flaherty.

"'Tisn't safe not to look where ye're going, lass." He dropped his hands and took a step back from her.

It had been days since she'd seen him, and longer than that since he'd willingly spoken to her. Staring at the top button of his waistcoat, she murmured, "I knew where I was going."

His snort of derision had her bracing for the harsh words that would surely follow. When he remained silent, she dared a glance up and caught a look of abject misery in the depths of his sapphire eyes. Was it pain from his injuries, or had something happened to his brothers? Caro and Prudence had been filling her in on the men who made up the duke's private guard when she joined them in the nursery daily to watch the twins and keep Millie company.

Hoping to ease some of his troubles—not add to them—she placed a hand to his forearm and felt the muscles tense. Before she could form the words, he said, "Surely ye understand that knowing and looking are not the same."

"Yes. I understand." She pinched herself, needing to know that she wasn't in the middle of a daydream—Flaherty was speaking to her. Pippa wished the chasm between them were not so wide. With each day that passed, his refusal to speak to her had cut deeper. It wasn't that she wanted to be absolved, but she wanted him to accept her apology. Without that, she would never be able to move past the hurt she had caused him.

"Mr. Flaherty, I'm—"

"'Tis just Flaherty."

The depth of his voice and the heat pouring off him scattered her thoughts. She blinked and tried to recall what she had been about to say. Drawing in a deep breath to clear her mind, she found herself distracted by the scent of him. Hay, leather, horse and... Pippa inhaled again, this time holding her breath to untangle and discern each scent. Ah, yes, rosemary, with an underlying hint of sandalwood...

Strong hands gripped her upper arms. "Breathe!"

She blinked and realized she'd been concentrating so hard on identifying the layers of scent that she'd forgotten to exhale. She did so, but then had trouble inhaling again.

"For the love of God, woman, breathe!"

"Can't," she rasped, pounding on her chest, hoping that would help.

"Bloody hell!"

The room darkened around the edges until there was just a tiny pinpoint of light in front of her before the darkness swallowed her.

CHAPTER SEVEN

FLAHERTY SCOOPED THE lass into his arms and held her to his heaving chest as Mrs. Green bustled into kitchen and gasped. "What happened to Miss Pippa?"

"I have no idea. We were having a conversation, then she stopped, drew in a breath and, I swear to ye, 'twas as if she forgot to exhale."

The cook stared at Pippa's chest. "She's breathing now. Hartshorn should bring her out of her faint." She reached into her apron pocket and drew out a small vial.

Flaherty was grateful that the cook had taken to carrying a vial around with her after the first time Lady Phoebe fainted unexpectedly—before it was discovered she was expecting. Relieved, he asked, "Should I set her down?"

"That's not necessary. If you would just hold still for a moment?" Mrs. Green opened the vial and waved it beneath Pippa's nose. Her dark lashes fluttered for a moment and then she slowly opened her eyes.

"Ye scared the life out of me, lass. What made ye forget to breathe?"

Pippa closed her eyes and shook her head in answer.

He was about to order her to tell him when the cook suggested, "Carry her to the room at the end of the hallway. She can gather her composure there without prying eyes."

"Will ye be staying with her to ensure she's not going to faint again?"

The cook shook her head. "I've got to pull the scones out of the oven, put the next batch in, and prepare the midday meal." As an afterthought, she said, "Pippa has been tired these last few days. It's either from the strain and worry she's been under, or her loss of appetite."

"I can't just leave her there. What if she stands too quickly, becomes dizzy, falls and cracks her head open?"

Mrs. Green studied him for a moment. "You're right. You should stay with her until you are assured that she is steady on her feet. Should only take a half an hour or so."

Flaherty wondered why Pippa wasn't opening her eyes. Her breathing appeared normal, not rushed or unsteady. "Lass?"

She scrunched up her face and squinted, but did not answer or open her eyes.

"Fine. I'll take her to the room next to the pantry. But ye'll need to tell O'Malley or his lordship where I am and why I'm not at me post."

"Thank you," Mrs. Green said. "Everyone has been so concerned about Pippa. A little time to herself may be just the thing she needs."

Flaherty felt the lass tremble, and his protective nature snapped into place. 'Twas his fault she'd been reduced to a state where she was not eating. Could lack of food affect the brain to the point where a person couldn't remember to breathe on their own? Had the lass been sleeping at night, or lying awake worrying?

Garahan was right. He needed to speak to the lass, and though it scraped his pride to do so, he'd forgive her...and mean it.

He heard the telltale hitch in her breathing—a prelude to a bout of tears—as he carried her down the hallway. "Hold on, lass. We're almost there. Ye can cry all ye want once I close the door."

Her eyes shot open. "Oh, but you cannot close the door! There is no chaperone. What will people think?"

"If they've half a brain, they'll be thinking ye fainted, need yer rest, and no one else is available right now to watch over ye but meself." He stared at the woman. She'd been the bane of his existence since he stopped to lend aid. Now he was starting to wonder if there wasn't more to what he felt for her. Had his stiff-necked pride been ignoring what his heart had been trying to tell his brain?

"Servants talk," she whispered. "I cannot have a blot on my reputation and still protect Millie and little Roarke. By association, her reputation will be ruined, too, and that I cannot allow. Millie is my dearest friend. Losing her husband nearly broke her strong will. For the last few weeks, I have watched her blossom as a mother. Her darling babe is gaining weight and filling out. He's thriving. They both are. I cannot do anything that will bring harm to them physically, emotionally, or to their reputation. She needs a strong man to protect her, though she refuses to accept that she does. Mayhap she doesn't need a man protecting her because she has me."

"What about what *ye* need?" Flaherty asked as he shoved the door open with his shoulder and strode into the room. "Ye obviously need a keeper, if ye aren't eating." He gently laid her on the cot and noticed the dark circles beneath her eyes. "Aren't sleeping either, are ye?"

"Whether I am or not is hardly your concern."

"I'm thinking ye need someone strong to protect ye, too."

Pippa bit her lip and closed her eyes. A lone tear slid from the corner of her eye, followed the curve of her cheek, before it disappeared beneath her ear. When the second tear clung to her lashes, Flaherty pulled his handkerchief out of his waistcoat pocket and blotted her tears. "Don't cry, lass. Surely yer da will have arranged a marriage for ye by now. Ye have to be at least seven and ten summers."

Instead of soothing her, his comment had the reverse affect. She snorted and opened her eyes. "Twenty summers."

"Are ye now? What of suitors? Sure and ye've had them lining the block in front of yer home waiting for a chance to offer for yer hand."

The lost look in her eyes unmanned him. Had the lass been ignored? With her curves, faery eyes, and angel hair, how was that possible?

"Is yer father holding out for a man with a title for ye?"

"I'm tired." She started to close her eyes to avoid answering him.

But Flaherty wasn't having it. He needed to know if they should be expecting her intended to arrive at any given moment. "Ye'll answer me question. 'Tis a matter of courtesy to his lordship and her ladyship to know if yer intended will come knocking on their door demanding to know if we've been taking care of ye while he searched for ye."

She shifted on the cot and pushed herself up. Crossing her arms beneath her generous bosom—distracting him—she grumbled, "If you must know—"

"I must."

"I do not have an intended. My father has been speaking to two titled gentlemen, but I won't have either one of them."

"Why not? What's wrong with them?"

"Both are nearly thrice my age. One is cadaverously ancient, the other so overweight that I cannot imagine a marriage to either gentleman lasting six months before I'd be a widow."

"Ye have a wild imagination, lass. What da in his right mind would marry off his beautiful daughter to a man three times her age?"

"Mine," she rasped. "Papa wants to see me settled with a man who is older and of some consequence..." She added in a soft whisper, "And able to tame my wild heart."

"I didn't catch that last bit, Pippa-lass. What did ye say?"

She clenched her jaw.

"Come now, lass—if I'm to be of any further help to yerself and Millie, we need honesty between us. What did ye say?"

Pippa's gaze shifted away from him. She answered, though

her voice wavered, "And able to tame my wild heart."

He leaned close and cupped the side of her face in his hand. "Wild hearts are courageous and loving. Ye have me word that if ye were married to me, I wouldn't try to change ye, lass."

Her eyes widened and her lips parted. Need shot straight to Flaherty's gut. He pushed past it to find the honesty the lass deserved from him.

"Why would I, when I think ye're perfect the way ye are…well, except for the small matter we already agreed not to discuss again."

She lifted her gaze and studied him for a few moments. "You mean that, don't you?"

"I always say what I mean. Tell me now, what do ye want, lass?"

"Truthfully?"

His gaze locked on hers. In that moment, he made a decision—even if someone should discover them alone together behind a closed door, he would marry her. "Aye, lass. We'll only have the truth between us."

She hesitated, then rasped, "Love."

"I take it ye don't love either of the two men ye mentioned." At least, he hoped she didn't, because she would belong to him. His mind was made up—he just needed to find the right moment to tell the lass they would be married to save her reputation, thereby saving Millie's and her son's as well.

Pippa's ire returned with a vengeance. "I do not! They only offered for my hand because I have a dowry and am young—they plan to use me as a broodmare."

Flaherty nearly choked on his laughter.

"It is not a laughing matter!"

"Then ye'd best find another way to describe yer meaning. Ye could say both prospects are 'wanting a family.'"

She shook her head, but did not say anything, leaving Flaherty to wonder if that was her way of disagreeing.

"Do ye always speak plainly?"

"I do try."

"And there have been no other men that have come court-ing?"

The lass's face flamed. She clenched her hands in her lap and stared down at them. "With four older brothers who found fault with every man who even looked at me with interest? If anyone did come courting, they soon forgot about asking for my hand, facing the wall of sibling disapproval."

He placed a knuckle beneath her chin, urging her to look at him. "Then 'tis a good thing yer brothers are not presently in Summerfield-on-Eden."

"If they were, they'd have ganged up on you and knocked you unconscious by now."

Flaherty smiled. "Ah, they could try, but they'd never make it past the perimeter guard—which is either meself, Garahan, or O'Malley. Have no fear, lass, we'll protect ye." He paused and held her gaze, "I'll protect ye with me strength, me heart, and me name. Marry me, lass. I know someone who'll obtain a special license if I ask. Then ye'd never have to worry about yer reputation, nor Millie and Roarke's."

Her blank expression had him wondering: had no man gotten close enough to press a kiss to the back of her hand, or her cheek?

"Yer angel hair and faery eyes draw a man's attention, lass. Yer curves are a distraction. I'm man enough to admit ye've turned me heart and me head—despite the blow to me pride."

To his consternation, tears welled up, magnifying her eyes, before spilling over. He placed the handkerchief he still held into her hands.

"Dry yer eyes and tell me the whole of it, for I'm not believ-ing there's a man alive who would not go in search of ye."

"I'm overweight."

He snorted. "Sure and that's a lie. I've held ye in me arms, lass. Did ye not hear what I said about yer curves causing a distraction? God help me, Pippa, yer curves would slay a man at ten paces. There's not a bit of ye that is overweight."

She shook her head. "If I were only five inches taller, my figure would be acceptable to Society. I may even be able to catch the eye of a man under the age of forty."

"Sure and ye've caught me eye, lass. Would ye discount me opinion because I'm closer to thirty than forty?"

She pinned him with her gaze. "You do not have to make fun of me, Flaherty. I know what I look like."

"I'm not having a laugh at yer expense. Once I got past the ill-fitting coat ye were wearing as part of yer disguise, I had to concentrate *not* to notice yer curves. Ye've the figure of a goddess, the face of an angel, and the lips of a temptress."

"You're mad!"

He leaned in close and slid an arm around her. "I'm thinking ye may be right. If I am, 'tis yer fault. Shall we test yer theory?"

Pippa furrowed her brow. "And just how do you intend to do that?"

Eyes locked on hers, Flaherty lowered his lips until they were a breath away from hers. "Like this." He molded his mouth to Pippa's and drank from the sweetness of her lips. Need slashed through him, urging him to taste more thoroughly. He traced the rim of her mouth with the tip of his tongue. She gasped at his touch, giving him the access he needed to explore the flavor, and test the texture, of her mouth. Passion wrapped in determination, forged in the fire of her convictions... That was what Miss Phillipa Stanhope was made of.

She slid her arms around his neck and leaned into him. The fullness of her breasts pressed against his chest and shattered his control. He pulled her onto his lap and crushed her to him, kissing her until she went slack in his arms.

"Bloody hell!" Flaherty rasped. "Don't faint again!"

"That's what I was going to say," a familiar voice said from the other side of the room.

Without looking over his shoulder, Flaherty grumbled, "Go away, Garahan."

"I've been sent to tell ye Mrs. Green's preparing a tray for the lass, but it appears that she may be needing more hartshorn."

He looked down into the dazed expression on Pippa's face. "She's made of strong stock and didn't faint. Just a bit overwhelmed by me manly form."

"Is that what ye're calling it now? When I approached the room, it looked as if ye were trying to swallow her whole. Though me eyes could have been deceiving me. Either way, I'm thinking ye'd best be ready to do right by the lass and marry her."

Flaherty ignored his cousin to tuck a silken lock of hair behind Pippa's ear.

"According to Mrs. Green, ye were worried about the lass regaining her equilibrium after passing out," Garahan said. "Last time I checked, kissing the breath out of a lass tends to have the opposite effect. Though now I'm thinking ye had another intention entirely. Have ye asked his lordship for the special license?"

Unable to bring himself to let go of her, Flaherty stayed where he was with the lass on his lap, her head resting against his heart. "To answer yer second question, I will. As to the first question, I have watched her and tended to her, just as I told Mrs. Green I would. Can ye not see the roses in her cheeks?"

Garahan sighed. "I have. Are ye blind, Flaherty, or do ye realize what's just happened?"

Flaherty pressed his lips to the top of Pippa's head and inhaled. *Heather.* The scent suited her as well as the lavender had when she'd stood defiantly in front of the broken-down carriage garbed as a coachman. He reveled in the taste and feel of the woman in his arms. "I've just kissed Heaven."

Garahan snickered. "Ye'd best prepare yerself, boy-o."

Pippa stirred in Flaherty's arms. "We Flahertys are always prepared," he grumbled.

Garahan grinned. "Well then, I'll be telling his lordship that ye want him to procure a special license for ye."

Flaherty felt the spit dry up in his mouth. "Just because I kissed the lass and mentioned marriage, does not mean I plan to marry her right away!"

One moment Flaherty was holding the lass on his lap, the next, she was standing in front of him with her hands on her hips, while his ears were ringing, and the side of his face stung.

"Well then!" Garahan chuckled. "Now that that's been settled, I'll be telling his lordship he'd best put a rush on the special license."

The stinging slap to the side of his face should not have been a surprise. The lass may be tiny, but she packed a wallop, and he admired her, though he truly had not meant to insult her with his comment about not marrying her immediately.

Before he could tell her as much, her fiery temper was let loose. "You rogue! You cannot just kiss a woman until you've muddled her mind, and in the next breath state that kissing doesn't lead to marriage! I was raised to believe that it did."

Flaherty took a moment to gather his wits about him—but would not admit that that was what he was doing. "'Tisn't what I said at all. I said—"

"It is what you *meant*."

"Faith, ye're going to be a handful." He stared at her until his guts untied and a feeling he had not experienced before filled him. Flaherty couldn't find the words at first, and then he realized it was euphoria—his heart was filled to overflowing with respect, admiration, and love for the lass. Truth be told, there was a healthy bit of lust as well. "I'm thinking ye've gotten the better of me too many times, lass."

Face flushed, eyes bright, Pippa narrowed her eyes to glare at him. "I have no idea what you are talking about."

Flaherty held up one finger. "First ye shoot me." She started to speak but fell silent when he held up a second finger. "Then ye try to bribe me with coin to protect yer friend and her babe."

"That is not what—"

He all but shoved three fingers in her face. "Then ye're slapping me face and telling me what ye think I said—which ye heard all wrong." When she continued to stare at him, he sighed. "Tell her, Garahan."

"I'm not getting in the middle of yer argument." His cousin turned his back on them and strode from the room. "I'm going to speak to his lordship about the license!"

"'Tis a discussion…not an argument," Flaherty called after him.

"What are you talking about?" the lass demanded.

Flaherty gambled with the fates and took a step closer to her. "When a beautiful woman, like yerself, bests a Flaherty, there's only one thing to be done." The fire in her eyes confirmed what he'd discovered the moment their lips met. There was passion simmering beneath the surface, just waiting for him to fully unlock it.

"Oh, and what is that?" Pippa asked.

"Ye'll have to marry me." Before she could disagree with him, he pulled her into his arms and kissed her again. This time lingeringly…tenderly. "If ye haven't figured it out yet, lass, I've been fighting with me pride. Though I've already apologized for it, I'm adding that I'm sorry to have been avoiding ye. A man's pride is important to him. Flahertys have it in spades."

When she didn't speak, he kissed her forehead, her cheeks, and the end of her nose before capturing her lips once more. This time, he kissed her until his desire for her had him by the bollocks. Pippa melted against him and sighed. "If you stop talking, and communicate with your drugging kisses, I may let you convince me."

He held her close and rasped, "I forgive ye for shooting me, lass, and should have told ye that weeks ago. Can ye let yerself forgive me for holding on too tightly to me pride, when I should have been listening to me heart?"

She cupped his cheek. "Do you promise that you do not hate me and won't hold what happened against me?"

"Ye have me word, lass. I could never hate ye—I could be mad at ye for a time, but never would I hate ye."

"And?" she prompted him.

"Ye have me word of honor that I will not hold what happened against ye." When she stared at him, he smiled, and this
time he prompted her, "And?"

Pippa blinked. "And what?"

He shook his head. "Faith, I'm thinking yer head is as hard as
mine. Say yes."

"Yes?"

He kissed her breathless. "Ye'll be a beautiful bride."

"Bride?"

"Did ye not just say yes?"

She frowned. "You asked me to."

Flaherty grumbled, "Have ye forgotten me question already?"

"Which one?"

"The one where I asked ye to marry me!"

Pippa shoved out of his embrace, put her hands on her hips,
and reminded him, "You told me you would *have* to marry me."

"I asked ye, lass."

"No. You did not. Your exact words were, 'Ye'll have to marry me.'"

Flaherty blinked and could not feel the top of his head, sure
and that was a sign he'd lost his mind. "Well now, 'tis the same
thing."

Pippa put her hand in the middle of his chest to keep him
from wrapping his arms around her again.

"Ye *are* going to marry me, lass. Aren't ye?"

"Not truly a proper proposal, but much closer," she said.

Flaherty put his hands around her waist, pulled her flush
against him, and nipped at her lips. "Will ye, lass?"

"Will I what?" she whispered.

"Will ye put me out of me misery and marry me?"

"I will not let my pride dictate my thoughts or actions like
some other people. But since you asked nicely, I will consider
your offer."

"I told ye we should not have left Flaherty alone with the
lass," Garahan grumbled, returning with O'Malley. "He mucked

it up and will need more time convincing her."

"Well now," O'Malley replied, "he's nearly healed and will be going back to his duties. I'm thinking once everything begins to settle down around here, Flaherty will have a chance to ask her again."

"I won't be needing advice from either of ye buggers!"

"But she didn't say yes," O'Malley reminded Garahan.

"Ah, but the lass did say she'd consider it," Garahan pointed out.

"Can't a man have a private discussion—" Flaherty began, only to be interrupted.

"I waited until ye were through kissing the lass," Garahan said.

Flaherty scrubbed a hand over his face. "Could ye not have waited longer?"

Garahan's incredulous expression was his answer. "Given the way ye were kissing her, I'm thinking I asked his lordship to get yer special license just in time."

Flaherty raised a hand to wave his cousin away. "Forget I asked. Now then, lass—"

"Ye should be calling her by her first name, if ye're intending to ask for her hand," O'Malley said.

Flaherty was resigned to the fact that his cousins were there to see that he would marry the lass to protect her reputation. Even the baron's loyal servants would talk—he had to promised to protect her with his name. Letting his frustration show, he told her, "Flahertys don't beg, lass." The hint of temper in her eyes pleased him. He added, "And I won't be waiting long for yer answer."

"Pippa!" The fear in Millie's voice had them all turning toward the woman running toward them.

"What's wrong?" Garahan asked.

"Is it yer babe?" O'Malley added.

"Easy now, Millie," Flaherty said. "Take a moment to catch yer breath."

Pippa pushed past the men and grabbed hold of Millie's outstretched hands. "What's happened?"

Millie stopped crying long enough to answer, "Roarke's gone!"

CHAPTER EIGHT

PIPPA COULD NOT believe the change that came over the three men. It was as if someone had snapped their fingers. As one, the men reacted. Gone were the congenial cousins who had been teasing Flaherty. In their place were hard-eyed, determined men who were ready to take action to find the intruder and rescue Millie's babe.

Holding on to her friend to steady her, Pippa listened as O'Malley gave orders. Garahan and Flaherty listened, and immediately sprang into action. Garahan strode outside to alert the stable hands trained to protect and defend Summerfield Chase. Flaherty left to organize the footmen who had been trained to do the same from inside the manor house.

Once he'd given the orders, O'Malley approached Millie. Tears streamed from her eyes, but she didn't make a sound. It broke Pippa's heart to think of the agony her friend was suffering. She tightened her hold on Millie.

"While the men are mobilizing the staff and stable hands we've trained, I need ye to tell me exactly what happened—what ye remember." O'Malley pulled a handkerchief out of his pocket, handed it to Millie, and waited until she dried her eyes. "Can ye do that?"

Millie nodded. "I had just fed Roarke," she rasped. "He let out the loudest burp and closed his eyes."

"Then what happened?" O'Malley asked.

"I laid him in the cradle and needed to sit for a few minutes. I must have fallen asleep because the next thing I knew, I heard him crying—but it sounded as if he was in the hallway!"

The glint in O'Malley's eyes was fierce. "Did ye wake up then?"

"Yes."

Pippa was proud of Millie for maintaining her composure. She was still grieving for her husband, and now this! She wanted to tell O'Malley to get moving and find Millie's babe now. Whoever stole Roarke could have already left the baron's estate. But she held her tongue, sensing that it would only delay the men finding the babe if she interrupted.

"What did ye do next?"

"I checked the cradle—he wasn't there." Millie paused. "The door had been closed because I didn't want Roarke's cries to disturb her ladyship. But now it's open."

O'Malley clenched his jaw. "Did ye hear footsteps or yer babe crying again?"

She shook her head. "No, but I cannot imagine whoever took him would have gone down the main staircase."

Pippa could not help but add, "Unless he had half a brain."

O'Malley surprised Pippa by turning to her, asking, "Who would have reason to steal Millie's babe?"

Without hesitation, Pippa answered, "Her brother-in-law."

"Her ladyship shared yer story with us, but not who ye were on the run from. As her ladyship's condition has been delicate because of the injury she received…" O'Malley fell silent, cleared his throat, and continued. "'Tisn't me place to discuss how or why with ye. But because of what happened a few months ago, involving Garahan's wife's family, Garahan, Flaherty, and I have been vigilant in protecting her ladyship. Which is also the reason why the baron or the baroness should have us told us the crucial bit of information of who would try to steal Mrs. Trentchester's babe!"

Pippa and Millie shared a glance. "We were only thinking of the baroness, and your wife—Garahan's too," Millie said.

"By not telling us who is headed our way? No one has managed to slip past our guard," O'Malley said. "The only servants hired recently were footmen hired by his lordship!"

Millie reacted as if she'd been struck. Pippa was not about to let the giant of a man intimidate Millie, and snapped, "We have our reasons for believing he would not be able to follow us here. Your temper, and Flaherty's, have convinced us that our decision was sound."

"Sound?" O'Malley bit out.

Pippa shifted her hold on Mille, grabbing her by the hand, as she eased her friend behind her, once again taking a protective stance, shielding her from O'Malley's anger. "How dare you raise your voice to Millie! She did not want Flaherty to bring us here, but because of his injury, she agreed. Only in the last few days has her strength returned to normal. And now…now, when the only reason Millie has for carrying on without the husband she adored—their babe—has been taken from her, you let loose your anger? It would have been better if Flaherty had left us to our own devices!"

O'Malley reared back as if he been struck. He tensed, and Pippa could all but feel him reel in his temper. His expression smoothed to a neutral one as he raked a hand through his hair and blew out a breath. "Forgive me, Millie. I reacted without thought to yer condition or what ye'd been through these last months, and specifically the time ye have been with us."

Millie squeezed Pippa's hand and moved to stand beside her. "You are forgiven, Mr. O'Malley, on the condition that you think first before you speak."

"Before you agree with Millie," Pippa added, "I have another condition. You will only confide in Garahan and Flaherty, and—" O'Malley opened his mouth to speak, and Pippa raised a hand. "I'm not finished." He fell silent, though his eyes and the set of his shoulders indicated his frustration. "Given the closeness we observed between the baron and baroness, I have a feeling Lady Phoebe already confided in her husband. You must understand that it could do more harm than good if you speak Millie's brother-in-law's name freely."

Millie nodded. "Servants—even well-meaning ones—are wont to talk with their contemporaries on their free afternoons or days off. His name could be overheard at the inn in the village, or the blacksmith's shop, or at the vicarage. Word travels fast via the mail coach, and those of the *ton* with nothing else to do to while away their hours repeating the latest *on dits* they hear. We cannot take the chance that if he has not already reached Summerfield-on-Eden, that he will be en route after hearing the mention of his name."

O'Malley waited a moment and glanced from Millie to Pippa and back. "Ye have me word of honor. Before ye think to ask, I'll be telling ye me cousins and meself have sworn an oath to the Duke of Wyndmere to protect his family with our lives. His Grace's sister and brother-in-law are under our protection."

Millie's voice quavered as she thanked him. Pippa's didn't as she asked O'Malley, "How well do you know the men and women serving on the baron's staff?"

He started to answer and then hesitated. "Most have served the baron before he wed the baroness. After Percy and Phineas came to live here, there was a footman from their father's household who was hired on shortly thereafter. Why?"

"It was a question that came to mind just now," Pippa answered. "I am quite certain yourself, Garahan, and Flaherty have been vigilant in your protection of the baron and baroness." O'Malley held her gaze without speaking, prompting Pippa to add, "We shall hold you to it. Millie and I will not rest easy until we hear the same from Garahan and Flaherty."

In answer, the guard grunted. He bowed, spun on his heel, and stalked along the hallway.

"Thank you, Pippa."

Pippa hugged Millie, undone by the tears flowing freely now

that Millie did not have to put on a brave face and hold them back. "Have faith. O'Malley and the others will find Roarke. Do you hear the footsteps above us? They do not sound frantic, but purposeful. O'Malley and Flaherty will lead the footmen searching inside the building, while Garahan and the stable hands search the grounds."

Millie used the handkerchief O'Malley had handed to her to blot her tears. "I do not intend to stand back and wait while everyone else looks for Roarke. I intend to help—but where do I start?"

"Where do *we* start," Pippa said. Then she had an idea. In a heartbeat she knew it would be an untapped resource the men had not mentioned. But with what she had observed in the short time she'd been at Summerfield Chase, there were two little boys would be eager to lend a hand—always in the thick of things, they were bound to have seen or heard something. "I have an idea."

"Tell me!"

Pippa shook her head. "'Tis best if we keep it between us. Follow me—we'll use the servants' staircase."

Millie followed. When Pippa paused to listen at the bottom of the stairs, Millie paused. And did so again, halfway up, and at the top. Pippa opened the door a crack and stopped. Millie waited.

Pippa grabbed hold of her friend's arm. "Hurry." As they were reaching for the door to the largest of those dedicated to the nursery—the schoolroom—it opened.

"Psst! In here!" a young voice urged.

Pippa pulled Millie inside the room and closed the door behind them.

"We know who took your babe," Phineas said. Something about the boy's demeanor had Pippa wondering if he knew more than just who had taken Roarke.

"And where he was headed," his brother added. There it was again, that slight shifting of eyes away from Pippa when both boys spoke to her.

Resolved to get to the bottom of what they were hiding,

Pippa quietly studied the boys' faces. "Tell us what you know."

"Then you can show us where he went," Millie said.

Pippa was surprised at the sudden change in her friend. Gone was the uneasy woman who'd let O'Malley lash out at her verbally. The old Millie was back now. And Pippa was so proud of her. They fell in line and followed behind the brothers.

"I will be forever in your debt," Millie told the twins, "if you can help us find my son."

The boys left the schoolroom and stopped in front of the door to the servants' staircase leading to third floor. "He went in here," Phineas said.

"The staff have rooms on the floor above us," Percy added. "I don't think Flaherty and the others know about the hidden passageway, though. You can only get there through the fireplace."

"In the room at the front of the house," Phineas said.

"How do you two know about the hidden passageway?" Millie asked.

"Or where it leads?" Pippa's belly churned with worry as she and Millie followed the twins through the door and up the staircase.

"We explored the whole house the first few days we were here," Phineas bragged.

"We weren't scared of the spiders or the dark!" Percy added.

Pippa stopped halfway up the stairs. "Spiders?"

"Dark?" Millie asked.

Phineas reached for Pippa's hand at the same time that Percy reached for Millie's. "Don't worry," Phineas said.

"We'll protect you," Percy assured them.

In the lead, Phineas reached the top, and slowly twisted the knob before pausing to put a finger to his lips. When everyone signaled that they understood, the boy opened the door a few inches and peered through the crack.

Pippa did not want the boys to come to harm if it was indeed Trentchester who was hiding upstairs with Roarke. "If you and

Percy wait here, I'll go to the room at the end of the hall."

"You are not going to search for my son without me," Millie declared.

"How will you find the passageway in the fireplace without us?" Phineas demanded.

"It's hidden!" Percy reminded them. "Besides Phineas and me, only one…"

Pippa knew then that someone else knew about the passageway. She'd bribe the information out of the boys later, with teacakes if she had to. Pretending disinterest, she said, "We cannot all go. We'd make too much noise and cannot afford doing anything that would startle whoever has kidnapped Roarke—someone has to go for help."

Phineas and Percy shared a telling look before they put their heads together and whispered furiously. Finally Percy said, "Fine, but I get to be the leader next time!"

"All right," his brother agreed.

"Promise?" Percy asked.

"On my honor."

The look on young Phineas's face, and the tone of his voice, reminded Pippa of the duke's guard. She knew then that, despite their youth, these two were determined to help find the missing babe. The only worry was whom were they trying to protect.

Percy held out his hand to Millie. "My brother and I agreed that you should stay behind with me. Phineas wanted to go alone, but decided that Pippa should go with him."

Millie protested, "But I'm Roarke's mother."

"And more likely than Pippa to gasp or cry out when you see your son," Percy said.

"How did the two of you come to that decision?"

"Shush, Millie!" Pippa warned. "He'll hear you."

Phineas looked from Millie to Pippa and back. "Never mind that now. Percy will stand guard, while Millie goes for help."

"But I'm his—" Millie began, only to close her mouth when both boys shook their heads.

"Mums are more protective of…" Phineas's voice trailed off and shoulders slumped.

Percy put his hand on his brother's shoulder. "*Most* mums."

Pippa sensed there was a sad story here. It would explain why the boys were in the care of their cousin Prudence, living with the baron and baroness. She would wait until Roarke was found and ask another time. "Millie, the longer we stand here debating, the longer Roarke is being held captive. Please do as the boys ask. Go for help. If you do not run into Flaherty on the second floor, just go into the nearest room and tug the bellpull. Then go into the next room, and the next, and next, and do the same."

Millie stared at Pippa for a moment before catching on to the plan. "The men will know something is wrong if all at once the servants are being summoned from all of the rooms on the second floor. The baroness is normally resting at this hour, and you and I usually stick by one another's side."

"Exactly," Pippa said.

"Cousin Prudence and Caro have become thick as thieves since O'Malley married Caro. They are always together too," Percy told them.

"Hurry, Millie," Pippa urged. Without another word, Millie slipped through the door. Pippa had to strain to hear the sound of her friend's footsteps.

"Follow me," Phineas said, leading the way along the hall until they reached the door to the last room. Unlike the others, it was open. He beckoned Pippa to lean close and whispered, "Stay behind me, and don't talk."

The confidence the boy exhibited warmed her heart. It encouraged her and gave her hope that they would find the man responsible for stealing Roarke—and more importantly, Millie's sweet babe! "I will."

Phineas stealthily lead the way into the room. Once they realized it was empty, they made their way over to the fireplace. "Duck," he ordered her.

Pippa obeyed, avoiding smacking her forehead. Once they

were inside the fireplace, she was able to stand. "What do we do now?"

Phineas didn't bother to answer her question. He ran his hands across the bricks until one moved, and a soft click sounded. Pippa's mouth hung open as the back wall of the fireplace swung in. "This way!" he announced.

She marveled at the boy's bravery, dashing into the darkened passage. She wished for a moment that she were the same age as the twins, and that *she* had discovered the secret passage. But no time for those thoughts now—she could hear the faint sound of an infant crying.

"Hurry!" Phineas rushed along the passageway.

Heavy footsteps sounded behind them. "How close are we to the other end of the hallway?"

"More than halfway."

Relief filled her as she hurried to keep up with the boy. "Those footsteps behind us must be help arriving. What if they can't get to us in time?"

Phineas sighed. "They won't reach us before we get to the kidnapper." He grabbed hold of her hand. "Listen!"

Roarke was screaming. Her heart ached for Millie's babe, who was letting his abductor know at the top of his lungs that he was ready to eat. "He's hungry and knows whoever has him is not his mum!"

"That's in our favor," Phineas replied. "Percy and I have noticed how Roarke squirms when he's screaming to be fed. He seems too young to be able to move like that, but he does."

"You have spent a bit of time getting to know Roarke if you have noticed that." Pippa was beyond grateful to have their assistance. "The kidnapper will have to stop or he'll lose his grip on Roarke, and trust me, he won't want to do that."

Phineas stared at her, looking as if he were going to ask a question, then the boy's expression changed. "We have to hurry, then!"

As young as Phineas was, he must have realized the reason

the kidnapper would not harm Millie's babe…money! Pippa picked up her skirts so she wouldn't trip and rushed after the boy, wondering if he was holding back vital information. The sight ahead of them in the passageway nearly stopped her heart—she recognized the man as one of the baron's footmen! Pippa knew she had to not only rescue Roarke, but protect young Phineas from harm. But how?

Her worst fears were realized when the man cocked his head, spun around with Roarke in his arms, and slowly smiled. "My cousin told me to expect you, Miss Stanhope." He let his gaze sweep from the top of her head to the tips of her half boots. "You are not even half as pretty as this babe's mum." Staring at her breasts, he added, "Though you are endowed where it counts."

Mortification heated her face, and she felt Phineas shift beside her. Hoping the boy didn't know half of what the man insinuated, she placed her hands firmly on the boy's shoulders. He trembled beneath her touch. She sensed it was anger—not fear. Needing the brute to know she was not cowed by his slur or suggestion, she demanded, "Give me that babe."

The miscreant tilted his head back and roared with laughter. "I like my women fiery!" It echoed down the passageway, and Pippa prayed it had been heard by their rescuers. Roarke's eyes widened as he cried louder. The kidnapper had the babe tucked in one arm while he lunged for Phineas. He missed when the boy shifted out of the way.

Pippa felt the large hand, and crushing grip, squeeze her upper arm. He yanked her toward him. Fearing for Millie's babe, and the boy, she yelled, "Go! Get help, Phineas!"

The man laughed again, watching the boy dash along the passage. "We'll be long gone by the time they reach this spot." He shoved Roarke at her. She pulled the babe protectively to her breast, whispering nonsense words to soothe him. Amazed that he quieted so quickly, she was about to say something, but the kidnapper held a knife in front of her face. "You'll do as a hostage." He leaned closer. "Know this: I'll gut you if anyone tries to stop us."

The terrifying fear that gripped her ebbed, in its place acceptance that she would give her life to protect the babe in her arms. In that moment, she fully understood the vow Flaherty, Garahan, and O'Malley had promised the Duke of Wyndmere, and the wherewithal it took to give it. Without hesitation, she would do the same for Millie and her babe.

"As long as you let me care for Roarke, I will do whatever you say."

The man snarled. "Start walking and don't stop until you reach the door at the end of the passage."

"Then what?" she asked.

"I'll tell you when we get there!"

Pippa tamped down the fear of what would happen to the precious babe in her arms, should she fail. Resolved that that would not happen, she prayed for the strength and fortitude to do so. A calm settled over her, and she knew her prayer had been heard. As they reached the door, shouts and the sound of pounding footsteps could be heard from somewhere behind them.

The knife pricked against her shoulder—the kidnapper was tall, or she would have felt it nearer her waist. He urged her into the enclosed staircase. In that moment she fervently prayed to Roarke's namesake—his father—and to the archangels: Michael, Gabriel, Raphael, and Uriel. Surely her prayer would be heard by those fierce warrior guardian angels! Her mum had told her that the angels carried huge swords in the battle to defeat Lucifer and the powers of evil.

Partway down the stairs, her gown slipped from her hand, and she nearly lost her footing. Tucking Roarke tight against her, she curled herself around him, prepared to fall. At the last moment, she was saved by the kidnapper, whose huge hand clamped on one shoulder. A heartbeat later, she felt the painful reminder—the tip of the blade—that she was under his control. But Pippa refused to let him get away with stealing her best friend's babe! She shifted to loosen his hold on her, and the blade sliced through the fabric of her gown, into her shoulder. Shock had her gasping for breath, while the pain intensified when he yanked the knife out of her.

"You'd best watch your step," he warned, "unless you'd rather I gut you now."

She managed to catch her breath, and bit the inside of her cheek to keep from crying out. It took the rest of her reserves of strength to say, "I… I'll be careful."

They reached the bottom of the steps, but she couldn't reach for the door without dropping her precious burden. "I can't open it. The babe… My shoulder…"

He shoved her aside. "I'll open it!"

Pippa felt another shaft of agony and the warmth of her blood where he pressed against the wound. She fought to hold on to consciousness as he shoved the door open.

Her captor cursed as he was yanked off his feet and hauled through the doorway.

"Bloody hell! Curtis? Hang on to the bleeding bugger, Garahan, while I grab hold of the babe and the lass!"

Flaherty's voice sounded farther away. He wouldn't just leave. Would he? "Flaherty, please don't leave us."

"Ah, lass, I'll not be leaving ye in this lifetime." Hands tried to dislodge the babe from her arms, but she'd managed to tighten her grip.

"No! You cannot have him." Her strength was ebbing along with her grip. She sank to her knees and cried out, "Millie!"

"Where is she?" she heard her friend ask. "Where's Pippa?"

Flaherty knelt by Pippa's side. "Here now, lass. Let me have Roarke—he's wanting his ma."

"Pippa! It's Millie. Thank God he's safe. You can let go now."

At the sound of Millie's voice, Pippa let Flaherty take the babe from her.

"Thank you, Lord," Millie rasped. "And you too, Pippa!"

"Phineas and Percy helped." It was a chore for Pippa to speak.

Her head swam, and her stomach churned. "Don't feel good."

"Dear Lord," Millie cried out, "is that blood? Flaherty, Pippa's bleeding!"

FLAHERTY FELT THE warmth of the lass's blood where he'd touched her upper back and fought the urge to roar in anger. The blackguard would pay for stabbing Pippa! He lifted his gaze from the woman in his arms and met Garahan's. The anger in his cousin's eyes settled his own, allowing Flaherty to question the footman who been hired by the baron six months ago, thinking it would be a comfort to Percy and Phineas to see a familiar face among the staff. He struggled against Garahan's hold, but was unable to break it.

"If ye cooperate and tell us how you know about Pippa, Millie, and her babe, we might ask the constable to go easy on ye."

Curtis shrugged.

"Did Trentchester hire ye?"

"Thinks he knows everything," the footman scoffed. "My cousin and I had a plan to blackmail him." He glared and Flaherty and Garahan. "Would have worked too, if not for the squire's brats and that meddling woman!"

"As God is me witness," Flaherty growled, "whatever ye did to the lass, ye'll suffer threefold."

"Ye're a traitor," Garahan murmured. "And ye planned to double-cross the man who hired ye."

"Trentchester didn't hire me—my cousin works for him and has been robbing him blind for the past few months, while the man was busy planning to get his hands on that babe!"

Flaherty had to ask, "Does the squire have anything to do with this?"

"Another toff who thinks he's smarter than those of us who shine his shoes."

"Ye're no smarter that Trentchester or the squire," Garahan murmured.

"Ye'll pay the price for kidnapping Millie's babe, and the attempted murder of Baron Stanhope's daughter."

Garahan cracked his knuckles. "Before we turn ye over to the constable, we'll be teaching what it means to honor a vow."

The man stilled, but to his credit, did not quail. Flaherty touched his right hand to his heart, leaving a bloody handprint that he'd swear he could feel, but it wouldn't show against the black. No matter—he'd felt the warmth of the lass's blood, and knew that Garahan saw and recognized his gesture. "We'll need Mrs. Green and Mrs. Chauncey's help. Someone has to fetch Dr. Higgins."

"Aye, Dillon."

"And get that bloody blackguard out of me sight before I rip his heart out!"

"Done!" Garahan dragged the would-be kidnapper down the hallway.

"Lass, can ye hear me? The blood has spread from yer shoulder near to yer waist. Tell me where he stabbed ye, so I can stop the bleeding!"

Praise be to God and all his angels, she was still conscious. "Left shoulder. Hurts…" Speaking must have been more than she could handle. Fear's sharp talons grabbed hold of Flaherty as she went limp in his arms. He yanked the two spare cravats out of his coat pocket, folded them, and pressed them to her shoulder. Her weak cry told him she wasn't unconscious—yet—just dazed with pain from her wound.

The twins rushed to his side, each boy placing a hand on one of Flaherty's shoulders. "Is she hurt bad?" Percy asked.

"Bad enough," Flaherty answered honestly.

"I wanted to stand at her side and fight," Phineas whispered. "She told me to go for help…I should have stayed, as neither one of us trusted Curtis—but he said he'd…"

Flaherty looked at Phineas. "A man of honor knows fear isn't the way to earn a man's—nor lad's—trust. We know what's in yer hearts, lads. Ye saved yer cousin, and then the baroness, a few months ago."

"But it was our father—"

"Ye're not responsible for the actions of yer da, nor yer ma. Remember that." Flaherty pulled one foot out from beneath him, and the boys dropped their hands as Flaherty levered himself to his feet. "Ye two brave lads best come with me. Ye can tell me the rest of what ye know later. I need to carry the lass down to the healing room."

"By the pantry," Percy said.

"Aye, lad. Open the staircase door," Flaherty ordered him. "Quick, now."

Percy did as Flaherty asked and clattered down the staircase with Phineas hot on his heels. Unease settled into the marrow of Flaherty's bones. He could still lose the lass. If not from blood loss, infection. He needed to see the blade the bastard used on Pippa. He doubted Curtis had had the time to wipe it clean, but what was more of a worry was whether it was rusted.

The bloody blackguard—Squire Honeycutt's former servant—had obviously threatened the two lads into silence during the few months he'd been a part of the baron's staff. Garahan would want to take a sizeable piece out of the man. Flaherty would let him have a turn…after he beat the truth out of him.

When they reached the bottom, he sent the footman standing guard by the rear entrance to tell Garahan he needed to see the blackguard's blade.

"We spread a clean bed linen on the cot," Phineas said as Flaherty carried Pippa into the room.

"Mrs. Green already put two pitchers of water on the long table over there," Percy added.

"Good lads." Flaherty carefully laid the lass on her side, but when she started to slump over onto her back, he shifted her until she lay on her stomach. "Bring a handful of those linen squares here, lads. We need to keep pressure on her wound."

Percy's eyes filled, and a tear escaped Phineas's guard, as they handed him a few of the cloths. Ignoring the sight of her blood on his hands, Flaherty shook his head. "I've got the order all wrong, lads. One of ye fetch the large bowl from the sideboard. Hurry now."

"Why?" Percy asked.

Frustration filled him. He wanted to be two places at once. Here with the lass, putting pressure on her wound—and in the outbuilding beating the shite out of the footman who'd stabbed her, thinking he could steal Millie's babe!

"Hold the bowl still. I need to put the sodden cloths in the bowl. There's a lad, Percy. Don't be afraid, and don't be touching the blood now."

"You are," Phineas reminded him.

"That I am, but I'll be washing up soon." Flaherty nodded to Phineas. "I'll take those cloths now. Thank ye, lads. Ye've done a grand job." Their worry washed over him, adding to his, but Flaherty dug deeper to find his own calm. "I've handled wounds like this more than once. Don't worry about Pippa—'tis the loose weave of the fabric of her gown that allowed the blood to spread so far so fast. She'll recover and be just as feisty as she was before."

"Promise?" Percy asked.

"On your honor?" Phineas added.

"On me honor, lads." Footsteps hurrying down the hall had Flaherty thanking the boys. "If ever I need help catching another kidnapper, the two of ye will be the first I enlist. I'm in yer debt."

Phineas nodded. "Can both my brother and I can ask a special favor of you?"

"Aye, lads—later, though."

"Anything?" Percy asked.

"Ye have me word"—Flaherty saw Phineas open his mouth, and knew what lad would ask—"of honor."

The boys hesitated when Mrs. Green asked them to go and wash their hands in the alcove off the kitchen. "We have to tell

Pippa something first," Phineas said.

"It's important," Percy added.

"Very well, but hurry," the cook said. "Miss Pippa needs that wound cleaned!"

Flaherty's heart filled with pride as first Phineas and then Percy quietly approached the lass, whispered something, and kissed the top of her head. "We're trusting you to protect her for us, Flaherty," Phineas said.

"It's me duty and me pleasure, lads." Their worry was a living, breathing thing, and Flaherty wanted the brave lads to remember their part in the rescue. He reminded them that without their help, there was no telling how far away the blackguard would have gotten with the babe and Pippa. What was more, they'd identified the kidnapper and his connection to the man Millie and Pippa feared enough to risk both Millie and her babe's lives on their desperate journey to the Borderlands.

Before Mrs. Green ushered them out of the room, they approached him. Flaherty thanked them again, pleased that they'd finally begun to trust that Flaherty knew what he was talking about, and that Pippa would recover. He said to them, "I could use yer help in the personal matter that involves the lass. Can I count on ye?"

"Yes!" Percy said.

"Depends on what it is," Phineas replied.

Flaherty studied the young boy's expression before adding, "'Tis important to the lass's future and me own."

Phineas finally answered, "Then you can count on me, too."

"I've asked the lass to marry me, but she said she's thinking about it. Will the both of ye put in a good word for me for the next fortnight—or however long it takes her to heal and say yes?"

The two grinned. "Every day!" Percy repeated.

"For a fortnight," Phineas said. "I think she's sweet on you."

"Do ye now?"

"Boys!" Mrs. Chauncey entered the room and motioned to the twins. "Beth is in the kitchen ready to help you wash up before you have your tea and cake."

"Thank you, Mrs. Chauncey! Bye, Flaherty!" the twins chorused, then departed.

Mrs. Green sighed. "They mean well and are good boys."

"We have them to thank for noticing the footman on the nursery floor. They're heroes and deserve more than tea and cake."

"And I have just the thing in mind," the baron said from where he stood in the doorway.

"So ye heard?"

The baron nodded. "I trust you were going to fill me in."

"Aye, after Pippa's been tended to." Flaherty waited a moment, then asked, "What kind of a surprise do ye have in mind for the twins?"

"A surprise of the four-legged variety—Phoebe and I discussed giving each of them a pony with Prudence, who thought it was a wonderful idea." Sensing the tension in the room, Summerfield asked, "How bad is it?"

"'Tisn't good, but I won't know how deep she's been stabbed until Mrs. Green lends a hand with cleansing the wound."

The cook frowned at Flaherty. "You will not be in here while I do," she told him. "It would not be proper—I need to expose her back."

"As she's going to be me wife, it *is* proper," Flaherty insisted.

"That's wonderful," Mrs. Green said.

The baron smiled, and asked, "When did she accept your offer of marriage?"

Flaherty shrugged. "As soon as she wakes up."

CHAPTER NINE

"BLOODY HELL!" FLAHERTY said. "She's coming around."

"Almost finished," Dr. Higgins remarked. "Keep her still."

"Don't move, lass, just a few more stitches to go." At her guttural cry, Flaherty wished God had listened and allowed them to trade places while she was unconscious. He'd been stabbed more than once, clubbed, shot… The list of injuries was long. His body was meant to protect and defend. The lass's wasn't.

"Last three, Miss Stanhope," the physician said. "Try to hold still."

The hand gripping his own was wet with the lass's tears. "Phineas and Percy wanted me to tell ye they're each saving an iced teacake for ye," he said.

PIPPA TRIED TO smile at the thought of those two little boys saving cake for her, but needed to clench her jaw to keep from crying out again. She held it inside until the physician tied off the last knot. Her stomach roiled as the buildup of bile churned up her throat.

A large bowl appeared in front her and Flaherty urged, "Get

rid of it all, lass. Ye'll feel better for it."

She was in too much pain to be embarrassed as she cast up her accounts. Now they were even—although she'd only heard Flaherty heaving and had not witnessed the deed. When a cool cloth was offered, she wiped her mouth and deposited it in the smaller bowl that magically appeared in front of her face.

"Are ye ready for a sip, lass?"

"Of water, yes. Please."

"Whiskey or brandy first?" the Irishman asked.

"Whiskey." It took more strength than she had thought required to shift around so she could sip from his flask and not spill it.

"Are ye wanting another sip?"

"No, but thank you. Is the doctor still here?"

"Aye." Flaherty rose to his feet. "Dr. Higgins, yer patient would like a word."

Dr. Higgins finished washing his hands and toweled them dry. Rolling down his sleeves, he walked to her side. "You were fortunate that the blade did not go as deep as Flaherty feared— given the amount of blood. Though the detailed list that I will leave with Mrs. Chauncey—"

"I'll be taking that list, as Miss Stanhope is me intended. We're to be married as soon as she's on her feet again."

Pippa looked from the physician to Flaherty and narrowed her gaze at the blue-eyed warrior angel who had stayed with her while she was being sewn back together. "I thought you heard me say that I needed to think about it."

"That ye did, lass. But before Dr. Higgins arrived, ye thanked me for taking care of ye and how much ye enjoyed the kisses we shared."

She gasped. "You were not supposed to mention that in mixed company."

"Words were not necessary, lass. 'Twas easy to discern how much ye enjoyed kissing me back."

"That is not what I meant, Flaherty. Could you *please.* stop talking about kissing?"

"I do believe Miss Stanhope should be on her feet in a few days, but should not attempt to get off the cot, or chair—even if she feels well enough to sit in one—without assistance," the doctor interjected. "A fall could do extensive damage to her injury, not to mention the additional blood loss."

"I shall see to it that the lass will stay put. I'll be acting as her nurse—"

Pippa stared at Flaherty. "Are you mad? The only way that will happen is when I marry you."

Flaherty grinned. "There, Dr. Higgins. Ye see, the lass is madly in love with me and cannot wait to marry so I can take care of her injury."

Pippa wanted to smack the hardheaded man. "Flaherty?"

The auburn-haired giant ignored her.

Dr. Higgins chuckled. "I can see that. These are special circumstances indeed."

"Exactly what I mentioned to his lordship when he told me he's obtaining the special license for us."

She called his name a second time. Again, Flaherty pretended not to hear her.

"Congratulations, Miss Stanhope," the physician said. "I know you and Flaherty will be very happy. Just be sure to listen to him and do exactly what he says."

"I most certainly will not!" She needed the stubborn man to listen to her. "I have no intention—"

Dr. Higgins was pulling on his frockcoat, but paused. "I cannot have you countermanding the instructions I'm leaving with Flaherty and Mrs. Chauncey. The chance of infection and wound fever is quite high, given the state of the blade that was used on you. I do not believe he wiped the blade clean recently. It was crusted with a combination of blood and matter I could not identify without much closer inspection and a special glass lens to magnify—"

Pippa put a hand to her mouth as the whiskey sloshed in her

belly and churned up more bile. Grateful Flaherty was quick on his feet, she emptied the contents of her now-aching stomach a second time. When she tried to lie back on the cot, he helped her do so, shifting her onto her side. "Thank you, Flaherty."

He handed her a damp cloth to wipe her mouth, and used another to bathe her face. "Try to rest, just for a bit, lass. Yer poor belly must still be tender. I'll be stopping in later to check on ye." His expression changed from caring to neutral. "I'll be heading out to our quarters to extract information from the blackguard who dared to stab me wife."

"But—"

He bent and brushed the tips of his fingers along the line of her jaw, interrupting her train of thought. "Mrs. Green will return in a few moments with the herbal she's prepared for ye."

"I have left instructions and the dosage for the laudanum," Dr. Higgins reminded them. "Use it sparingly."

"Aye, doctor. Thank ye." When the physician left the room, Flaherty asked, "Do ye need a dose now, lass?"

Pippa didn't dare put anything else in her stomach. Her heaving had pulled at her stitches. The ache went deep. She couldn't decide which was worse, casting up her accounts or the pain in her shoulder. "Mayhap shortly. Not right now."

He pressed a kiss to the top of her head. "Try to sleep, lass. I'll return in a few hours."

Pippa grumbled, "I'm not in the least bit sleepy."

Flaherty shifted to the side as Mrs. Green entered the room. He nodded to the lass and stepped into hallway. She heard his deep, rumbling voice and knew he was speaking to one of the footmen stationed by the rear door. A few moments later, she heard the rear door open and close and knew Flaherty had gone—he had duties to attend to.

The past few hours seemed like a blur. So much had happened, some of it unreal. From all that she had heard about the duke's guard, she would not have thought anyone would be able to sneak past them to get to Millie's babe. When Pippa saw the rough-looking man, she realized he had not had to get past the duke's men…he was already here! There was one thing she now knew for certain—Grant Trentchester had hired him to steal Millie's babe.

By the time she had replayed the events in her mind twice, she felt exhaustion weighing her down.

Mrs. Green brushed Pippa's forehead with the tips of her fingers. "Flaherty is right—you need sleep."

Pippa had too much to think about—sort out in her head—before she gave in to what her body needed. "I'm not sleepy," she whispered.

She drew in a breath, fighting the inevitable, but did not have the strength to keep her eyes open.

CHAPTER TEN

FLAHERTY NODDED TO the footman standing guard. "If ye need me, I'll be in the outbuilding near me quarters."

"Flaherty, wait!"

He glanced over his shoulder. "Mrs. Green, is there a problem?"

"Not at all," she assured him. "I wanted to let you know that Pippa has finally closed her eyes and is resting. Mrs. Chauncey and I will be taking turns sitting with her."

"Ye're a treasure, Mrs. Green, watching out for the lass for me—and keeping me cousins and meself in scones."

The cook smiled. "It is my pleasure."

While helping to hold the lass still for the physician, Flaherty had felt a burning anger tearing through him. He needed to make the footman pay for daring to harm Pippa. Now that the lass's wound had been cared for, he could concentrate on beating the answers out of him to confirm that Millie's brother-in-law had paid the man to kidnap her babe—and in the process use whatever force was necessary. Curtis would pay for stabbing the woman Flaherty loved.

"Bloody hell… How much time have I wasted while me blasted pride kept me from realizing what me heart was trying to tell me?"

He couldn't wait to get his hands on the man who thought to

steal a babe—for coin! The bloody bugger was fond of using a knife. Flaherty decided if the man wouldn't answer his questions, then he would threaten to use a knife on *him*—stripping off patches of the man's hide until he told them everything he needed to know.

He strode toward the outbuilding but stopped when he spotted O'Malley coming out of the stables. Before Flaherty could ask who was guarding the prisoner, O'Malley asked, "How is Pippa feeling?"

Flaherty answered honestly, "I thought 'twould be a blessing that she was unconscious while Higgins was sewing the wound closed…"

O'Malley grimaced and stated the obvious: "She woke up before he was finished."

"That she did. It gutted me that she was in pain." Flaherty scanned the area between the stables and the outbuilding. "Why aren't ye guarding the prisoner?"

Garahan shouted his name, and Flaherty turned to see his cousin striding purposefully toward him from the front of the manor house. Flaherty could not believe neither of his cousins were standing guard over the scoundrel. That was when he knew something had occurred while he was with the lass. He needed to question the man—nay, needed to beat on the man while he questioned him about who'd paid him to abduct Millie's babe.

"Unless ye want me to bash yer heads together, one of ye best tell me what in the bloody hell ye're thinking trusting the guarding of the prisoner to one of the men we trained. They weren't hired for that type of work!"

"I'll have yer word that ye'll not punch first and listen second," O'Malley said.

Flaherty raked a hand through his hair and gave it a hard tug. "I promise."

"The constable arrived. He and Summerfield are speaking to the prisoner."

"'Tis our job, not the baron's, to question the man," Flaherty grumbled. He pushed past Garahan and stalked toward the outbuilding.

"The baron feels responsible," O'Malley told him, matching Flaherty's stride. "He agreed to hire Curtis when the squire's household servants were let go pending the outcome of the trial."

"He doesn't look like a man I'd want spending time inside with *my* wife," Flaherty grumbled.

"His lordship said he feels responsible for Millie's babe nearly being kidnapped," Garahan added, catching up to his cousins. "His lordship hired the footman based on what me wife had to say, and because Percy and Phineas mentioned he treated them well, too. And before ye ask, aye, without allowing any of us the opportunity to meet the man and question him."

"Bloody hell," Flaherty grumbled. "Curtis didn't need to sneak past us into the house because he was already working here!"

"All the new footmen are trained by Timmons," O'Malley reminded him.

"What of it?" Flaherty asked.

"When I saw Curtis near the servants' staircase earlier, I didn't ask where he was headed. The man had been hired by his lordship, and had already been under Timmons's close scrutiny for the first few weeks he worked here. We've never had an issue before."

Flaherty wanted to shake O'Malley, but would do so after the matter of the fraudulent footman was resolved. "Well, we bloody hell have one now!" Flaherty growled. "The woman I love is lying inside, suffering in pain from being stabbed and having her wound sewn back together!"

The door to the outbuilding opened, and Summerfield walked toward them. "Summerfield Chase has been in an uproar since you arrived with Pippa, Millie, and her babe. And with Percy and Phineas spying on Curtis after they overheard him boasting of coming into coin for a small job that no one need find out about."

"How would Millie, Pippa and myself—or the rest of ye—not notice that Millie's babe was kidnapped?"

"Not what I meant," the baron replied. "Curtis planned to be long gone before anyone knew he was the one who absconded with Millie's babe."

"Well, Percy and Phineas noticed," Garahan said.

Flaherty grunted. "That they did. I'll be forever grateful to them—as will Millie and Pippa."

"I sent for the constable," the baron said. "He will escort the prisoner to the village." When Flaherty remained silent, the baron continued, "This was my doing...my fault. I handled the matter."

"Like ye handled the matter when Lady Phoebe told ye her plan to let herself be kidnapped in order to lure that bastard Stillman out of hiding?" Flaherty asked.

At the baron's incredulous expression, Garahan spoke up. "It may sound like a strike at yer pride, yer lordship, but 'tisn't. Flaherty's brother Seamus, and me brother James, told the tale of what lead to the abduction of her ladyship, and the capture of Stillman's thugs. They were impressed that ye managed to climb on the back of yer horse at all, given yer head wound at the time."

Summerfield inclined his head and rasped, "I would give my life for Phoebe's. What worries me is that she has proven more than once that she is all too willing to do the same."

"Ye're a fortunate man, yer lordship," Flaherty said. He wasn't certain he should ask the question burning in his brain.

His facial expression must not have been as neutral as he thought, because Summerfield said, "Whatever is on your mind, Flaherty, just ask."

"'Tis plain to the lot of us—and our brothers who were assigned to protect Lady Phoebe at the time—that ye have a deep and abiding love for one another."

"Aye, we do," the baron replied.

"When did you know for certain that her ladyship had captured yer heart?"

Summerfield chuckled to himself. "I mistakenly used the word *obey* in the same sentence as the words *cease prattling*."

Flaherty's eyes widened. O'Malley coughed to cover his laughter, while Garahan snorted and said, "Faith, but ye're a lucky man, yer lordship."

"And well I know it," the baron said in a perfect imitation of their Irish brogue.

Flaherty grinned. "And she forgave you right away?"

"Hardly," Summerfield replied. "It was my insistence on riding with the duke's men to rescue her, and apologizing with the offer to strike the word *obey* from my vocabulary, that earned her forgiveness."

"It was that simple?" Flaherty did not think that would be the case with the lass.

"Nay, but we bumbled along until we came to an agreement. We agreed that in the future, we would have a conversation before either one of us left in a huff, or put ourselves in a dangerous situation without first discussing it with one another."

Flaherty's shoulders slumped. "Do ye think there's hope for me?"

The baron placed a hand on his shoulder. "Where love exists, there is always hope. Talk to her. Apologize. Beg her pardon."

"And if that doesn't work?" Flaherty asked.

The baron grinned. "Haul her into your arms and kiss the daylights out of her."

Flaherty may not have liked the idea of apologizing at first, but agreed the last bit of advice was something he could embrace wholeheartedly.

"Take half an hour and go seek her out now. Garahan and O'Malley will find someone to cover the rest of your shift."

"Thank ye, yer lordship."

"Lass?"

"Mmm?"

"Ye need to wake up and drink more of the herbal."

Pippa opened her eyes and stared at the worry on the handsome visage before her. When had she started thinking of him as handsome instead of an irritation? "Did you forget something and have to come back so soon?"

"I'd never forget anything concerning yerself, lass. Did ye sleep well?"

Momentarily confused, she murmured, "I wasn't sleeping."

"I see. I suppose it was someone else in the room snoring when I arrived."

The throbbing in her shoulder intensified, but instead of moaning, she snapped at Flaherty, "I do not and have never snored!"

"Do ye have a sister ye shared a bed with?"

Confused, she frowned at him. "No. Did you forget that I told you I have four older brothers?"

He stared at her for a few moments as if weighing his words. "Why were they not able to come to the aid of Millie and her babe?"

Pippa sighed. "Three of my brothers are serving the Crown—one in the Royal Marines, one in the navy…the other in a capacity he is not at liberty to divulge. My eldest brother is studying estate matters, working closely with my father's estate manager."

"While yer father is in London."

The discussion was taxing, draining what little energy she had left. "Yes. He and Lord Haybrook travel together whenever Parliament is in session."

"Then how do ye know ye don't snore?"

He was back to that question? Lord, his smile irritated her. "I just know."

He chuckled. "I love yer fiery attitude, lass. We'll be a good match, make a good life, and babes between us."

How had he guessed that in her heart of hearts, she wanted a strong man by her side and babes to love? Mayhap he wanted a family too. Though she could not imagine how they would manage it, if the two of them were at cross-purposes more often than being in agreement with one another.

She shook her head. Flaherty was putting ideas in her brain. Because of her overprotective brothers, she had never entertained thoughts of marriage—or a family of her own—before.

"We can marry tomorrow evening if ye're up to it, lass."

The dark and desperate look in his eyes had her wondering just what the man was thinking. The memory of her response when his mouth met hers swept through her. She'd actually moaned and encouraged him! Shaking thoughts of kissing him free, she sniffed, then answered, "I will not marry you until I can stand beside you when we repeat our vows."

Had she lost her mind and said that out loud? She covered her mouth with her hand.

His eyes sparkled and his grin widened. "'Tis fine with me, lass. Ye don't need to look shocked. I'm certain between O'Malley, Garahan, the baroness, and meself, we can quell the talk in the village."

A feeling of dread settled into her bones. "What talk?"

"Ye were in and out of consciousness and fought against anyone but meself trying to hold ye still while Dr. Higgins stitched the wound closed."

Pippa had no idea what to say.

Flaherty inclined his head and continued, "Well then, if ye don't mind that talk has already reached the village—possibly the inn—ye won't mind what they're saying."

She had to concentrate to keep her voice steady when she asked, "What *are* they saying?"

He shrugged. "Mostly the fact that ye were obviously partial to me, as no one else could manage to quiet ye while the physician tended to ye. Then there's the fact that ye did not seem to mind in the least that I've seen yer upper back unclothed."

"I don't remember you holding me. Did you say my back was..." She could not say the word aloud... *Unclothed?* Logically, it must have been more expedient to cut the top of her gown and her chemise off her to tend to her wound. Why couldn't she recall? Uneasy under his potent gaze, she grumbled, "People always assume the worst! I have nothing to hide. My reputation is spotless. Should they not be speaking about that fact that I was stabbed, trying to rescue my friend's babe?"

"That they should," Flaherty genially agreed. "I'm not certain how the details of yer gown being cut from neck to waist made its way to the village. Mrs. Green and Mrs. Chauncey were insistent that they would see to whatever the physician needed to preserve your dignity and reputation."

She struggled, but managed to get her elbow beneath her and lift herself up enough to meet his gaze. "Please tell me that you're joking! Talk like that would be scandalous—we're not married."

"Aye, that is part of what's being said about us. Though the rest no one really credits. After all, your injury was grievous, and I am an honorable man."

"I am honorable, too."

"Aye, lass, that ye are, with a brave and loving heart. Tell me, did ye speak to Millie? Are ye no longer worried about her reputation?"

Her heart sank. How could she forget about Millie and Roarke's reputations? "I must have closed my eyes for a bit longer than I thought." She could not believe she'd fallen asleep. "I haven't seen Millie recently."

Flaherty squatted down beside her cot and tapped the tip of his finger to the end of her nose. "That's because yer lovely faery eyes have been closed for the last four hours."

"Impossible."

"Well now, ye can ask either Mrs. Green or Mrs. Chauncey. Both have taken turns sitting with ye."

There was no use arguing. Pippa had obviously fallen asleep. "Forgive me for arguing with you, Flaherty."

"Call me Dillon."

"Of course…Dillon."

"I enjoy arguing if it ends with yerself in me arms. How would ye feel about sitting up, propped in a chair?"

"I'd like that. I'm thirsty and my stomach is empty."

"Excellent. We'd best let everyone know that ye're awake and wanting yer cup of broth and calves' foot jelly."

Pippa grimaced, managing to swallow her irritation. It warred with feelings of helplessness. She was used to being the one in control and being depended upon by Millie—not relying on a man, *especially* a hardheaded Irishman with eyes that saw through her carefully crafted façade to her very soul. "Thank you, Flaherty."

He swept his arms beneath her and carefully set her on the chair by the cot. Mindful of her injury, he wedged a quilt behind her and urged her to lean her uninjured side against it. "There ye are, lass. How does that feel?"

His attention and careful treatment of her was so unexpected that tears welled up and spilled over. Flaherty brushed them away and kissed her as if she were fragile.

"'Tis a good thing his lordship expects yer license to arrive midday tomorrow," Garahan mumbled from the doorway. "Ye need to let the lass rest, else it'll take twice a long for her to heal."

Mrs. Green arrived with a small tray, and Garahan stepped aside so she could enter the room. "Should you be out of bed?" she asked.

"The lass is hungry," Flaherty answered. "She's ready for the next dose of yer herbal."

"Well now, that is surprising but wonderful news. Would you help hold the cup for her, Flaherty?" the cook asked. "We want her to drink all of it."

"That I can." He locked gazes with Pippa and rasped, "Open yer pretty mouth, lass. Drink every drop."

She didn't bother to argue with him. He seemed to enjoy it too much. The thought lingered along with a question: Did she truly want to marry the man for reasons other than wanting to escape her father's plans for her to wed either one of his elderly contemporaries? Searching her heart, she realized that her feelings for him went far deeper than she had realized. Protecting Roarke from his kidnapper, and vowing to protect the babe with her life, had opened her eyes and forced her to see beyond her stubborn pride.

Yes, she wanted to marry Flaherty…but had more questions.

Did Flaherty truly have feelings for her? He'd seemed to enjoy the kiss he initiated, but given the way females acted around the man, it would not have been his first kiss—though it was hers. She sighed, accepting that she would have to wait until they were alone again to ask one last time if he was serious about marrying her. Then, and only then, would she ask what she needed to know: Where they would live? How many children did he want? Pippa hesitated, worried over the last and most important question in her mind: Would he agree to her unusual terms, or balk when she asked him?

Worry settled on her shoulders, draining her. What other choice would she have if the rumors swirling around the village traveled to the Lake District, where she lived? What would her father say? Would he immediately obtain a special license and marry her off to Lord Hinchman or Lord Ives? There was no other choice for her. Because she and Millie had neglected to inform their fathers of Millie's situation, they had fled without a chaperone, nor escort. Her brothers were bound to find out what she had done, but it would take time to reach them. When they received word, would they pull strings to rush home? And whom would they side with, their father, or herself and Millie?

Faced with the same situation, she would not hesitate to thrust herself to the fore, in a bid to rescue Millie's babe. Supporting her friend and her unborn son had been Pippa's mission from the moment the missive arrived with the news of Captain Trentchester's death. When Millie had confided the veiled threats from her brother-in-law, Pippa's support switched to protection. They had been friends far too long for her to simply ignore the situation. She'd had to do all in her power to continue to protect and defend Millie.

Given the circumstances, what other choice did Pippa have? She would have to agree to marry Flaherty, but only if he agreed to her terms. She intended to see to Millie and her babe's protection *permanently*. What better way to accomplish that than to have Flaherty promise to open his home and extend his protection to include Millie and Roarke? If he agreed to that, Pippa would do whatever Flaherty asked.

Lifting her gaze to meet his, she hesitated until he said, "Ask whatever is weighing heavy on yer mind, lass." He traced the tip of his finger across her forehead. "'Twill give ye wrinkles otherwise."

She licked her lips and tried to ignore the way his eyes turned a deeper shade of blue as he stared at her mouth. He'd definitely enjoyed their kiss as much as she had. "If you can agree to my terms, we could marry tomorrow."

"I'll agree to whatever terms ye want, lass."

"You will? Without knowing what they are?"

"Aye, lass."

"Th...thank you, Flah—er...Dillon. I was uncertain, but hoping you would." From what she knew of the man, she knew he would honor his word. There was something about him that called to her on an elemental level. It began when he'd ridden up next to their disabled carriage and offered his assistance. The size of him, combined with his confident presence, had overwhelmed her, had her defenses going up. His kisses had muddled her mind and stolen her breath. But what would he think once she laid out the terms? Could they build a life together based on that, or would he hold her accidentally shooting him over her head for the rest of their lives?

Pippa knew then that she could not live with her conscience if she did not tell him what her terms would be. There was a slight chance that he would come to care for her, if his kisses were any indication. Mayhap she should try it again, to see if she still had the same overwhelming reaction to his mouth being pressed to hers. "Would you kiss me to seal your promise?"

Flaherty's eyes deepened to the color of a midnight sky. He molded his mouth to hers, sending sparks careening from her mouth to her fingers, from her breasts to her toes. "'Twill be me pleasure to kiss ye, lass, every day. Every morning, midday, and evening for the rest of our lives."

Pippa had to tell him. She eased out of his embrace and licked her lips, savoring the potent flavor of him. When he leaned toward her, she struggled to compose herself. Finally, she put a hand to the middle of his broad chest. "Before you turn my mind to mush, you should know my terms are not negotiable. I will marry you, but you must agree to allow Millie and Roarke to live with us and extend your protection to include them. There is a chance that at some point, Millie will want to live with her father, but until then, I'd like your word that you won't pressure her to to do so."

Flaherty stared at her, as if trying to discern whether she was testing him. "From what I've gleaned while ye've been living here, I do not believe ye would issue such terms without good reason."

Thank God he had not refused outright. "I would not."

"And 'tis clear that Millie fears her brother-in-law."

"He cannot be trusted." Needing to win him over, she added, "You must have noticed that the change in Millie as she recovered from the birthing. Under the protection of yourself, O'Malley, and Garahan, she has started to relax and seem like her old self again. Her babe is thriving, and the fear and the hunted look have vanished from her eyes."

When Flaherty remained silent, Pippa urged, "I know it is a huge favor to ask, but I cannot in good conscience leave her to her own devices. I know the moment I let my guard down, Trentchester will move in and whisk Millie and Roarke away. I could never live with myself if I had the chance to protect my very best friend and her babe and did nothing."

"What about her husband? Is there no chance that he is injured and missing in action?"

Pippa replied, "We have asked our fathers to visit the War Office—they have contacts there that would have the information we seek. Millie has been informed that he died. Not where, nor when or how."

Flaherty nodded. "It would seem that whatever regiment her husband was attached to was involved in something crucial." He paused, studying her face without speaking. Finally, he said, "I think Millie should have a say in this as well. We'll speak to her together. If she agrees, then I will offer a permanent place in our home for Millie and her babe for as long as she wishes. Will that be agreeable to ye, lass?"

Tears welled up and spilled over. "Aye, Dillon. Thank you."

"I could never turn away someone in need—especially yer friend and her infant son. Can ye not understand that I'd do anything for ye, lass?"

"I am beginning to."

He gave a brief nod. "Well then, there's just one more thing, Pippa-lass."

"Oh?"

His lips were a breath from hers when he whispered, "I'll be thinking of ways ye can thank me later, lass."

Pippa blinked, but Flaherty's devastating smile remained on his too-handsome-for-his-own-good face. Needing him to understand that she was not afraid of him, she warned, "I'm no pushover, Dillon."

The intensity in his blue eyes deepened. He slipped a hand behind her head, tilted it back, and stole her breath with a kiss that set off a conflagration inside of her. Dear Lord, what had possessed her to think that she could ever control the man?

When he ended the kiss, an inadvertent sound of distress escaped before she could think to contain it.

"Ah, Pippa, ye have no idea what ye do to me. Do ye?"

Unable to articulate any one of the myriad thoughts trapped in her brainbox, she opened her eyes to stare into the ones she would see first thing in the morning. Every morning. The sculpted lips that lifted into a devastating smile the longer she stared at him. Would he smile at her while they sipped their morning cup of tea before sharing their meal? He would be far too busy with his duties to the baron and the duke to see her midday…or even at teatime. Pippa trembled, thinking of gazing at Flaherty during their evening meal before he took her hand, guiding her to the bed they would share…

"Pippa?"

The sound of her name snapped her from her reverie. This man was dangerous in ways she'd never even considered. How was she supposed to be diligent in protecting Millie and little Roarke if her mind was muddled with thoughts of kissing her husband—well, her husband-to-be—instead of watching for another attack from within?

Warm lips pressed to the middle of her forehead had her sighing. "Forgive me. I was woolgathering," she said.

His self-satisfied smile held the knowledge that he knew what she had been thinking. "If that's what ye'd prefer to call it, I won't be arguing with ye. Now then, lass, shall we tell Millie that ye're awake? She'll be wanting to speak to ye."

Pippa nodded. "You are right. It would only be right to ask Millie—not tell her—what we have in mind. I know for a fact the payment was coming due on the cottage she and Roarke rented."

"Did she not have the coin to pay?"

Pippa bowed her head, murmuring what she feared, but Millie had never confirmed: "The payments Roarke arranged before he left to join his regiment have stopped."

His expression turned lethal for a heartbeat before all emotion was wiped clean from his face. "I have connections through His Grace. We will get to the bottom of what has happened. Until then, Millie and her babe will be under me protection, and therefore that of me brothers and cousins in the duke's guard. All told, there are sixteen of us—including meself." Eyes suddenly ablaze with emotion, Flaherty placed his hand to his heart. "Ye have me word, Pippa-lass, on me honor, me heart, and me life, that neither yerself nor Millie and her babe shall ever be fearful again. Ye will never be cold, nor will ye go hungry again."

"How can you be certain? I have heard and witnessed how dangerous your duties are."

Flaherty brushed her cheek, gently, reverently. "Did ye not hear that ye'll be a part of me family and under their protection as well? I have three brothers, two older—Seamus, Rory—and one younger, Fenton. Four Garahan cousins—including Ryan, whom ye've met. Eight O'Malley cousins—including Thomas, whom ye've also met. Shall I name the rest of them for ye?"

She leaned against him, felt the play of the powerful muscles in his broad chest as she let her body all but melt into his. "No. I did hear you, but my worry got in the way. How could you be so honorable? So willing to take on my vow to my dear friend to protect her and her son? Why are you being so nice to me, when I am the person who shot you?"

Flaherty chuckled. "Well now, lass, ye have a number of attributes that bear exploring…sampling…tasting—once we've wed."

Her mouth fell open, but not a sound emerged. Flaherty was laughing when he called out to the footman in the hallway that Pippa wanted to speak with Millie.

By the time Pippa closed her mouth, and the stain of embarrassment had faded from her cheeks, soft footfalls approached from the kitchen.

"Are ye ready to ask yer friend if she'll accept me protection and offer of a home?"

Pippa studied him for a moment before asking, "Do you *have* a home?"

CHAPTER ELEVEN

London War Office

LORD HAYBROOK PLACED his hands on the Secretary at War's mahogany desk and leaned forward. "I'll have your explanation now, Palmerston! What in the bloody hell happened to my son-in-law?"

Viscount Palmerston rose from his seat. "As it happens, I have news I was about to send to you via private messenger."

"Is this connected to whatever mission you have sent my son Winston on?" Lord Stanhope asked. "I have not received a missive from him in weeks—part of the understanding we had when you strong-armed me into agreeing to buy my second son's colors. You know full well that Winston will be my heir apparent, God forbid, anything should happen to my eldest son, George."

Palmerston frowned. "You know I am not at liberty to divulge certain information without the express approval from the Secretary of State for War and the Colonies."

"Bathurst is a blithering idiot," Haybrook murmured.

Stanhope agreed. "Those of us in the House of Lords, who have sons in the military, know that you are the man who runs this office and Bathurst is the figurehead."

Haybrook was visibly vibrating with anger. "My widowed daughter is about to give birth—"

Stanhope interrupted, "She may already have done so, Haybrook."

"We need to know what happened to her husband, Captain Roarke Trentchester."

"Bathurst advised that word had been sent to his widow," the Secretary at War replied.

"She needs to know when his body will be released to her for burial," Haybrook said.

Stanhope turned to glare at the viscount he had been acquainted for more than a decade. "For God's sake, Palmerston, your daughter is married to a captain in the king's navy! Would you not demand the same information for her should your son-in-law perish in battle?"

Palmerston raked a hand through his hair, making it stand on end.

Haybrook shared a telling look with Stanhope, then inclined his head. Stanhope knew his friend grieved for his son-in-law as if he were his son by blood. They had agreed on the way to the War Office that Stanhope would take the lead in the questioning, if the situation warranted it.

It did.

"You may still send the missive to Haybrook, but tell us the contents now," Stanhope said.

"Lower your voice, Stanhope. I'll not have the men in the outer offices listening to you berate me!"

It took a supreme measure of will to rein in his temper, but Stanhope managed it. "Beg pardon, Palmerston. It isn't just Mrs. Trentchester who is of concern here."

"Is it not?" the viscount asked.

"Nay. You may not know it, but aside from my four sons, I have a daughter, Phillipa."

"She is like a sister to my daughter," Haybrook added. "And moved in with her months ago when she received the news about Roarke. I have no idea how Millicent would have navigated her grief without Phillipa."

"I see," Palmerston murmured, though Stanhope could see that the man was rapidly losing interest in the change in topic.

His next words confirmed Stanhope's suspicion. "What does that have to do with the captain's death?"

Stanhope and Haybrook exchanged a glance before scanning the area to ensure they were alone. "It has come to my attention that there have been threats made against my daughter," Haybrook said.

"My daughter has been acting as her protector!" Stanhope ground out. "Neither of our daughters realize that we have been made aware of the dire situation—"

Haybrook interrupted, "Nor that we have recently heard rumors of threats to take my daughter's babe from her the moment she delivers!"

"What's this? What you are intimating is criminal!" the viscount exclaimed. "Who is this person, who would dare such a thing?"

Haybrook's shoulders slumped, and Stanhope replied, "Grant Trentchester—the captain's elder brother."

Palmerston squared his shoulders, and the tone of the discussion changed radically. "I have a contact—retired from the Royal Navy—Captain Gordon Coventry, good friend and London man-of-affairs to His Grace, the Duke of Wyndmere," he said. "He has formed the beginnings of a private force of retired military men, after successfully forming the duke's sixteen-man private guard. The guard is responsible for protecting the duke's immediate and extended family. There are men stationed at the duke's various properties and that of his cousins. From here in London to Sussex, and north to the Lake District, to Cornwall and the Borderlands. Just say the word, and I shall contact Coventry, who will have men dispatched to protect your daughters."

Haybrook was the first to admit, "I did not think you would offer to help in that regard. I was hoping for answers as to my son-in-law's death."

The Secretary at War straightened to his full height—a head shorter than Stanhope and Haybrook. "Though it may seem as if we are ignoring the situation," he said, "we are aware that it is not only our brothers and sons who have returned from war missing limbs, or an eye—or have given their lives in valiant protection of our sovereign king. Their wives and children also suffer from our lack of foresight in doling out back pay, or half pay for widows. We owe it to their families to make up for this lack."

Haybrook extended his hand to Palmerston, who shook it. Stanhope did the same.

"Now then, I'll tell you what I know about Captain Trentchester."

CHAPTER TWELVE

PIPPA WAS GRATEFUL for the quilt that cushioned her back, and wondered when the shards of pain streaking through her wound would begin to fade. She was desperately trying to maintain a modicum of control—but who could, really, after being stabbed?

"I came as soon as Mrs. Green let me know that you were awake. How are you feeling?"

Millie's voice had her looking up. One glance and fear sliced through Pippa. Her friend was here…alone! "Where is Roarke?"

Millie's concerned expression slowly eased into an indulgent smile. "In the nursery with Prudence and his new self-appointed protectors, Percy and Phineas."

"Those lads are crafty," Flaherty added. "They've managed to get the better of meself and me cousins on more than one occasion. Millie's babe is safe with them. Tell yer friend what's on yer mind, lass."

"But I thought you would," Pippa replied.

Millie glanced from Pippa to Flaherty and back. "Well, since I'm here, one of you should." Her easy demeanor changed instantly. "Oh Lord, It's Trentchester, isn't it? He's found us!"

Millie spun, and was about to leave when Flaherty stepped around her, blocking her exit. Reaching for her hand, he gave it a gentle tug to get her attention. "'Tisn't Trentchester. He is not here. Ye're safe and have nothing to worry about."

Pippa rose from her seat, and Millie waved at her. "Please sit down. I'm sorry to have jumped to the wrong conclusion."

"Given all you have been through, you have every right to react in a panic," Pippa replied. "I know I would have if our places were reversed." When Millie remained silent, Pippa beckoned her friend to come closer. "Dillon and I have news."

A ghost of a smile appeared on Millie's face as she sat in the empty chair next to Pippa. "I knew there was more between you than misplaced pride."

"I have no idea what you are talking about," Pippa grumbled.

"Oh, I think you do. We have been friends far too long for me not to suspect what was really bubbling beneath the surface between you and our handsome protector," Millie said. "When's the wedding?"

Pippa's jaw dropped, but she recovered quickly. "What makes you think—"

"I have eyes, Phillipa Rose Stanhope."

"So do I, Millicent Alison Trentchester!"

Flaherty grumbled, "I'm not telling either of ye me middle name—even if ye threaten to torture me."

The gruff expression on his handsome face loosened the knots of worry in Pippa's belly. He would not take no for an answer, and would protect Millie and Roarke with or without Millie's consent.

His next words confirmed it: "Just ask her, Pippa-lass."

Millie gave Pippa her full attention. "Ask me what?"

"Pippa has given a request to me concerning yerself and yer son. I have agreed upon the condition that she ask ye herself. No one should have their lives upended without their consent."

Pippa frowned at Flaherty. "Isn't that what you had in mind when you asked me to marry you?"

"I knew it!" Millie crowed. "Will you wait for the banns to be read?"

"Nay, not with the possible threat still lurking around yerself and yer babe, and thereby me hardheaded bride-to-be—yer self-proclaimed protector," Flaherty said.

Millie waited, but Pippa didn't know how to ask without her friend thinking it was out of pity. Then she decided she would lead with that. "We have never lied to one another."

Millie nodded. "Our friendship is based on trust and the truth."

"As it should be," Flaherty interjected.

Pippa sighed. "I have grieved the loss of Roarke with you, Millie, and have never pitied you. The love the two of you shared was a beacon of hope that I have held in my heart, praying that I would find the same, if only my father would relent in his bid to see me married to an older gentleman."

Millie's eyes welled at the mention of her husband, but she blinked the moisture away at the mention of Pippa's marriage prospects. "Elderly…not older," she corrected her. "I do hope my father talked yours out of arranging a marriage between yourself and Lord Hinchman." Millie grimaced. "Or Lord Ives."

Pippa shuddered, and Flaherty walked over and gently placed a hand on her uninjured shoulder. "Baron Summerfield has obtained a special license on our behalf. We're to be married—as the lass has informed me—as soon as she's recovered enough to stand on her own two feet."

"Tomorrow, then." Millie's knowing look should have irritated Pippa, but her friend knew her far too well.

Flaherty chuckled. "Aye, Millie, tomorrow. But there is the matter of yer safety…and that of yer babe."

"Er…yes." Pippa rushed on, "I accepted Dillon's proposal on the condition that you and Roarke will live with us and will be under his protection for as long as you wish."

Before Millie could refuse, Flaherty added, "With me protection comes the added benefit that me brothers and cousins will add yerself and Roarke to those they protect."

Millie's frown deepened. "But I haven't met your brothers."

"I haven't either," Pippa said, "but Dillon has assured me that should anything happen to him"—she paused to lift her gaze to meet his—"and Lord willing it won't, his three brothers and twelve cousins would protect me with their lives." When her friend remained silent, Pippa added, "I cannot, and will not, marry Dillon unless you and Roarke accept my terms, too."

"Pippa, you do not know what you are asking of Flaherty. He has every right to enjoy your marriage without interference. You have witnessed that my son has a strong set of lungs and would no doubt raise the roof before either of you are ready to begin your day."

"I grew up in a small cottage with me three brothers, da, ma, and grandma," Flaherty said. "Family takes care of family."

"But I'm not your family," Millie reminded him.

"Yerself and yer son will be after Pippa and I wed. Ye're the sister of her heart, and Roarke is her adopted nephew. Don't let yer pride get in the way. Search yer heart, and let it guide yer answer."

A tear escaped, and then another. "Mayhap you should ask Garahan and O'Malley—"

"Ask me what?" Garahan said as he entered the room. "O'Malley and I heard there was a situation brewing that we needed to know about."

"'Tis the same situation I agreed to without having been asked ahead of time the day the both of ye wed," Flaherty said.

"That ye did, Dillon," O'Malley replied. "Caro and I are grateful."

"I never said I wouldn't agree," Garahan grumbled. "The twins were the ones who overheard yer discussion earlier and told me wife."

"And Prudence told ye," Flaherty finished for him. "Then ye agree?"

Garahan walked over to stand in front of Pippa and Millie. O'Malley did the same. They nodded to Flaherty, who put his hand over his heart.

"I pledge to love and protect ye, lass, and will gladly add

Millie and her babe under me protection—and will do so with me life if that is what God demands of me." He nodded to his cousins, who put their hands over their hearts.

Garahan was the first to echo the pledge. O'Malley second.

"Our brothers and cousins would add their vows if they were here," Flaherty added.

"But why? They don't know me either," Millie insisted.

"Ah, but they know Flaherty," O'Malley said. "And if he has pledged his heart and his life to the lass, and his protection to include yerself and yer babe—"

Garahan interrupted, "That is enough for us to add ours as well. Accept our pledge."

"And accept Flaherty's," O'Malley added.

Millie rose from her chair and threw her arms around Flaherty first, then Garahan and O'Malley. "Thank you all, though I will never fully deserve—"

"I'd stop at thank you," Pippa told her.

Millie smiled. "Thank you. What time is the wedding?"

"Aren't you going to ask where we will live?" Pippa asked.

"It doesn't matter where we live, as long as you and Flaherty are happy. Roarke and I will be happy and try to stay out of your way."

Flaherty shook his head. "I'm partial to babes"—the sound of a scuffle coming from the hallway beyond the door caught his attention, and he grinned—"and irascible, interfering twins. Come inside, lads, and hear me good news!"

Percy and Phineas ducked into the room and gave a cheer. "We knew you were stuck on her," Percy said.

"Stuck?" Flaherty asked.

Percy shrugged. "You stare at Pippa all the time."

"And?"

Phineas grinned. "You are either smiling at her, or frowning and grumbling. We noticed Garahan did that when he fell in love with our cousin Prudence."

"O'Malley acted the same way with Caro," Percy added.

"Well, there ye have it, lass." Flaherty grinned as he handed Millie his handkerchief. "The experts on marriage have spoken."

Millie dried her eyes and blew her nose before asking, "Are you certain? I'd rather you change your mind now than after when you have had a chance to live with Roarke and myself."

"I won't be changing me mind." He bent to press his lips to the top of Pippa's head. "I've a feeling the lass will be strong enough to stand by me side tomorrow. All I need to do is speak to his lordship. He said he'll send word to the vicar. We'll exchange vows then."

Pippa reached for Flaherty's hand and held it tight. "Are you certain you will you be able to set aside time to marry me tomorrow afternoon? And that Garahan and O'Malley will be there, too?"

Flaherty raised their joined hands to his lips. "I'm certain. Faith, I'd move the sun and the moon if ye asked it of me, lass."

Pippa snuck a glance at Millie and then looked up into the brilliant blue eyes of the man who had stolen her heart. "You already have, Dillon."

CHAPTER THIRTEEN

PIPPA WAS NOT used to the hustle and bustle that occurred immediately after the men left the room where she'd been resting. Whisked upstairs without being asked, she wondered what reason the baroness had for doing so—not that it was not her right. After all, it was her home. She just was unaccustomed to *not* having any say in the matter. As it appeared was to be the case as far as having to accept charity in the form of another gown to wear.

"Thank you for the offer, but I have yet to wear the other two gowns you lent me," Pippa protested.

"The three gowns I had Beth place in your room are far different—each one would be quite suitable to wear when you marry Flaherty tomorrow." Pippa drew in her breath to object for the second time, and was immediately cut off by Lady Phoebe. "Millie's trunk was delivered late last night," the baroness advised. "Did you think to stitch half a dozen clouts together to wear in place of a suitable gown?"

She wanted to respond that of course she would not think to do so—those were for Millie's babe. Then there was another matter to consider…her voice tended to take on a tone that her father referred to as *petulant*. Pippa was never petulant. On occasion, she had been perturbed, irritated, and incensed—but *never* petulant.

Millie spoke up. "It was my fault. If Pippa wasn't so concerned about spiriting me away from my brother-in-law as quickly as possible, we both would have thought to pack more than a spare chemise and stockings."

"I have slept in my chemise more than once," Lady Phoebe admitted, "when I've been too tired to change into my nightrail. It would make sense to pack that along with the lovely gowns you sewed for your babe. I am not talented with a needle and thread and made a muck of the gown I tried to sew for *our* babe."

"I'd be happy to sew one for you," Millie said. "Do you have any fabric left over from when you made the gown? Batiste would be ideal. Such a soft fabric, and easy to clean."

Lady Phoebe smiled. "Yes, there is quite a bit of unused fabric. That would be so lovely. I haven't thought to make the time to speak to the seamstress in the village about clothes for our babe…"

She trailed off. From her hesitation, Pippa wondered if the baroness would confide what had happened to her.

"I have been…recovering," Lady Phoebe finally added.

Millie spoke before Pippa could. "You do not have to confide what happened. Pippa and I both understand how"—she paused to clear her throat—"er…circumstances and events affect one's sleep and life."

"Please do not feel the need to confide in us," Pippa added.

Percy and Phineas knocked loudly on the open door to the nursery. "May we come in?" Percy asked. "Mrs. Green was telling us that babes grow bigger every day."

"And," Phineas said, "we wanted to know if we could begin measuring Roarke every day and keep a record of it!"

Percy grinned. "For scientific purposes."

"That would be up to his mother," the baroness replied.

"Percy! Phineas!" a voice called out. "Where are you two scamps?"

"Uh oh, it's Prudence!" Percy whispered to his brother.

"She must have discovered the pillows and blankets that we

lumped up on in our beds aren't us," Phineas said.

The boys put their fingers to their lips, slipped into the room, immediately opened the wardrobe that stood in the far corner, ducked inside, and closed the door.

"Are they hiding?" Millie asked.

Lady Phoebe smiled. "It's what those dear boys do."

"Often?" Pippa asked.

The baroness nodded.

Garahan's wife stood in the doorway, an expression of frustration marring her brow. "Have you seen Percy or Phineas? It's time for their writing lessons."

"Yes, actually," Lady Phoebe replied slowly, deliberately. "Though we have been chatting and I do not recall how long ago it was. Five minutes? Mayhap twenty."

Prudence sighed. "If you do see my cousins, please tell them I am looking for them and that we need to start their indoor lessons."

Owing the boys for helping to find Millie's son, Pippa spoke up. "Have you checked the stables? They told Millie and me how much they enjoy their job feeding carrots and apples to his lordship's horses."

Prudence placed a hand to her belly and sighed. "I did, actually, but am feeling a bit peckish this morning."

Pippa rushed to her side and looped her arm through Prudence's. "Come, please sit. You are a bit pale."

Millie laid her son in one of the cradles and walked over to Garahan's wife. "Any discomfort in your abdomen? Cramping?"

"Nothing like that," Prudence answered. "I feel like I'm dragging my feet lately." Lady Phoebe giggled, and Prudence murmured, "Do not ask me—"

"I would never dream of discussing something so personal as to whether or not your husband kept you up…instead of letting you sleep."

Pippa gasped, and Millie covered her mouth, but the merriment in her eyes gave away the fact that she was laughing!

"Millie!" Pippa scolded her.

"Do forgive me, Prudence," the baroness said. "I meant no disrespect, but we are all married ladies here—" She glanced at Pippa. "Well, Pippa will be as of tomorrow afternoon."

Prudence plopped down on the settee beside Lady Phoebe. "If you must know, it wasn't Ryan's fault at all." She slowly smiled. "It was mine."

The baroness patted her on the arm. "It *is* so difficult to keep one's lips to one's self when married to a man who is far too handsome for his own good. Was it the desire in his dark eyes, or when he started to unbutton his frockcoat?" Before Prudence could answer, Lady Phoebe sighed. "Marcus knows removing his frockcoat calls attention to his broad shoulders. His eyes never leave mine as he unbuttons his waistcoat, and by then, I'm unable to string even a simple sentence together. He knows full well his appeal and uses it to his advantage!"

"Ryan knows it's when he removes his cambric shirt over his head and then flexes his pectoral muscles. It positively puts me in a trance, and I'm unable to move while he slowly walks toward me and…" Prudence trailed off.

Pippa suddenly remembered the twins were hiding in the wardrobe. "What you need is tea. Don't you think, your ladyship?"

The baroness turned to look at Pippa, who turned her head toward the boys' hiding place and back. "I could do with a cup and something sweet myself," Lady Phoebe said. "Would you mind giving the bellpull a tug for me, since you are closer? Mayhap Mrs. Green has baked a batch or two of her iced teacakes. It is such a shame that Percy and Phineas aren't already ready and waiting for their morning lessons, Prudence. I would of course have ordered extra and invited the three of you to join us."

"That would have been a welcome distraction," Prudence said. "Even I have to admit that everyone knows how much the boys enjoy their outdoor lessons and try to avoid the indoor ones."

The baroness laughed. "They are definitely outdoorsmen in the making. I can see them with a stable of horses and packs of hounds—though not for hunting." Lady Phoebe turned to Pippa and Millie, explaining, "They love all animals and creatures, especially foxes."

"And since the last time they went to the pond without me…they have been extra cautious around bodies of water," Prudence added.

Pippa did as she was bidden to, and returned to her seat. She was intrigued by the conversation, and interested in hearing more about the boys' hesitance around water, but did not want to upset Prudence in her present condition. Millie had been quite emotional during her pregnancy, and Pippa did not want to cause any distress to Garahan's wife by asking her to explain the reason for the twins' caution.

Millie, on the other hand, apparently wasn't as circumspect. "Forgive me for asking, if you do not wish to speak of it, but as the mother of a son who will be apt to explore all manner of things with or without my express permission, would you mind sharing why Percy and Phineas are cautious? Pippa and I found them to be quite courageous."

Lady Phoebe responded to the knock on the door and requested the tea and sweets.

Prudence glanced at the cradle and then back at Millie. "It was a nightmare, and one I do not care to have to live through again…but I will tell you because I have come to realize that most, if not all, young boys are apt to get into scrapes that only their guardian angels—or one of the men in the duke's guard— can rescue them from."

Interest piqued, Pippa scooted to the edge of her seat, prepared to listen. The tale that unfolded had her glancing at Millie. Her friend's expression was one of resolve and determination. Millie would absolutely dive into a pond after Roarke—when he was old enough to sneak off on his own—if he managed to fall into one!

"And Garahan found you?" Millie asked. "And pulled you both out?"

Prudence nodded, while Lady Phoebe shook her head. "Not at the same time. Really, Prudence, you'll have Millie and Pippa believing the duke's men guarding us were inhumanly strong, able to swim while at the same time rescuing yourself and Percy from the water. Don't forget that Killian O'Ghill arrived in time to help."

Pippa listened to the rest of the story, to how Prudence dove into the water knowing that her gown would weigh her down, hampering her strength. Then of Garahan's rescue of Percy after she had swum across the pond to reach him as he was going under. Then Garahan had had to save Prudence! O'Ghill arrived in time to keep an eye on the boys and helped bring everyone safely back home.

"You love Percy and Phineas, enough to save them at all costs," Pippa observed.

Prudence's eyes glistened with unshed tears, and Pippa had her answer. "As I understand it, you feel the same for Millie's infant son. You took a blade in the back for Roarke."

The knock on the door allowed Pippa the time to swallow past the lump in her throat to reply, "Millie is more than a friend—she's like a sister to me. I would protect her and Roarke with my life if need be."

Lady Phoebe nodded to the footman who delivered the tea tray, then thanked him. "You and Millie share a quality I noticed Prudence and Caro have with myself, and I have with my sisters-in-law—Persephone and Aurelia—and our closest friend, Calliope."

"Oh? What would that be?" Pippa inquired.

"Your are as strong, brave, and true as the men we have married."

"But Dillon and I aren't married—"

"Yet," the baroness said with a smile as she poured out cups of tea. "This time tomorrow you will be." Their conversation was interrupted by another knock on the door. "Enter."

Caro stuck her head inside the room and asked, "Have you seen Prudence?"

Lady Phoebe smiled. "Caro! There you are, and just in time for tea."

Caro smiled, but shook her head. "I need to find Percy and Phineas before I run out of energy."

"Do join us," the baroness said, glancing over her shoulder at the wardrobe again. "I made sure we would have enough for you to have tea with us."

Prudence frowned at the direction of Lady Phoebe's stare, and then slowly smiled. Pippa wondered if she had finally caught on to the fact that her cousins were closer than she realized.

Prudence's next words confirmed that she had. "It is such a shame that we have two large plates of iced teacakes and my poor little cousins are going to be missing out on the scrumptious treat—"

The door to the wardrobe burst open and the boys spilled out on to the floor one on top of the other. Pippa could not contain her laughter at the sight of Percy and Phineas scrambling to their feet, brushing their hands down their clothes, and rushing over to their cousin. "You knew we were here all along, didn't you, Cousin Pru?" Percy asked.

"Of course she did," Phineas answered for her. "You heard the way she raised her voice mentioning scrumptious iced teacakes."

Percy smiled at his brother. "She knows we love them." Turning to the baroness, he asked, "May we join you?"

"We promise to use our best manners," Phineas added.

Lady Phoebe's eyes were damp with tears that she quickly blinked away. It was obvious to Pippa that she held great affection for the twins. "We would love for you two gentlemen to join us, wouldn't we Pippa? Millie? Caro?"

Millie scooted over in her chair and patted the cushion. "There is just enough room if one of you wants to sit with me."

Percy dashed over to sit beside her.

Pippa moved to make room for his brother. "And I have a spot for you, too, Phineas." Once he sat, and the boys had been served half cups of tea with cream and sugar—as the baroness explained, the cups were otherwise too full and easy to tip over—Pippa noticed that all three of the woman who were carrying their first babes were sniffing back tears. The love and caring in the room for two little boys who were not their own, the realization that these three women—from different levels of society—had formed a friendship, humbled her. The lines were blurred. She would feel comfortable here at Summerfield Chase and could imagine life here with Millie and Roarke, Lady Phoebe, Prudence, and Caro as friends…married to Dillon Flaherty.

"Pippa?"

"Hmm?" She glanced at the teacup in her raised hand and blinked. Had she gotten lost in her thoughts while taking a sip of tea? Embarrassed and bit surprised, she lowered the cup to its saucer and placed it on the table in front of her.

Phineas patted her on the arm. "It's all right, Pippa. Cousin Pru did that a lot before she married Garahan."

Percy grinned at his brother. "She still does!"

Prudence laughed. "That's enough of that kind of talk, you two. You are far too young to speak of such things."

Phineas snickered. "Like what we heard you say about Garahan's pectoral muscles?"

Prudence gasped and nearly choked on her tea. Caro patted her on the back, while Lady Phoebe was clutching her belly, laughing so hard she was crying.

"Mind if I ask what is going on in here?" Summerfield stood in the doorway for a moment before striding into the room and over to his wife. "Phoebe!" He went down on one knee next to her. "You're crying. Where do you hurt?"

Instead of answering him, she wrapped her arms around him and held tight.

The baron grumbled, "You'd best answer in the next three

minutes, or I shall be forced to summon Dr. Higgins."

"It's my fault," Phineas said.

"It is!" Percy agreed. "He was the one who reminded Prudence that she mentioned Garahan's pectoral muscles."

Pippa put her hand over her mouth to keep her laughter contained.

The baron eased back and stared down into his wife's smiling face, then brushed the tears from her cheeks and sighed. "I hope you did not add anything to that particular conversation."

"She said it first," Phineas told him.

"Yeah," Percy added. "Do you really stare at her when you take off your frockcoat, unbutton your waistcoat, and—"

Prudence interrupted, "I think you two should finish one last teacake and head to the schoolroom for lessons."

When they ignored her, and Percy opened his mouth to continue, Caro spoke up. "Why don't I just put a few cakes on this plate? The two of you can come with Prudence and me to the schoolroom."

"Er…yes, boys," Prudence agreed. "Lady Phoebe looks positively worn out. I'm certain she could do with a nap."

Percy tugged on Phineas's arm and grumbled, "I don't think she rests at all whenever the baron joins her."

"If you want another teacake, you'll be quiet and come along," Prudence ordered them.

Millie nearly snorted her tea, quickly grabbing a napkin to cover her face.

"I do believe those two hooligans have been hanging around our private guard too long. Don't you, Phoebe dear?" Summerfield asked.

Pippa did not quite know what to say. She had picked up quite a few interesting ideas from the married women, and wondered what her reaction would be when Flaherty removed his frockcoat and unbuttoned his waistcoat. Would his pectorals engender a similar reaction from her?

"Don't you agree, Pippa?" Millie asked.

"I beg your pardon. I was woolgathering."

Summerfield pressed a kiss to the top of his wife's head and rose to his feet. "If you are finished with your tea, my love, I think you should rest."

The boys had just walked through the door, but obviously were still in hearing range. "I told you so," Percy said.

"We should ask Garahan what he thinks," Phineas added.

The baron's mouth was still hanging open when Lady Phoebe slipped her arm through his. "I cannot imagine life before the twins moved in with us. Can you, darling?"

Summerfield shook his head. "Do you think our son will be as precocious and outspoken as those two?"

Lady Phoebe sighed. "Oh, I do hope our son or daughter will be just like Percy and Phineas."

Millie and Pippa shared a look as the baron and baroness followed the others out of the nursery. "I have no doubt that Roarke will be a younger version of those two," Millie predicted.

"Growing up under the same roof as Dillon, I would have to agree," Pippa replied.

"Why don't you have a look at the three gowns her ladyship said she had delivered to your bedchamber? It's quiet now, and I could use a few moments to close my eyes while Roarke is still sleeping. His appetite won't let him sleep too much longer."

"I still feel so bad that we are reduced to accepting charity—"

"It is not charity," Millie said. "I don't think they feel loaning us gowns to wear, or providing a roof over our heads and food in our bellies, is a charitable act. I believe it is out of the goodness of their hearts. We should accept their friendship and all that it includes graciously, and promise in turn to help those *we* see that are in need."

"You have a much kinder heart that I, Millie Trentchester."

"Ah, but I'm rubbing off on you."

Pippa smiled. "You will let me know if you need me, won't you?"

"I will—now run along and see which lovely gowns the baroness has found for you to try on." Millie waited until Pippa had her hand on the door to the room before adding, "You will be a lovely bride."

Nerves had Pippa's skin tingling, her heart beating faster. "I hope Dillon thinks so."

Millie was smiling when she motioned for Pippa to keep walking. "I have no doubt on that score."

Pippa wondered if she was ready to be in the same room with Flaherty when he removed his frockcoat—let alone his waistcoat or anything else! "Dear Lord, what have I gotten myself into this time?"

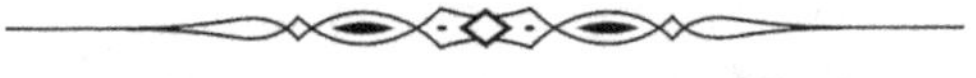

CHAPTER FOURTEEN

GARAHAN LOOKED UP at the sound of his name. "Well now, lads, aren't the two of ye early to be handing out carrots and apples in the stables?" When neither Percy nor Phineas answered, he added, "I thought ye'd be elbow deep in books and computations right now."

Percy elbowed Phineas. "It's hot today. I can hold your coat if you want to take it off."

Wondering what was going on in the minds of the brothers, Garahan chuckled. "Sure and 'tis warm, but His Grace likes us to dress appropriately despite the heat."

"I can hold your cravat," Percy offered.

"Thank ye for offering, but I'll be needing to wear it until the end of me shift." When they stared at him, Garahan urged, "Off with ye now. Flaherty's on the roof and may be amenable to answering a question or two."

Phineas shoved his brother. "Let's go!"

Percy responded by trying to trip Phineas. "I'll race you!"

Garahan shook his head watching the two lads run toward the side of the building until they disappeared around the side.

Hold yer coat. Take off yer cravat. I wonder what the devil those two are about now." Garahan settled into the saddle and guided his horse onto the long drive that wound around to the front of the building. His mind was already on his duty, patrolling his surroundings as he rode toward the village.

FLAHERTY HEARD TWO young voices calling him, but as he was currently patrolling the perimeter from the roof, he did not answer right away. He heard their mumbling and grumbling when the breeze shifted.

"I bet we could get Flaherty to do it."

"What if he won't?" he heard Phineas ask his brother.

"We'll think of something," Percy said. "We have to find out which muscles are the pectoral ones."

"And why they distract Cousin Prudence."

A movement across the distance to the south caught Flaherty's eye. He shrugged his shoulder, sliding the rifle off it and into his hands. Scanning the area, he saw a deer step out of the wood, lift its head, turn around, and disappear between the trees.

"Flaherty?"

The possible threat had evaporated, so he answered, "Aye, lads?"

"Isn't it hot up there?"

"As a matter of fact, 'tis," he replied. What did heat have to do with pectorals? Realizing he'd never know what was on the lads' minds until he asked, he called down, "Me shift will be over in half an hour. Why don't the two of ye see if ye can help Old Ned with a few chores in the stables, since it seems ye've free time on yer hands."

"He'll tell us," Phineas said loud enough for Flaherty to hear. He grinned and waited to hear what Percy would say.

"We will!" Percy answered for the two of them.

"Be off with ye now. I've the entire perimeter to guard."

The pounding of footsteps headed off toward the stable had him muttering, "Have the lads been studying musculature? I'll have to ask Prudence and keep up on what to be teaching me own son." Flaherty grinned. "Though 'tis the making of our son that I'll have the pleasure of seeing to first."

He was still smiling half an hour later when O'Malley climbed the ladder and stepped onto the rooftop.

His cousin stared at him for a moment. "I take it that look is anticipation of tomorrow."

"Ye'd be right then, and in fact 'twas those two hooligans who put the thought in me head."

"Did they now?" O'Malley asked. "How?"

"Ye know how sound carries when the wind blows from a certain direction."

O'Malley nodded.

"I heard them arguing about who was to ask me about pectorals. Then they asked me if I was hot. Do ye know what they may be up to?"

O'Malley snorted. "The wee devils overheard a conversation not meant for their ears."

"About chest muscles?"

"Aye—and more. Summerfield has been trying to get to the bottom of the situation, but apparently me wife, and Garahan's, have been avoiding his direct questions."

"As only a woman would do. Do ye know anything else?"

"I've been trying to listen, rather than ask questions and demand an answer. I think it has something to do with the time Prudence was looking for the lads, who were not in the schoolroom where they were instructed to be this morning."

"Ah," Flaherty said. "Hiding out on the third floor, no doubt."

"I have a feeling they might have been hiding in plain sight," O'Malley said.

"Well now, as they're to meet me at the stables, where I'll be saddling up me gelding to patrol to the village and back, I'll extract the information and let ye know."

O'Malley was laughing when Flaherty climbed down the ladder and disappeared around the corner of the building. His mind on his duty, O'Malley set aside all thoughts of the twins and concentrated on keeping a lookout for intruders.

CHAPTER FIFTEEN

TRENTCHESTER IGNORED HIS initial reaction to the man's face and stared at the man sitting across from him in the back corner of the tavern. "What have you discovered?"

The man with the slashing scar from forehead to chin waited a beat before answering, "The man you hired has been taken into custody."

Trentchester checked his impulse to pound on the table and demand to know what in the bloody hell had happened. "I see." He knew from their previous meeting that he would have to pay for additional information. "Do you have anything else for me?"

The dark-haired man sitting across from him stared until Trentchester felt the urge to shift on his seat. Digging deep to ignore the involuntary reaction, which he considered a sign of weakness, he reached into his waistcoat pocket and withdrew a small leather bag of coin. He placed it in the middle of the table between them, but did not let go of it. "I want to find out how closely watched Millicent Trentchester and Phillipa Stanhope are." He thought about the new information he'd gleaned, extremely pleased that what he'd learned had led to the arrest of his informant—cousin to one of his footmen—who'd apparently stabbed the irritating Phillipa Stanhope. "The duke's guard has a reputation for closing ranks when necessary. There must be some point during the day when she is left unguarded at the baron's estate."

"Rest assured, I shall find out and relay the information."

The rough edge to the scarred man's voice pleased Trentchester. Here was a man who would find out what he needed to know. The price was less than he thought he'd have to pay.

He frowned. From the looks of the man opposite him, there *was* the worry that he may escape being caught and talk. Nevertheless, Trentchester let go of the concern and the bag, shoving it toward the man. "How soon will you have the information?"

"Three days." The man rose to his full height and left without a backward glance.

"Bloody bugger had best get the information I need," Trentchester muttered.

⇻⇻⇻≻⇺⇺⇺

CAPTAIN COVENTRY WAS waiting in an alleyway, a fifteen-minute walk from the seedy tavern. "Well?" he demanded of Tremayne.

"Trentchester hasn't a clue who I am. He can't seem to stomach or get past my scar."

The captain shrugged. "There are those who will only ever see the scars that mar us, Tremayne. Never the heroic actions, nor orders followed serving king and country to have earned these scars."

Tremayne sighed. "There are times when it gets beneath my skin, like a sliver of wood, and stays there—a constant reminder. You seem to have conquered that. I have come to the conclusion that it is because you have found a treasure of a woman, Coventry. You have a strong son, whom you've helped to raise, since you kept your promise to your friend to watch over his family should he give his life for the Crown. A strong lad who is following in your footsteps and enlisted in the navy. A beautiful wife and daughter. Mayhap I shall be able to do the same if, and when, I ever meet someone who can see past my scar. The only women, aside from your wife, who are able to see past the reminder of the cavalry sword that nearly ended my life have been the wives of the men in the duke's guard. Are there no others capable of such a feat?"

Coventry smiled. "Miranda is a gem among women. Each and every one of the women who have married one of the O'Malleys, Garahans, and Flahertys is cut from the same cloth. It may be the adversity and hardship that have helped to form their character—some with visible flaws, some hidden. My gut tells me it is the mutual love and trust of the men they married that have completed their transformation into the diamonds of the first water they have all become."

Tremayne grinned. "You're waxing poetic, Coventry. The only other time I've heard you do so was when Miranda..." He paused and stared at the captain, who broke into a wide smile. "Am I to congratulate you?"

Coventry chuckled. "Aye. Miranda is pregnant again."

Tremayne shook his head. "You are a bloody lucky son of a bitch."

"I could not agree more. Unfortunately, right now, Miranda is in no mood to share in my delight. Though as soon as these first few months of sickness pass, I expect she'll be glowing."

"Ah, instead of the green complexion she had for the first few months when she was carrying Emma."

"Aye." The captain's expression changed to one of neutrality. "How soon can you reach Summerfield Chase?"

"Making use of one of the duke's stallions that he keeps stabled nearby, and at inns dotting the way north, I will arrive by early afternoon." He patted his waistcoat pocket. "I have the note from His Grace granting permission to utilize his horses."

"Excellent. The missive I received from Summerfield indicates that Lord Haybrook's daughter Millicent Trentchester and his infant grandson, and Lord Stanhope's daughter Phillipa, have been rescued from an incident with their carriage and been brought to safety at Summerfield Chase."

"Who found them?"

"Flaherty—he was on patrol to the village." Coventry's lips twitched as he fought to contain a smile. "Word is that he was accidently shot for his trouble."

"By a sharpshooter?"

Coventry was quick to answer, "Nay. It was an accident, and before you ask, yes, it was Stanhope's daughter. Summerfield advises that she was protecting Haybrook's daughter and grandson."

Tremayne snorted. "Are you predicting what I think you are?"

The captain's expression remained neutral. "It is too early to tell."

Tremayne chuckled. "Knowing Flaherty, his head's been turned by the woman who shot him."

Coventry did not disagree, though a hint of laughter lingered in his eye.

"Has he returned to duty yet?"

"Aye, and apparently Summerfield has applied for a special license for Flaherty."

"The men in the duke's guard are both honorable and predictable to a fault," Tremayne said. "Just because you rescue a woman, does not mean that you have to marry her before your heart is engaged—especially one who misinterpreted your intentions and thought you were the enemy!"

Coventry did not comment on that. Instead, he returned to the topic at hand. "Be certain to send word as soon as you arrive, and confirm that the two women currently ensconced at Summerfield Chase are indeed Mrs. Trentchester and her son, and Miss Stanhope—and not imposters."

"Is there reason to believe that someone would impersonate them?"

"Given the request I received from my connection in the War Office to see to the protection of the two women, and the fact that Mrs. Trentchester has recently given birth?" Coventry said.

"Aye. It is inconceivable that she would be in any shape to travel, let alone travel as far as the Borderlands."

Tremayne asked, "Do you have a miniature of either woman?"

Coventry sighed. "Unfortunately, no. Mrs. Trentchester has dark hair and amber eyes, is of medium height and on the slender side—before pregnancy. Miss Stanhope has light-blonde hair and blue-gray eyes, and is a bit shorter and curvier."

"It could well describe any number of women. But I will have to be enough to go on. Do you have any other information or pertinent facts that I could use to confirm their identities?"

"Both of their mothers are deceased. Mrs. Trentchester is the earl's only child. Miss Stanhope is the youngest of five by a decade, and the only female. That is all I have at present."

"You did not mention Lord Stanhope's title."

"Baron. His four sons are each nearly a year apart. His eldest son, and namesake, George is currently working closely with the baron's estate manager, as is to be expected as the heir. Next in line is Winston, Colonel Stanhope. He has recently returned to London and the War Office and has not been with his regiment for some time." Coventry paused and locked gazes with Tremayne before adding, "His current assignment is unknown."

"A spy," Tremayne remarked. "Interesting."

"Stanhope's third son, Randolph, is a captain in the navy. Lastly, Miles, the youngest son, is a lieutenant in the marines. Confirmation has been requested by his lordship, as I have it on good authority that Miss Stanhope's brothers currently serving in the military are being granted special leave to aid in finding their missing sister and her infant son. Captain Stanhope will be on shore leave in a matter of days, as will Lieutenant Stanhope. They serve on different vessels."

"What about his older brother?"

Coventry lifted his chin. "Colonel Stanhope's whereabouts are not openly acknowledged or discussed by the War Office. Although I have heard scuttlebutt that he has been on a mission to locate Captain Trentchester. Apparently they have been friends for years."

"I thought Trentchester was reportedly killed?"

"Rumors of his death have been greatly exaggerated," Coventry said.

"Does his family know?"

"For the sake of all those involved, I do not believe so."

Tremayne nodded. "Then the captain's wife Millicent and her very good friend Miss Stanhope are completely in the dark."

"Aye, given the matters the elder Stanhope is involved in, and information from the War Office being leaked, it is for their protection that they do not know. How soon can you leave?" Coventry asked.

"At once," Tremayne replied.

"Watch your back, Tremayne."

"Aye, captain. Watch yours."

HOURS—AND HARD MILES—LATER, Tremayne stopped to change horses at another of the inns on North Road. He was making excellent time, thanks to the note he carried.

With a slightly longer stop to fill the empty hole in his belly—and more than a pot of tea to add a fire to it without muddling his head—Tremayne set out for the last leg of his journey.

It was just past eleven o'clock the following morning when he rode up the winding drive to his destination—Summerfield Chase.

He braced for, and was glad to hear, the first shrill whistle and echoing response. He pulled gently on the reins to bring his horse to a stop. "We'll wait for the men to come to us."

His horse waited patiently while one man raced toward him on horseback from the stables. Another ran toward him from what Tremayne knew was the side of the house that had a ladder leading to the rooftop. The third man rounded the building from the back, joining the other two a moment later.

O'Malley dismounted. "Tremayne! Is Coventry involved in

this matter?"

"Is there trouble in London?" Garahan asked.

"'Tis either Pippa or Millie and her babe," Flaherty stated.

"Aye, the captain is involved, and it is connected to trouble in London," Tremayne answered. "You're also right, Flaherty. It does involve Miss Stanhope and Captain Trentchester's wife and son. I'm given to understand that you have a vested interest in the matter."

"That I do. The lass and I are to be married in just a few hours."

"Then congratulations are definitely in order. But first, I bring news from Coventry—with the caveat that I must first confirm the identities of the two women claiming to be Miss Stanhope and Mrs. Trentchester. Where is his lordship?"

O'Malley frowned, but did not gainsay Tremayne. "Come with me."

Garahan shared a look with Flaherty, but remained silent.

Flaherty, on the other hand, squared his shoulders and lifted his chin. "Are ye saying that the lass and her friend have lied to us?"

"Not at all. I'm saying I have been tasked by the captain to verify that they are who they claim to be because of the delicacy of the situation. Though I suppose we can wait a few days, until two of Miss Stanhope's brothers arrive."

"Why haven't they been protecting the lass all along?" Flaherty demanded.

"Captain Stanhope has been given special leave from the Royal Navy. His younger brother Lieutenant Stanhope, with the Royal Marines, has been given the same."

"And you believe there will be charges filed against the two women we have been protecting if—though there is no question in me mind whether either woman has lied to us"—Flaherty paused, trying to contain his anger—"Miss Stanhope's brothers arrive ready to rout out who their family believes are imposters."

"That sums it up," Tremayne said. "Lead on, O'Malley. I'd

like to question the women as soon as possible. Coventry is waiting for the missive from me confirming their story." When Flaherty and Garahan fell into step behind them, Tremayne paused. "I do not want to upset either of the women by questioning them with all three of you present."

"As the lass is going to be me wife in a few hours, I'll bloody well be there when ye question her," Flaherty replied.

"We have come to hold Miss Stanhope and Mrs. Trentchester in high regard," Garahan added. "Ye'll have the three of us, as the guard responsible for protecting His Grace's sister and her family."

O'Malley nodded. "Garahan has the right of it, Tremayne. We've made a vow to His Grace. We'll be with ye when ye question the women. We're bound by blood to protect Flaherty's bride-to-be, and have said as much."

Tremayne stared at O'Malley. "I have no problem questioning the women separately."

"Like hell ye will." Flaherty's eyes blazed with anger. "Pippa has promised to protect Millie with her life, and gained me pledge to take in Millie and her babe and protect them with *me* life."

Tremayne shook his head, but before he could speak, Garahan added, "We've given our word to include Millie and her son under our protection. Ye'll include the three of us in yer questioning, or we'll be going a few rounds in the outbuilding."

God, Tremayne loved working with these men! Their word was their bond, and their vow of honor would never be broken. "Alert whoever on staff will be taking over your shifts...and an hour or so afterward while I go a few rounds—starting with you, Flaherty."

Flaherty grunted.

Garahan nodded, and O'Malley called to the stable lad, who approached. "Take care of Tremayne's mount, and tell the stable master we'll be in a meeting with his lordship. Have the men assigned to take over our shifts do so immediately."

Stalking toward the back of the building, O'Malley yanked

open the door and barked at the footman, "Let Timmons know immediately that Garahan, Flaherty, and I will be in a meeting with his lordship."

"Aye, O'Malley." The footman rushed off to do his bidding.

As the men strode toward the kitchen, two footmen rushed past them, heading outside. With a nod to the cook, O'Malley paused to ask, "Mrs. Green, where are Mrs. Trentchester and Miss Stanhope?"

The cook brushed the flour off her hands and glanced nervously at Tremayne before answering. "They were going to be trying on gowns to wear to the wedding this afternoon."

Her tremulous smile had Tremayne wanting to reassure the woman. "Lieutenant Tremayne, at your service, Mrs. Green. I'm here on behalf of Captain Coventry."

The worry in her gaze was replaced by curiosity. "It's a pleasure to meet you." Turning to O'Malley, she said, "Please let his lordship know that I can have a tea tray ready in a trice."

"Thank ye, Mrs. Green. I shall pass along yer message."

Tremayne hoped he would be able to allay the fears of any other of the household staff as easily as he had the cook's, who was not unduly upset by his scar. As he followed O'Malley and the others, he hoped the women were who they claimed to be—for everyone's sake.

CHAPTER SIXTEEN

THE BARONESS PAUSED at the knock on her sitting room door. "Come in!" She smiled when she saw her husband standing in the doorway. "Marcus, we've found the perfect gown for Pippa—What's wrong?"

"Lieutenant Tremayne has arrived." The baron glanced from Pippa to Millie. "A situation has arisen that needs to be resolved at once."

"Can it not wait until after the wedding this afternoon?"

"I'm afraid not, Phoebe. Tremayne has ridden straight through from London. It is urgent." Again his gaze settled on Millie and Pippa.

"I see. Whatever the issue is, I wish to be included in the discussion…or will it be the *questioning* of our guests?"

"If you would let me explain—" Summerfield began, only to be interrupted by his wife.

"I will not countenance anyone meeting with either Millie or Pippa unless I am present," she said. "Have I made myself clear?"

"Quite," the baron replied. "If you had not interrupted, I would have agreed." Turning to Pippa and Millie, he continued, "I do not want either of you ladies to feel uncomfortable. And yes," he added, "the situation warrants a few simple questions. Tremayne has assured me it will not take long for him to ascertain the veracity of your claims."

"Veracity?" Phoebe exclaimed.

"Yes, love. Tremayne has come at the behest of Captain Coventry."

Millie sighed, and Pippa grumbled, "I take it by 'claims,' you mean that this Coventry doubts Millie and I are who we say we are?"

"It is merely a formality," the baron told the women.

Pippa asked Millie, "Did I not tell you that you should have told your father what Trentchester had threatened?"

"You did—but you were there when he..." Millie trailed off and fell silent.

Summerfield urged, "When he what?"

Millie shook her head and changed the subject. "I need to feed Roarke soon. Can it wait until after I do so?"

The baron did not hesitate to respond, "Of course. Forgive me for not taking your babe into account."

Lady Phoebe suggested, "Pippa, why don't you go with Millie to the nursery? I'll have a tea tray sent over. After you feed Roarke and tuck him in his cradle, Millie, have Pippa send for Caro and Prudence to sit with Roarke."

"I will. Thank you, your ladyship," Millie rasped. Pippa slipped her arm through her friend's and led her from the room.

When they were out of earshot, Phoebe rounded on her husband. "I do not like the way this is being handled. Who does Captain Coventry think he is to order about a new mother who has been terrorized by her brother-in-law and forced to leave her own home with only her best friend as her protector? Pippa has suffered equally, having been stabbed by the squire's former footman...that blackguard who tried to kidnap Millie's sweet babe!"

The baron reached for his wife's hand and gave a tug.

Lady Phoebe resisted at first. "Do not try to distract me with any of your soft words or kisses, *Summerfield*. I am extremely vexed with you!"

"You know I love the challenge of changing your vexation

into something a bit more...pliable." Summerfield enfolded his wife in his arms. He rested his chin atop her head and sighed. "Trust me, Phoebe. I will not let any harm come to Pippa, Millie, or her babe. Tremayne has not met either woman yet, and once he speaks to them, there will be no doubt that they are indeed who they say they are. Now then, shall I escort you to the nursery? I am quite certain you will feel more at ease after you have had your tea and cake."

"You know me too well." Halfway to the nursery, Phoebe paused. "I'll have your promise ahead of time that you will not let Tremayne raise his voice to either Millie or Pippa."

"You have my word."

"I have heard tales of stressful situations curdling a new mother's milk."

Summerfield's mouth gaped open for a moment before he collected himself enough to close it. "Let us hope for everyone's sake that it is merely a tale, mayhap a warning to keep all fathers vigilant in retaining order and civility in their households for the sake of his heir and his wife."

"Yes. Let us hope so." As he knocked on the nursery door and waited to be admitted, Phoebe added, "I hope a father would do the same for his daughter."

Summerfield pressed his lips to the top of his wife's head. "He would without question, my love."

The door opened, and he bade his wife to rest until Millie's babe had been fed and put down for a nap. Phoebe lifted to her toes and kissed his cheek. "I'm so very glad I answered that ransom note. I'd do it again in a heartbeat."

"Armed with a handful of ribbon-wrapped hatpins and a paperweight?"

His wife smiled, entered the room, and glanced over her shoulder. "I didn't really need the paperweight."

Summerfield quietly closed the door behind her and strode to the staircase. It was time to get to the bottom of what had happened to the women Flaherty had brought to Summerfield

Chase. Whoever they were, he'd given his word to add them to those under his protection. He intended to keep it.

FLAHERTY WANTED TO club the lieutenant in the mouth, but then he wouldn't find out what in God's name had precipitated Tremayne's riding through the night to question Pippa and Millie. He had to bury his anger deep to regain control of it. He met O'Malley's stare, then Garahan's, letting them know without words that he wouldn't lash out at the messenger they were meeting with in the baron's library.

"Ye'd best start talking now, Tremayne," he said.

"You already know why I'm here, and it's a simple matter—"

O'Malley snorted with derision. "If it were simple, ye wouldn't have arrived on one of His Grace's stallions."

"He's got ye there, Tremayne," Flaherty said. "Spill yer guts now, or we'll be dragging yer sorry arse outside to beat it out of ye."

Tremayne chuckled. "Is violence the only way you three communicate?"

Flaherty felt one of the tethers holding his temper in check snap. "It is when it concerns the woman I'm to marry in a few hours."

"How well do you know Miss Stanhope…if she is truly who she claims to be?"

Flaherty got in the lieutenant's face and growled. "Ye'll not cast aspersions against the lass or Millie unless ye fancy losing a few teeth." Tremayne held up a hand, and Garahan grasped Flaherty's shoulder. Both actions had Flaherty opening his right fist, relaxing it. "Faith, but I cannot wait to go a few rounds with ye."

"I have already said I would. You know that Coventry has never sent Bayfield, Hennessey, Masterson, or me to investigate a situation unless there was information that needed to be verified."

The cousins exchanged glances before O'Malley replied, "Ye have the right of it, but that does not change the situation. Ye understand that we've given our word to protect the women."

"No matter if ye're satisfied that they are indeed who they say they are," Garahan added.

Flaherty could not believe what he was hearing. Were Garahan and O'Malley hinting that *they* did not believe the horrific story they'd been told? "Tell me that ye aren't suggesting that Millie would venture out hours after giving birth if her life wasn't at stake?"

"I never said that," Garahan shot back.

"Ye're putting words in our mouths," O'Malley said.

"Pippa and Millie have been friends since before they could walk. Yet ye're ready to believe Tremayne's claim that they are imposters?" Flaherty said.

Garahan moved to stand on Flaherty's left while O'Malley stood on his right. "We're bound by blood, and our vow of honor to His Grace, and have been battered, bruised, and bled to keep it," Garahan murmured.

"We have been in yer boots, Dillon, and felt the bolt to our hearts," O'Malley added. "Meself when I rescued Caro, and Garahan when he rescued Prudence. Our hearts met the missing halves of ours, as ye recognized Pippa as the other half of yer own."

Flaherty glared at Tremayne before responding, "Coventry did not send Tremayne or anyone else to question whether or not Caroline was claiming to be someone she wasn't."

"True," Garahan replied. "But 'tisn't what matters here now, Flaherty, and ye know it."

O'Malley grunted. "When an O'Malley or Garahan gives his word, we keep it—same as yerself or any of yer boneheaded brothers, Flaherty."

Flaherty felt as if the breath had been knocked out of him,

and with it his anger. Had it been his imagination, or had his Uncle Patrick O'Malley reached from beyond the grave to whack some sense into him?

"Felt that, did ye?" O'Malley asked. "I've had it happen to me once or twice. I'm thinking Uncle Patrick is more involved with our being hired on by the duke than any of us realized."

"Aye," Garahan agreed. "It started with Uncle Patrick's oldest son and namesake. Then yer brother Sean was hired, O'Malley."

"One by one, the rest of the Cork O'Malleys, Uncle Patrick's sons, were hired, then his nephews, meself, and me brothers from Wexford," O'Malley added.

"Then the Garahans and me brothers," Flaherty said. "I'm wondered how we got out of some of the scrapes and untenable situations, when it seemed all hope was lost."

Garahan grunted, then locked gazes with Tremayne. "Me brother told me how the two of ye worked together to lift Finn O'Malley once the lever was pulled and the trapdoor opened beneath his feet. I'm thinking yerself and James had a little help from Uncle Patrick keeping the hangman's noose from snapping Finn's neck."

Tremayne cleared his throat, and the men turned as one. "It is something to think about. But back to the issue at hand. I have given my word to the captain, and I intend to keep it. As soon as his lordship arrives, I have a bit of pertinent information about Captain Trentchester that I have been given leave to share, once I verify the identities of the women under your protection and report my findings to Coventry. That is all I am allowed to say until after I interview the women."

Flaherty knew the lieutenant wanted him to acquiesce. And from the elbow to his side, he knew that O'Malley expected him to. "Fine then, I'll"—he looked to O'Malley and then Garahan—"*we'll* listen."

"That's all I ask." Tremayne rubbed his hands together and grinned. "Afterward, I'll take all of you on...one at a time."

Flaherty nodded. "I'll accept for the lot of us." He narrowed his gaze on the lieutenant. "I go last."

Tremayne was laughing when Summerfield walked into his library.

"Mrs. Trentchester is feeding her son, and will be down shortly. While we're waiting, Tremayne, let's hear the reasons Coventry sent you."

Flaherty listened intently. He was surprised to learn that three of Pippa's brothers were in different branches of the military—her eldest brother was Baron Stanhope's heir and involved in the running of the baron's estates. The youngest and closest in age to her—ten years her senior—was a lieutenant in the marines. The next eldest was a captain in the navy, and the second eldest of the brood was a colonel in the army—but at present the regiment he was attached to was not disclosed. Bloody hell—he was probably a spy.

"And no one knows the whereabouts of Colonel Stanhope?" Summerfield asked.

"I would assume someone in the War Office is aware, though not at liberty to say," Tremayne answered.

Garahan shook his head. "And ye think the navy captain and marine lieutenant will be landing at the docks any day?"

"Aye."

"What ye haven't said is whether or not they plan to make their way here," O'Malley said.

"I'll not have them upsetting the lass or Millie," Flaherty bit out.

"We are getting ahead of ourselves," Summerfield interjected. "We will of course welcome the men. Though why Pippa and Millie did not tell their fathers of their situation is still a question that must be answered."

"Aye," Flaherty agreed. "One I'll be asking Pippa meself."

"I'll be questioning the women first," Tremayne reminded them.

"Not without meself," Flaherty growled.

"Nor me," O'Malley announced.

"And me," Garahan added.

The baron sighed. "Apparently, my wife will also be on hand during the interview. We'd best adjourn to the sitting room—it's larger and has more places to sit."

Tremayne immediately agreed. "Whatever will make her ladyship and the women comfortable."

"Miss Stanhope and Mrs. Trentchester, ye mean," Flaherty said, deliberately reminded Tremayne that he believed the women were who they claimed to be.

The lieutenant met the intensity of Flaherty's gaze. "I always say what I mean."

The knock on the library door had all conversation ceasing "Enter!" the baron called, and the door opened. "Ah, Timmons, are the ladies ready for to join us?"

"Yes, your lordship. Her ladyship has asked that you join her in the sitting room."

"Thank you, Timmons." Summerfield turned to the men. "Come with me."

The men filed out and made their way to the sitting room. The door was open, and Flaherty wasn't surprised to see the tension on the faces of the three women. He knew at once that he needed to help set the tone for the interview and put the ladies at ease.

"Well now, let's get this meeting over and done with so the lass and I can marry and get to the good part."

Pippa's face flamed. Millie covered her mouth, but not before a snort of laughter escaped. Lady Phoebe laughed openly. "Flaherty, you are a scoundrel, but a handsome one. I should chastise you for such a declaration...but I won't."

Summerfield shook his head at his wife and frowned at Flaherty, who ignored him and kneeled at Pippa's side. "Ye haven't had a change of heart, have ye, Pippa-lass?"

Millie answered for her friend, "She has not."

"How do you know I haven't?" Pippa asked her friend.

"Because I can see right through to your heart, dear friend."

Millie turned to Flaherty. "None of us know how many days we'll be granted on this earth. Treat Pippa as the treasure of a woman she is—and do not let her brothers cow you. My husband was great friends with all of them. It was how I met Roarke. He stole my heart, and though he's gone…" She paused to compose herself, then continued, "I have the most precious gift he could ever have given me…our babe."

Flaherty swallowed against the lump in his throat. "I know most might not think I'm worthy of Pippa, but I'll protect her and cherish her always." He turned to Pippa and reached for her hand. "Remember what I promised ye, lass. If I die before ye, you will have the protection of me three brothers, Garahan and his three brothers, and O'Malley and his three, as well as his four O'Malley cousins."

"Don't be forgetting Killian O'Ghill, and the Fitzpatricks and the McGreevys," Garahan added.

"Aye. Ye'll never want for anything. Any children the Lord grants us will never lack for family." Flaherty met Millie's quiet stare. "Ye'd best not have forgotten our pledge to yerself and yer babe, Millie."

"Ye'll be protected always," O'Malley promised.

"And have more uncles for yer son than ye could ever want," Garahan said.

Summerfield handed his handkerchief to his wife. "Dry your tears, love. Tremayne, let's get on with the interview."

Flaherty kissed the back of Pippa's hand and rose to his feet. "Aye, we've business to attend to, and a family to start."

"Shut yer gob before the lass turns purple with embarrassment!" O'Malley ordered him.

"He has a point," Garahan added.

"Gentlemen, do be quiet and let Tremayne get to it," Lady Phoebe urged. "I'm hungry."

"I thought you had a tea tray sent up to the nursery—" Summerfield began, only to be interrupted.

The baroness glared at her husband. "I would not finish the

rest of that statement, Summerfield."

While the women gawked at the baroness, Flaherty and his cousins kept their mouths closed. They had been guarding the couple long enough to know when to speak…and when not to.

"Shall I ring for tea, then?" the baron asked.

Lady Phoebe turned and asked Tremayne, "Just how many questions do you have for Millie and Pippa?"

Tremayne's eyes shifted from the baron to the baroness. "A few—mayhap half a dozen."

The baroness sighed. "Very well. Marcus, please do order tea for us."

Flaherty was grateful that Lady Phoebe was unintentionally setting the tone for the interview. Bless the Summerfields' cook for always having the water hot and sweets ready to be served. Tea arrived promptly. Though he did not ask for any, a teacup and saucer were placed in his hands—and that of the other men.

"Drink up, gentlemen," the baroness urged. "We have a wedding to finish preparing for this afternoon."

And there was the heart of the matter, as far as Flaherty was concerned. He turned to look at Pippa and found she'd anticipated him. She slowly smiled, and he knew all would be right with his world the moment they said their vows. This feisty woman would be his wife, Lord willing, would bear his children and make love to him every night for the rest of their lives—mornings too, if he could convince her to wake well before dawn so he wouldn't be late reporting for duty.

"You're embarrassing the lass," Garahan remarked.

"Nay," Flaherty replied. "'Tis a promise I'm making…without need for words."

Millie's eyes welled with tears and Tremayne—who was closest to her—handed her his handkerchief.

"Now then, mayhap we could begin with Mrs. Trentchester's reason for leaving the safety of her home hours after giving birth."

Pippa set down her cup and saucer and reached for Millie's

hand. Flaherty recognized that the two women drew strength from their bond of friendship. He and his brothers and cousins did the same. "Shall I answer for you, Millie?" Pippa asked.

Millie wiped her tears and said, "It would be best if I start at the beginning." Turning to Tremayne, she sighed. "It all started when my brother-in-law realized I was expecting…"

As Millie recounted the number of veiled hints of what the elder Trentchester brother intended to do with her, should reports of his missing brother change and his death be reported, Flaherty clenched his jaw. As the hints became threats, and increased in number and frequency, his gut iced over. A glance at his cousins showed they were having the same reaction.

Tremayne's expression never changed, though Flaherty noted his green eyes faded to piss-yellow and hardened. Whether or not the lieutenant would believe Millie was who she claimed, the man would be seeking justice for what she had suffered.

"Do you have any idea why Trentchester would threaten to take you and your babe?" he asked.

Millie started to answer, but her voice broke. Pippa reached for her hand, held it, and looked Tremayne in the eye, her expression lethal. If she'd had the blunderbuss in her hands right now, Tremayne would be saying prayers to his Maker for forgiveness!

Flaherty shifted his stance, and Pippa spoke up. "Trentchester had been obsessed with Millie before she and Roarke married— he intends to use her…" She trailed off and looked helplessly at Flaherty, who nodded.

"He plans to get her with child, doesn't he?" he asked.

Pippa nodded. "Until then, he wants her son."

Tremayne waited for Pippa to expound on her statement. When she remained silent, he asked, "Why?"

She looked at Millie, who shook her head, and Pippa slipped her arm around her friend. "Millie, we have to tell them everything, or else Trentchester will continue to try to steal your son."

Flaherty felt the woman's pain—not only was she a widow, but her despicable brother-in-law was after stealing her son! He watched, waiting, about to intercede and stop the questioning, but then he heard Millie rasp, "Tell them."

Pippa spoke of Trentchester's wife—and his three mistresses, all of whom appeared to be barren. "Not one of them could give him what he craves...an heir to his fortune and shipping enterprise!"

"Why his nephew?" Tremayne asked.

"He is a Trentchester by blood—"

Pippa was interrupted by Millie. "Roarke never liked his brother. In fact, he warned Grant to stay away from me before, and after, Roarke and I married."

"I take it something happened to have him warning his brother to keep his distance?" Tremayne asked.

"The blackguard cornered Millie in her sitting room, when he thought Roarke was out of the house," Pippa said. Millie stared at the floor, silent as a grave. Pippa continued, "Little did he know Roarke was in the library, heard the commotion, and rushed in to save Millie. He left three days later to rejoin his regiment."

"A few weeks later, I discovered I was carrying our son." Millie paused. "I'm not sure how his brother found out about our babe. I had confided our news in a letter to Roarke. I went for a few months without hearing from him—or reading any news about casualties his regiment suffered. And then the missive arrived saying that he was dead." She lifted her head to meet Tremayne's eyes and whispered, "Not when, nor where, nor how. No 'we're sorry to inform you of his passing,' just that he was dead."

Flaherty had been watching Millie's expression the entire time, and there was no doubt in his mind that she was Earl Haybrook's daughter, Millicent Haybrook Trentchester. He had no doubt about Pippa, but had calmed enough to listen without interrupting when Tremayne turned to her and asked, "What can you tell me about your family?"

Pippa shot a glance at Flaherty, who silently urged her with a look to just answer the question. She rolled her eyes at him—which had him silently chuckling—and asked, "Shall I start with the death of my mum when I was little, or would you like to know the rank and file of my decade-older brothers? Mayhap you would like to know my father's title—as if you don't already know he is a baron."

"Tell me about your brothers, if you wouldn't mind," Tremayne replied.

Flaherty braced himself as Pippa's gaze rested on Tremayne's forehead for a brief moment before following the length of the scar that bisected the side of his face. He hated knowing that the former lieutenant in the king's dragoons had to deal with the injury that ended his military career and nearly his life.

"Thank you for serving our king and country, Lieutenant Tremayne. My brother Winston is a colonel in the army—but his regiment is not as distinguished as the dragoons you must have served with, judging from your grievous injury. Even though I take umbrage at your questioning my dear friend about her marriage and her babe, because of all she has been through, I will answer your questions about my life. It is far from exciting."

Garahan's snort had Flaherty rounding on his cousin. "I'm certain the lass was referring to her life *before* she met me."

"Don't ye mean before she *shot* ye?" O'Malley asked.

"Of course I meant before I met you, Dillon." Addressing Garahan, Pippa said, "Dillon believes that I was not shooting at him." Turning back to Tremayne, she explained, "I fell backward and the blunderbuss went off."

Garahan sighed. "We believe ye, but as cousin to Flaherty, 'tis our right to rile him."

"Aye," O'Malley said. "He's a formidable bare-knuckle foe when his temper's up."

"Why would that matter now?" Pippa asked.

"You will not beat on one another in this house!" Lady Phoebe proclaimed.

Flaherty grinned. "Sure and ye don't have to be reminding us of that, yer ladyship. We'll be going a few rounds in the outbuilding. After the lass and Millie have answered all of Tremayne's questions."

"A satisfying round or three of bare-knuckle with an able opponent clears the cobwebs out of yer head," Garahan said.

"Don't you mean a round or two?" Pippa asked.

O'Malley answered for Garahan, "Nay, it takes at least two rounds to get a feel for your opponent's strengths and weaknesses. The third round usually decides the bout."

"About your brothers, Miss Stanhope?" Tremayne asked.

"George is the eldest and has the makings of a fine baron, and will no doubt be a good and honest steward of the land and all that is entailed along with the title." When Tremayne waited, Pippa continued, "Winston is a colonel in the army, Randolph is a captain in the navy, and Miles a lieutenant in the marines. Though thankfully they serve on different ships, otherwise Miles would be in the brig constantly."

"I take it Miles and Randolph do not get along," Tremayne said.

Flaherty was surprised by the way the sunshine of Pippa's smile melted away the worry. "Er…yes. I suppose one would come to that conclusion. Though in truth, they just see everything from a different perspective."

"And your other brothers?" Tremayne asked without a hint of inflection in his voice.

"I have no other brothers."

"And you, Mrs. Trentchester, how old are your brothers?"

"I am an only child," Millie replied.

"And your mothers? How could they allow either of you to go off on such a journey without both of them accompanying you, with a wet nurse and midwife in tow?"

Pippa and Millie shared a look, and Millie replied, "If your Captain Coventry is planning to trip us up in answering questions about our families, he must be quite worried. What are you not telling us?"

Tremayne held Millie's gaze for a long moment before urging, "Answer my question, while I consider the ramifications of answering yours."

"Both Pippa's mum and my own died when we were but two years old. They had been visiting one of Father's tenant farmers who had been ill. First my mum and then Pippa's caught the same virulent fever and were gone a few days later."

"I am sorry for your loss, Mrs. Trentchester, Miss Stanhope."

Millie sighed and thanked him.

Pippa, on the other hand, spoke up. "We're waiting for you to tell us what you know that involves both of our families."

When Tremayne did not immediately answer, Flaherty asked, "Are they in immediate danger?"

"No more than five minutes ago," the lieutenant answered honestly. "I need to send a missive to Coventry to ask his permission to confide in you."

"Then we have answered your questions satisfactorily?" Pippa asked.

"You have, thank you, Miss Stanhope. Thank you, Mrs. Trentchester."

When he rose from his seat and was speaking to the baron, Pippa said, "We'd be honored if you would stay for our wedding, lieutenant. It will be a very small affair, but Mrs. Green has been baking a lovely cake for the occasion."

Flaherty added, "'Twould be a shame to have to leave before eating yer fill and enjoying a bit of wedding cake."

Tremayne stared at Flaherty. "Cake was mentioned twice. Did you happen to mention my weakness for cake in passing?"

Flaherty shook his head and turned to Garahan. "*I* didn't tell her."

O'Malley stepped in front of Garahan and crossed his arms over his chest. "As all of us know, you cannot resist any baked goods, though we know ye prefer cake. 'Twould be best to blame all three of us, as we are all well aware ye cannot pass a slice of cake by without having just wee taste."

"If that is all, gentlemen, please excuse Pippa, Millie, and myself. We have a wedding to get ready for," Lady Phoebe announced.

As the women swept from the room, Flaherty nudged Tremayne. "'Tisn't telling if ye're reading aloud what ye write in yer missive to the captain."

"He's got ye there," Garahan said.

"That seems like a bit of a whitewashed lie," Tremayne mumbled.

"Ah, so it is…and 'tis white and pure as the driven snow," O'Malley said.

Summerfield motioned to the men. "Let us adjourn to my library. Tremayne will find the quill sharp, the inkwell full, and plenty of foolscap to write on."

"If Coventry finds out that I told you—" Tremayne started.

"God, ye've a harder head than Garahan, Tremayne. We told ye, reading aloud what ye're writing 'tisn't the same as telling," Flaherty grumbled. "Now let's go—I have a flask to refill, and a tub of hot water waiting for me to sink into so I'll be presentable for me bride this afternoon."

Tremayne sighed. "Very well." He glared at Flaherty. "But it will be my turn to win the argument next time!"

Flaherty grinned. "Ye heard him, boy-os. 'Twill be his turn next time."

Summerfield just kept walking until he reached his library and walked to his desk. He pulled out a sheaf of foolscap and laid it on the desk. "Here's the quill and there's the inkwell. Start writing…and don't leave any detail out."

CHAPTER SEVENTEEN

PIPPA SMOOTHED HER hands over the delicate fabric of the gown's gossamer skirt.

"Oh, Miss Stanhope, you look lovely!" the maid exclaimed.

Pippa bit her lip and glanced at the looking glass hanging on the wall above the washstand. "It is a lovely, soft shade of blue. It reminds me of lying on my back in the grass, looking up at the early morning sky through wisps of clouds." She hesitated and folded her hands at her waist. "I doesn't feel right to be borrowing Lady Phoebe's best gown. Is there another I may borrow?"

The maid shook her head. "Oh, but her ladyship insisted that this gown is perfect, as it accentuates your coloring."

When Pippa bit her lip and was about to refuse, the maid added, "Her ladyship wanted me to remind you that you promised…in case you refused to wear it."

Turning from side to side, Pippa admired the cut and color of the gown. Resolved to honor her word, she lifted her chin. "Once a Stanhope gives their word, they do not break it."

"I have heard her ladyship say something quite similar about her family, the Lippincotts. Now then, have a seat, Miss Stanhope. A few strands of your hair have come undone. It won't take but a moment to add a few more hairpins."

The knock on the door startled Pippa, proof that she had let her guard down. Although she knew that the security around the baron's home would be difficult, if not impossible, to break through, the worry for Millie and little Roarke remained. Frustrated with herself for not paying attention, her voice was sharper than intended when she answered, "Come in."

The door opened slowly. The worried expression on Millie's face cut Pippa to the core. "Forgive me for disturbing you. I thought you might want company while you wait for Baron Summerfield to escort you downstairs."

Pippa rushed over to the door and pulled her friend inside. "Where's Roarke?"

"Prudence and Caro have him." Millie paused for a moment and clapped her hands together. "You look absolutely lovely. Lady Phoebe was right—that shade of pale blue highlights the blue-gray of your eyes. Flaherty will be tongue-tied when he sees you."

"I doubt anything could make Dillon lose his ability to speak."

Millie smiled. "I'm not so sure about that. Now then, is there anything you want to ask me about tonight?"

Momentarily confused, Pippa asked her friend, "Tonight?"

Millie sighed. "We both listened to the advice from your cook, Pippa, and most of it was spot-on."

Pippa watched a delicate blush rise from the base of Millie's throat to her cheeks. "Most of it? Is there something else to the marriage bed that Mrs. Beemish left out?"

Millie giggled. "Quite a bit, but nothing about what..."

Pippa's belly twisted into a knot. She was nervous enough about the marriage bed, and to have Millie tell her there was more than her family's cook had confided, right before she was to wed Dillon, wreaked havoc with her nerves. "What?"

Red-faced, Millie managed to continue, "About what goes where."

"I beg your pardon?"

"And so you should, Pippa! We have been friends since before we were able to talk, and you know how difficult it is for me to discuss such things."

"So you decided to come here now, right before I am to be escorted downstairs to marry Flaherty, and tell me there is—in your words—quite a bit that was left out of what goes on in the marriage bed."

"Aye."

"For Heaven's sake! Your babe is proof that you and Roarke did not spend the fortnight before he reported for duty sipping tea and eating berry tarts!"

Millie covered her mouth with her hands and murmured, "Who told you?"

Confused, Pippa shook her head. "Told me what?" She started tapping her foot in agitation. "Take your hand off your mouth and stop speaking in riddles. I have no time for that. I'm to be married in less than quarter of an hour to a man I barely know. You had a year to become accustomed to the fact that you and Roarke were to marry."

Millie's hands fell to her sides. "Forgive me. You are right." She reached for Pippa's hand and tugged her toward the settee. She didn't let go, even when Pippa sat beside her. "I want you to promise me that you will trust Flaherty to treat you with care tonight."

What did she mean by *that*? "He already promised never to hurt me—or you—and to protect us."

Millie sighed. "That is not what I mean. In the marriage bed, when it is just the two of you, consummation can be painful at first, but if you trust in your husband, he will do his best not to rush you and to see to it that the pain is minimal."

"Can you be a bit more specific?" Pippa asked.

"I knew I should have spoken to you before now. You always want more details that *I* would ever ask for."

"Well, what exactly can Flaherty do to minimize the pain of consummating our marriage?"

The sound of a throat clearing had Millie and Pippa's heads turning toward the door.

Millie shot to her feet. "Your lordship, we did not hear you knock."

Summerfield shook his head. "I knocked—twice—but apparently neither of you heard."

Pippa stood next to her friend. "We did not. Forgive us for not paying attention."

The baron put his hands behind his back. "Do you need more time to continue your discussion, or are you ready to put Flaherty out of his misery?"

Pippa could not contain her gasp of shock. "Misery?"

Summerfield chuckled. "All men forced to stand and wait for their brides-to-be cannot help but wonder if she has changed her mind. With each minute that passes, the worry increases. So yes, Pippa, he is presently in a state of agitated misery."

Pippa gave Millie a quick hug and rushed over to the baron's side. "We'd best not keep him waiting. Do hurry, Millie!"

The baron offered his arm. The solid strength of it was a reassuring anchor in the midst of her uncertainty. Thoughts of what would happen later—the pain, and the question of what exactly Flaherty would be able to do to ease some of it—added to the throb at the base of her skull. She hoped she did not embarrass herself when the time came to cleave unto her husband.

Pippa did the only thing she could think of to keep from turning into a trembling, want-witted woman—she prayed. *Lord, please don't let me embarrass myself tonight with Dillon.*

"I have three younger sisters," Summerfield said.

"Would you trade them for three of my brothers?"

The baron chuckled. "That might be to your detriment, as I understand one of the twins—Minerva, I think—has formed an attachment to one of Garahan's cousins. A McGreevy, I believe."

"I would love to meet your sisters, your lordship. Millie has been a sister to me all my life."

"I am quite certain they would enjoy making your acquaintance, too. They are over the moon now that Phoebe's time is drawing closer. They're looking forward to doting on their niece or nephew."

"Babes are so precious, and the closest thing to an angel," Pippa murmured.

"Anyway, I hope you don't mind my intruding—however, in view of the fact that I overheard the last bit of your conversation, I can arrange for you to have time to speak to Phoebe before Flaherty whisks you off to the cottage I had built at the same time I commissioned the other two."

"Other two?"

"Yes," the baron said, leading her slowly toward the sitting room, where Flaherty and the others were waiting. "Garahan was the first to marry, and I could see right away that he would need a cottage of his own. As a matter of fact, my cousin, William, and Phoebe's brother Edward both had cottages constructed for the married men in the duke's guard as wedding gifts. I had the finishing touches put on Flaherty's cottage the day after he brought the three of you here to Summerfield Chase."

"You are too kind, your lordship—thinking of Flaherty and the other men's comfort."

The baron stopped in front of the closed sitting room door. "I was thinking of their brides as well. Shall I ask Phoebe to have a word with you, while I ask Tremayne and the others to distract Flaherty?"

"Thank you for the offer, but I believe I shall do as Millie suggested."

"Oh?"

"I shall put my trust in Flaherty."

Summerfield patted her hand and smiled. "He will treat you well, or I shall know the reason why!" He knocked on the door the sitting room, and it swung open a moment later.

"She's here, Flaherty, so quit yer bellyaching!" Garahan called out.

Pippa knew that Millie had to check on Roarke before joining them for the ceremony, or else she'd have her friend find out what worries Flaherty had before she arrived. Letting her gaze sweep the room, she noticed the vicar first—he was standing in front of the window overlooking the garden. Sunlight glinted off the windowpanes, momentarily blinding her.

She blinked, and when her vision cleared, she saw Dillon standing next to the vicar. The sunlight glowed around him, emphasizing the width of his black-clad shoulders. But it was the way a sunbeam seemed to bring out the fire in his auburn hair that had her mesmerized by the handsome man she would wed.

"I'm so sorry to be late, Pippa," Millie said as she rushed in. "Roarke just would not settle down." The worry in her friend's eyes tugged at Pippa's heart. The sound of her babe crying drew closer by the moment. "I know it is not commonplace, but would you mind if Roarke joins us?"

"Not at all." Pippa turned, intending to ask Flaherty, but the man was no longer standing beside the vicar—he was striding toward where she and Millie stood with the baron. "I would be honored to have yer son attend our wedding. After all, ye'll be living with Pippa and me. We're a family, Millie, or did ye forget me promise already?"

She stepped around Pippa to hug Flaherty. "You are the dearest of men, and remind me of my husband. He would have liked you."

Flaherty patted her on the back. "I'm not sure if I would have liked him, but faith, a round or three of bare-knuckle and emptying a flask between us would have settled the matter in his favor."

"Thank you, Flaherty." Millie turned around and rushed into the hallway. The crying stopped, and she returned with her babe in her arms, taking her place next to the baroness, Caro, and Prudence.

Flaherty brushed the tip of his finger to Pippa's cheek and nodded. "Are ye ready to marry me, lass?"

Pippa's heart skipped a beat before settling back down. "I am, Dillon."

He nodded to the baron and strode back over to stand beside the vicar.

Pippa did not remember moving, but Flaherty was reaching for her hand, holding it firmly in his much larger one.

The vicar cleared his throat and began, "Dearly beloved…"

Thoughts of Flaherty's callused hands touching her intimately had her heart beating double time. She clung to Millie's wise advice and trusted that Dillon would not hurt her—he would do whatever it was that he could do to ensure the pain was minimal.

"Well?" Flaherty's deep voice sounded close to her ear. "Do ye, lass?"

Garahan snickered, and O'Malley spoke up. "I'm thinking 'tis the lass's nerves affecting her hearing, vicar. Best ask her again."

"Ahem. Very well, but I would *think* you would be paying attention at an important moment like this, Miss Stanhope."

"Forgive me, vicar." Pippa's gaze collided with Flaherty's, and the knowing look in the depths of his blue eyes had her mind going off on another tangent. She heard mumbling, but her mind was half a mile away, in the cottage the baron spoke of.

"As me bride appears to be having trouble paying attention, I'll answer for her." Flaherty slipped his arm around Pippa's waist and somehow pitched his voice to a raspy falsetto. "I, Phillipa Rose Stanhope, do promise to love, honor, cherish, and obey Dillon James Flaherty."

Pippa stared into the bright-blue gaze of the man who would not let anything stop them from marrying this afternoon—not Tremayne's interrogation, nor Millie's babe, who'd demanded to attend and then promptly fallen asleep as soon as he was surrounded by the people who had come to mean the world to Pippa and Millie.

Flaherty's high-pitched voice had everyone chuckling. She blinked back tears of joy. This man would cherish her, honor her, and love her… She slowly smiled as she realized neither one of them would easily *acquiesce* and *obey*. But they would try.

"Highly irregular, Flaherty," the vicar grumbled. "But it is Miss Stanhope who must finish her vows—and not your imitation of her."

Flaherty grinned at her. "Best get it said, and no letting yer mind wander where I know it has been."

She gasped, and he laughed in her face, but she managed to finish saying her vows. "I promise to love, cherish, and honor Dillon James Flaherty until the Lord calls me home. And I promise to fill our home with as many babes as the Lord blesses us with."

Flaherty kissed the breath out of her. "There's a lass."

"Ye're supposed to wait for the vicar to declare ye man and wife, Flaherty," Garahan reminded him.

"And well I know it, boy-o. I was just giving her a quick reminder of what's in store for her…later."

This time it was Tremayne who spoke up. "Best finish it, vicar, before Flaherty sweeps his bride off her feet and leaves."

Flaherty turned to Pippa. "Would ye mind, lass?"

Warmth swept up from her toes, settling in her belly and then filling her heart. "Not at all—" Her words were cut off when her husband swept her into his arms.

She finally managed to draw in a breath as the vicar pronounced them man and wife, and then was breathless again from another mind-bending kiss from her husband. When their lips parted, she sighed deeply and rested her head beneath his chin. "We're not staying for cake, are we?"

Flaherty was already crossing the threshold into the hallway. "I've asked Mrs. Green to set aside a big slice for us. She was preparing a basket of food for us to take with us in the carriage."

She lifted her head to ask, "Carriage?"

"Aye." He looked down into her eyes and smiled. "No wife of mine is walking a mile and a half on her wedding day. Though I wouldn't mind carrying ye the distance, lass. Yer curves feel like Heaven in me arms." He kissed her again and strode toward the butler. "Timmons, I shall see ye on the morrow."

"Congratulations, Flaherty, Miss Stanhope. I know you will be very happy."

"Thank ye. Is the carriage ready?"

The butler nodded and opened the front door. Flaherty grunted in response to whatever else Timmons said. A footman was waiting to open the door to the coach. Flaherty nodded to the man and all but leapt into the carriage, never letting Pippa go.

She landed with a jolt on his lap on the seat. "You could have set me down, and avoided tossing me around like a sack of grain."

He stared at her face without speaking.

"Well," she grumbled, "you *could* have."

"Ah, lass, but me arms weren't ready to let ye go. I'll try when we get to our cottage, but I'm warning ye, ye'd best prepare to be hauled out of the coach in a similar manner."

The carriage slowed down more quickly than she'd imagined it would—mayhap due to the fact that Flaherty was currently leaving a trail of kisses along the line of her jaw.

"Dillon."

"Save that thought, lass. We've arrived." The door swung open and the footman's cheeky look had Pippa's face heating. She barely heard Flaherty thank the footman or the coachman as he stepped down out of the carriage. True to his word, he never set her down as he strode to the cottage door.

"Welcome to our home." He took his time sipping from her lips, tasting her fully with his tongue until she felt lightheaded. "Open the door, Pippa-lass."

She turned the knob and stared at the beautiful interior of their home. There was a round table near the cooking stove with four straight-backed chairs. Two upholstered chairs faced one another by the fireplace. Across the room were three doors, two of which were closed. Pippa looked in the open door and saw a bed, adorned with a quilt in shades of green and cream, a chest of drawers, and a chair. "It's lovely, Dillon. A generous gift from his lordship and her ladyship."

He closed the door to their cottage with his foot and stopped halfway to the bedroom. "I'm going to try to hold off talking ye to that bed, but I'm warning ye, it won't be easy."

Pippa slipped her arms around his neck and pressed her lips to his. When he moaned, she mimicked what he'd done earlier with his tongue, earning a groan from Flaherty this time.

"If ye keep that up, I'll not be able to wait more than five minutes."

"It might take longer than that to do whatever it is Millie meant when she said you would do things to make it easier for me to bear the pain."

Flaherty eased her to her feet and pulled her into his embrace. "Ah, lass. I'll be as gentle as I can. All I ask is for ye to trust me."

Pippa tilted her head back and stared up into the face of the man she'd come to count on for more than the safety of Millie, Roarke, and herself. She'd leaned on his strength when the physician was sewing her wound closed, and listened to him speak of family, vows, and honor. Everything she knew about Dillon Flaherty up to this moment had her sharing what was in her heart. "I trust you with my heart and my body, Dillon."

"I promise to take ye to the stars, lass—more than once." He eased her out of his arms, removed his frockcoat, and set it on the chair by the bed. "Now then, the first thing we need to do is rid ourselves of these garments."

Pippa's mouth was still open by the time he'd shed his cravat, waistcoat, and cambric shirt.

Flaherty gently tapped beneath her chin until she closed her mouth. "Turn around so I can undo yer buttons."

She couldn't think of what to say, so she inclined her head and spun around. The feel of his hands on the back of her gown, opening one button at a time, had tingles shooting down her spine. His hands were warm on her shoulders as he turned her around to face him.

"Shall I help ye take off yer gown?"

Be brave, she told herself, and managed a strangled "Yes."

His eyes never left hers as he slowly slipped her gown up and over her head. He carefully laid it over his clothing on the chair. "Before I help ye off with yer chemise, have a seat."

"A seat?"

"Aye, I'll help ye off with yer half boots, then I'll remove me own." When he removed her footwear, he sat on the edge of the bed and took off his boots and socks.

"If you turn your back, I'll remove my stockings."

She waited for him to do so, but he grinned instead. "I'm thinking ye should leave them on."

Confused by his request, she muttered, "But I don't sleep with my ribbon garters and stockings on."

Flaherty pulled her onto his lap and watched her chemise slip off one shoulder. He nipped her shoulder, then kissed it. "Ah, lass, we won't be sleeping."

$$\diamond\!\!\!\diamond\!\!\!\diamond\!\!\!\diamond\!\!\!\diamond$$

CHAPTER EIGHTEEN

FLAHERTY WAITED FOR the lass to fully relax. Little by little, his nips and kisses elicited a delightful chorus of moans and groans from his wife—interspersed with her gasps of surprise as he slowly added kindling to the fire he planned to stoke inside of her. His goal was but one: to have the lass mindless to all but the pleasure his mouth, his teeth, and his tongue gave her.

"You taste of springtime. 'Tis like making love in a field of flowers." He gathered her to his heart and rose from the edge of the bed. "I'm trying to hold on, lass, but I'm not sure how much longer I can wait."

"Wait? For what?"

The confusion in her pleasure-dazed expression touched a part of him that he'd walled off years ago. He'd never planned to marry. The lass was messing with his concentration. He had a task to see to...to consummate their marriage for it to be legal. Had she forgotten that part of their vows? Cleaving unto one another? Her innocence was bone deep. 'Twas time to wake that up.

He spun around and placed her in the middle of the bed and stepped back, just to look at her. The longer he looked, the more he wanted. His desire for her eclipsed what he'd felt for any other woman. Was this what his brothers had felt? Unsure if it was simply desire for the woman who would bear his children, he shook his head.

"What's wrong?" The tremor in her voice grated over the questions in his mind. The raw need to bury himself inside of the curvaceous beauty that was his bride had him by the throat. But an unfamiliar emotion sweeping up from the soles of his feet had him clamping down hard on the need to take what lay before him.

Flaherty bit back the coarse words he had used with other women. They would cheapen what was between himself and Pippa. He refused to do that, but could not keep the grit from his voice when he answered, "There's more to what happens in the marriage bed, lass."

"I know, Millie said that there would be."

"Aye, ye told me that earlier when ye gave me yer trust. I'm thinking I'll start at the bottom and work me way up." The thought of skimming his hands and mouth from the tips of her toes to her woman's core had a tight grip on his bollocks. "I'm thinking we need to remove yer shift."

Flaherty leaned over her and brushed a featherlight kiss to her lips. Her chin. The base of her throat. Inhaling her scent, he groaned. "Ye bounteous beauty is a feast fit for a king." He lifted his head and stared into the blue-gray eyes that had darkened to the color of a storm cloud in the early spring. "But I'm no king, lass."

She reached up to touch his face. "And I have no title," she murmured as she traced the rugged shape of his cheek, the strong line of his jaw. "Unless you pen a missive to me, but I am far from honorable."

Flaherty stiffened and reared back. "By all that's holy, lass, ye're more honorable than most of the men I know—save me family and the men we serve." Seduction could wait. The need to help her understand how much he revered her strength as a protector of those weaker than herself roared to the surface. "Ye stood yer ground when I approached." Before she could disagree, he reminded her, "Though I offered me assistance, ye were right not to trust easily. Ye did not know me then, lass."

Her eyes glistened with unshed tears. "But I shot—"

"We both agreed 'twas an accident, lass. One ye need to forget."

She slid her hands to his sides and watched him closely. He didn't flinch. Truth be told, he barely remembered it, nor felt it. "Ye're the one who took a blade to the back… If it had been any lower, it could have skewered yer lung! And all to protect the babe of yer childhood friend."

He almost let it slip that there was a chance Millie's husband was reported as dead because of the mission he had been on when he went missing. But Flaherty had given his word to Tremayne along with the others. None of them would tell, but would be there when and if the man returned from the dead like Lazarus.

She slid her hands up his sides, around to his back, and onto his shoulders. "You are physically as strong as the heroes of old, Dillon. But it's not just your physical strength that I depend upon; it's the strength of your heart in your loyalty to the duke and his family—and your own. I know you will honor your pledge and protect Millie, Roarke, and me."

Her words smashed his youthful determination not to marry or give his heart to another. He relinquished it one inhale at a time as he drew the essence of her into him. In return, he would give her his strength and essence and prayed that it would plant the seeds of their love this night and bear fruit nine months from now. "Ye already have me vow, lass, pledged not an hour ago before God, the vicar, the baron and baroness, me family, and yer friend." Flaherty eased back, grasped the hem of her chemise in one hand, and slowly slid it past her knee. Pausing mid-thigh, he bent and kissed her, tasting her, tempting her to want more of him, because he was a hairsbreadth from losing control.

The scent of her, the feel of her beneath his hands, had him craving more—he wanted it all. He kissed her as if his life depended upon her responding to him. God help him, it did! She moaned into his mouth, shyly touching his tongue tentatively, then more boldly, as her hips lifted, seeking what she had yet to experience. In that moment, he felt himself fall the rest of the way in love with her. There would be no other woman in his life that would be able to reach into him and pull out the feelings the lass did. No other woman would grow round with his babes. He prayed to be the one to die first, but if the Lord took her before him, he would dedicate his life to the sons and daughters that the love between them would make.

When he could bring himself to stop kissing her, he whispered, "Let me undress ye. I need to see the beauty no one else ever will." He slid the chemise up to her hip on one side, waiting for her to acquiesce. "I need to ready ye to receive me, lass. I'm not bragging when I tell ye that it'll be a tight fit."

Her furrowed brow had him gently taking her hand and pressing it to the hot, hard length and breadth of him beneath the trousers he'd yet to remove. At her gasp, he sighed. "Faith, 'tis a burden to be so well endowed, but 'tis one I've accepted."

Her snort of disbelief irritated him at first, until he realized she had nothing to compare his cock to—and by God, she never would! "Ye'll have to be taking me word for it, lass, as yer searching for another man to compare me to is out of the question."

"You are outrageous! I would never even think to comp—"

Flaherty cut off her words with his mouth, climbed on the bed, and settled between her thighs. Using some of his weight, but not all of it, he pinned her into the mattress. Two more threads holding his libido in check snapped. When she shifted to cradle him with her hips, he ended the kiss and leaned his forehead against hers. "If I'm to ready ye, I need to do what I promised…starting at yer toes. I'm giving ye fair warning—I'm wanting a deep taste of ye, lass."

Confusion mixed with desire in her eyes. "Didn't you just do that when you kissed me?"

He shook his head and slid down her body until her dainty,

stocking-clad feet were within reach. "Another time, I'll peel yer stockings off." He kissed his way up to her knees and lifted his head, delighted with the dazed look in her eyes. "I'm wanting to remove yer chemise, lass, but can wait until after I taste yer honey."

Her shock had him deciding not to wait for her answer. He licked and nibbled a path up the inside of her thigh until he could bury his face between her legs. He gripped her hips with his hands and murmured against her core. "Ye're already wet, but I need more of yer essence—yer honey—if ye're to take all of me."

Her garbled reply was music to his ears. She was mindless to all but his tongue tasting her, delving into her core, testing for the softening he knew would indicate she was nearly ready. Though it killed him, Flaherty paused, lifted his head, and rested his chin on where his mouth had been. "I need to stretch yer opening. 'Twill ease yer pain."

The feisty lass frowned at him. "How?"

"'Tis easier to show ye."

She shook her head, and the hint of fear in her eyes undid him. He slid two fingers up over her knee to the top of her thigh. "I'll be using these."

Pippa bit her lip. He nuzzled her core, and she moaned. "Dillon. I ache."

"I'll be relieving that ache. Watch me eyes, lass, as I test yer core." He inserted one finger, and she lifted her hips. He groaned and put a chokehold on his lust. Flaherty set the rhythm he knew would tempt her to reach for what she did not know was waiting for her. He added a second finger, urging her toward the release he knew her body ached for. She stiffened and cried out his name as her orgasm ripped through her.

Flaherty was there to catch her when she fell apart in his arms. His fingers were still buried inside of her when she blinked and stared into his eyes. "What just happened?"

"Well now, I'm thinking ye've been to those stars I promised ye."

"Oh." She shifted beneath him. "Dillon?"

"Aye, lass, I'm thinking ye need a second trip to the heavens before ye'll be ready for me. Do ye trust me not to hurt ye?"

"I do."

"I'll be adding one more finger and me mouth." She shivered beneath him, and he whispered, "I'll not stop until ye drench me, lass. Then I'll be removing yer shift."

Eyes locked on his, she whispered. "Yes, please."

PIPPA FELT HER body tighten to the point where she ached, but the coil continued to build. Warm, firm lips licked and nibbled one thigh and then the other, while Dillon's masterful fingers worked their magic until she felt herself experiencing the same rush of feeling as before. When his fingers plunged deep, his mouth found her again. His tongue tormented, while her hips thrust upward, seeking more of the bliss her husband's mouth and hands gave her.

She felt a fullness she had not before and knew he'd added another finger. *Good Lord!* She couldn't decide if the ache inside of her was from the stretching or something else.

"You're almost there—open yer mind and yer heart. Take all that I'm giving ye."

His words and ministrations seeped into her, and she felt the ache burst inside. Unable to hold back, she lifted her hips off the mattress and screamed out his name. As the ecstasy still had her in its grasp, she felt her husband peeling her chemise off her. She reached for him, but he urged, "Not yet. I need to rid meself of these trousers."

And then his hot skin seared into hers as he wrapped his arms around her and settled himself between her legs. She could feel the heat of his shaft at her core and knew pain would follow, but she accepted that it would not always be so. Needing Dillon to know that she was willing, and grateful for his taking the time to ready her for his invasion, she shifted and wrapped her legs around his waist.

He cupped her backside and slowly entered her. She felt a pinch of pain, but heard his words of encouragement. "Ye'll stretch to accept me, lass. Know that I love ye, and think of the beautiful babes we'll make between us."

Heart full, body craving what it had yet to experience, she gave over to the wonder of their joining. Her reward was the tension she'd experienced before. This time she knew where it would lead her.

As he thrust into her with the rhythm he'd set earlier, with his fingers and tongue, he groaned, "Come with me, *mo chroí*."

She lifted her hips to meet each thrust, reveling in the sensations coursing through her body until she could no longer hold back. Dillon thrust deep and stiffened. Instinctively, she slid her hands to his muscled backside and held on for dear life, while her inner walls tightened around him.

"Phillipa!"

Her name on his lips was accompanied by a rush of warmth inside of her as his mouth found hers and he kissed her lingeringly until his body relaxed. The heavy weight of if set off tingles in places she had only just been introduced to. When he shifted, she was surprised that she wasn't ready to let him move just yet, but the warmth of him was lulling her to sleep.

The last thing she heard was the gruff sound of Dillon's voice. "*Mo ghrá.* I love ye, Phillipa."

"Mmm…I love you too."

CALLUSED HANDS STROKING from her shoulder to her wrist woke her. She slowly opened her eyes and smiled.

"There ye are, lass. I was wondering when ye'd wake up."

She blinked. "I didn't mean to fall asleep on you."

His deep chuckle had the more intimate parts of her waking up too. "I'm not complaining but need to take care of the parts of ye that I may have abused, though I tried me best not to."

Pippa trailed the tips of her fingers along his jaw. "You have whiskers."

He laughed. "Aye, they usually start making an appearance by nightfall."

"I never noticed them before."

"We've never spent this hour of the day together before—excepting when I was watching over ye after the physician took care of yer wound."

"Why didn't you have whiskers then?"

"I took the time to shave them off when I finished me shift so that ye wouldn't be startled by me unshaven face."

"Oh."

"Now then, *mo chroí*, I need to wash ye—and before ye refuse, 'tis me duty as yer husband to take care of ye. That includes washing the parts I intend to spend more time worshipping."

Pippa had never even conceived of having such an intimate conversation and had no idea what to say. She felt the bed shift as Dillon rose and—without a stitch of clothing on—walked over to the pitcher and bowl. After he poured water into the bowl, she watched as he dipped in a cloth and a round of soap.

She closed her eyes as he reached her side of the bed.

"Phillipa, love, do not be embarrassed. Please watch me tend to ye. Whenever ye think ye're ready, I'll be letting ye tend to *me*."

Her eyes shot open—and so did her mouth at the sight of his large hands gently washing her. That this giant of a man could tend to her so gently gave her hope that he would do the same for any babes they had. In her heart, she sensed that Dillon would be a wonderful father. She'd seen the way he treated Percy and Phineas, and little Roarke, too.

"Well now, that got ye to do as I asked. 'Tisn't out of the ordinary for married couples to take care of one another. We're one now, lass. And if God in His mercy grants me wish, we conceived the first of our thirteen children."

"Thirteen?" The number astounded her. Four, mayhap five like her parents had had—but thirteen? "Why thirteen?"

He changed the subject. "I'm looking forward to bathing with ye."

"With me?"

"Aye."

"In a tub?"

He was trying not to smile when he asked, "Would ye rather bathe in the stream near here?"

"Good Lord, no!"

"'Tis a bit chilly at certain times of the year," he admitted as he finished washing her, then returned the cloth to the washstand and returned with a large cloth. "Let me dry ye off. I'll be careful, as ye're bound to feel a bit sore."

When he finished and returned the drying cloth to the washstand, she knew in her heart that with their earlier vows and consummating of their marriage, something magical had occurred.

Pulling the covers up to her chin, she whispered, "Where once were two, now are one."

"Aye, Phillipa. Mayhap in a few weeks, proof of our love will start to show."

"Weeks?"

He stared at her. "Me seed could have already taken hold, lass. Though it may take a bit of time before ye notice yer body changing."

Embarrassed that her husband seemed to know more about the making of babes than she did, she ducked her head to her chest and shrugged. She felt the mattress dip under his weight as he sat beside her. The tip of one finger lifted her chin until their eyes met.

"I have suffered many injuries since becoming a member of the duke's guard, but none are deeper and no battle harder fought than when a woman gives birth. I grew up on a farm, and knew more than I wanted to about life, birth, and death by the age of five summers. Watching the three women under me protection suffer through the early stages of pregnancy, to where they are right now, I've picked up more than enough information to know what to expect."

"You probably know more than I do."

He shrugged. "'Tis possible. Sure and me cousins and meself observed the duchess when she was expecting the twins, before leaving Wyndmere Hall to man our assigned posts at the various estates the duke owns—and those of his distant cousins Baron Summerfield and Viscount Chattsworth. I'll be watching over ye more closely, lass. Never doubt that I will take care of ye and see that ye rest when ye should, eat when ye might forget or not be wanting to."

"I do not believe my father ever did that," she muttered.

"Ah, how could ye, if ye're the youngest in yer family? Don't discount what yer da may or may not have done."

"He never spent too much time around me until he heard that Millie and I were spending too much time in the stables, and riding bareback across the meadows."

"When ye were what, four and ten?"

She shook her head. "I believe I was two and ten...maybe three and ten. I honestly don't remember."

Dillon pulled her into his arms, apparently not concerned with his nakedness at all. She was very conscious of the play of muscles across his chest, and in his arms and shoulders whenever he moved. Tingles raced up her spine and she shivered.

"Cold?" Her face flamed, and he chuckled. "Ah, well now, I can do something about that without adding to any soreness ye may be having...if ye like."

Intrigued, she asked, "What kind of something?"

His blue eyes glittered with desire. "Well now, let me show ye what I have in mind."

He kissed a path from beneath her ear to her collarbone. Her breath snagged in her lungs when he licked and kissed his way to her breastbone, and took her breast into his mouth, suckling deeply.

"Is it permissible for a wife to kiss her husband in the same manner?"

He groaned. "Aye, Phillipa." Given license to do so, she tortured him by kissing the same path he'd used on her. Nibbling, licking, and kissing.

HOURS LATER, THEY had charted an intimate map of spots that tantalized and spots that tickled. Unfortunately, she had more ticklish spots than he had. But she now knew that scratching Dillon's back and his head relaxed him. Kissing and nibbling on his hip bone caused an instant reaction—one that she reaped the benefits of, and in the heat of the moment did not notice any tenderness.

As she fell asleep safe within his arms, she had a feeling she would experience discomfort tomorrow, but tonight, she felt loved. The way Dillon had slowed his pace and tempered his lovemaking made her feel wanted and treasured. Though she was inexperienced, she hoped he had felt the same.

Pippa could not wait until tomorrow to begin their new life together.

CHAPTER NINETEEN

EXHAUSTION HAD HER snuggling beneath the covers, but the sound of someone calling her name pulled her from sleep. She woke to find her handsome husband leaning over their bed, smiling at her. "Ah, the faery princess has awoken at last."

Pippa rubbed the sleep from her eyes, sat up, and immediately felt the chill. A glance down revealed what she feared—she was naked! She tugged the covers up to her chin. Belatedly, she remembered that she and Dillon had spent a good part of last night admiring one another's attributes—though she was too embarrassed by her reaction to a particular part of his anatomy to admit to it this morning.

From the knowing look on his face before he turned and reached for a garment on the chair by the bed, she knew he remembered it too.

He turned back to her and helped slip her chemise over her head. "Ye must be hungry after expending so much energy last night, lass. Though ye'll not find me complaining a bit."

"I...er...could eat." His self-satisfied expression irked as her embarrassment increased. "Are you enjoying yourself at my expense?"

Flaherty retrieved his frockcoat and wrapped it around her shoulders, then plopped himself next to her. She had to scoot her legs over to avoid being sat on. "I'm enjoying me wife's hesitation—not embarrassment. Ye were a joy to instruct last night, Phillipa. I'm looking forward to continuing tonight."

The sudden fear that she would be stuck alone in the cottage all day was not like her. Why was she all of the sudden unsure of herself?

"What's troubling ye, lass? It's to be expected that yer womanly parts would be tender this morning, but not overly so. Was I too rough last night?"

She could not seem to force the words past the lump in her throat. His concern eased the worst of her embarrassment, but his next words compounded it.

"I'd best take a look to see if I damaged ye."

Pippa put both hands on the covers by her hips. "No!"

For a second she thought she saw hurt in his expression. She blinked, and his concern had her immediately apologizing. "Forgive me, but I'm not accustomed to having a man examine me—there!"

"Well now, if ye had been, I'd be asking the man's name and taking a strip off his hide."

"You would… Wait a moment. What?"

"As yer husband, 'twould be me right to ensure the man wouldn't speak ill of ye." He tugged on her hands and pulled her onto his lap. "Ye have no fear that I'd ever speak of what happens in the sanctity of our home—especially the reason ye'll be exhausted. Though, I will confess, I'll be having a bit of trouble concentrating on me tasks today."

"You're expected at your post? I would have thought you would at least have a day or two to… Well, that is to say… Is it not normal to have a few days to celebrate one's marriage?"

His soft chuckle soothed her nerves. The strength of his arms as he enfolded her into his embrace, and the way he'd dropped his chin to the top of her head, told of the depth of his feelings. They had spoken of love last night, but he had said a few words she did not understand.

"What do *mo chroí* and *mo ghrá* mean?"

He eased back to brush his lips over hers. "'Tis the Irish for *me heart*, and *me love*."

Tears welled up and spilled over before she could stop them. Dillon kissed her gently…reverently.

"Never doubt for a moment that I love ye, Phillipa. Ye are *mo chroí*, and *mo ghrá*."

"And you are mine. I love you, Dillon. Are you certain that you have to leave soon?"

"As soon as I feed ye and help ye wash and dress. I've asked for a copper tub to be delivered before midday. I'm sure Millie and Roarke will be visiting with ye today. Mayhap Caro and Prudence, too. But I'd warn ye not to overdo and to ask that ye conserve some of yer energy—ye'll be needing it for tonight."

Her face felt as if it were on fire, and she had a feeling she knew what he meant from the desire in the depths of his blue eyes. She gathered her composure to ask, "I will?"

"Unless ye are too tender."

Pippa put her hands over her eyes and groaned. "Will I ever get used to your speaking of intimate things in the light of day?"

"Am I only to speak of them after dark?"

"Well, no." Frustration bubbled inside of her, making it difficult to put her feelings into words. "I mean, that is to say… Botheration! I don't know."

He kissed her deeply. "Ye are a joy to rile, lass. I'm looking forward to later. Now then, I've put the kettle on and laid out what Mrs. Green packed in the basket for us last night."

She smiled. "I wouldn't mind eating cake for breakfast. I won't be lazy tomorrow morning—and if you were wondering, I *can* cook."

"Can ye now? I hadn't thought to ask, but will appreciate having a meal ready and waiting for me during me dinner shift. Me cousins and I take our meals at different times, so that we can rotate the men we've trained to cover for us on a daily basis to take our posts. They get the experience they need, and Garahan and O'Malley—and now meself as well—have a home-cooked meal with their wives."

He tucked a lock of hair behind her ear and brushed his hand over her hair. "'Tis like moonlit silk. May I brush if for ye tonight? I'm afraid I don't have enough time this morning."

Her heart fluttered in her breast as she asked, "Are you certain they cannot spare you? You did mention that you have men who are trained to take your place."

"Ah, Pippa-lass, if ye knew how much I want to stay home, wrapped in yer arms—even if 'tis only to sleep—I cannot. We're expecting visitors—"

He broke off and scrubbed a hand over his face. "Bloody hell! I gave me word not to say anything…but ye're me wife now and… I'll ask Tremayne if I may tell ye." When she opened her mouth to speak, he held up a hand. "Me word is me bond. Don't ask me to break it."

"I would never do that. I feel the same as you. And before you ask, once a Stanhope gives their word, we keep it."

"Ye've the soul of a warrior, lass. As feisty as any Irishwoman I know. Me ma will love ye." He set her on her feet and smoothed the covers up and over their pillows before placing his hand at the small of her back.

The heat of his hand had her thinking of things best left until later. When he pulled out the chair for her, she sat and immediately shifted on her seat. Without a word, Flaherty walked over to their bed, retrieved one of the pillows, and motioned for her to stand up so he could place the pillow on her chair. "Should I be asking for that tub to be delivered earlier?"

"Thank you for thinking of my comfort, but I'll be fine. As a matter of fact, since you will be busy with your duties, I believe I see where *I* can be useful today." When Flaherty stared at her, she shrugged. "I'm not used to being idle, husband."

Flaherty poured her tea, while she set out thick slices of cake. He smiled and had a forkful of cake to his lips when she asked, "When do you expect my brothers to arrive?"

The cake missed his mouth and fell back onto his plate. He

carefully placed his fork beside it. "I beg yer pardon?"

"My brothers, Randolph and Miles. I assume they are the visitors expected today. After all, Tremayne has ascertained that Millie and I are telling the truth, and I'm quite sure he passed the information on to Captain Coventry—wasn't that his name? My eldest brother George is always tied up with the estate, and I haven't had a letter from Winston for months—that leaves Randolph and Miles. Though last I heard, they were both at sea."

She pushed his cake plate toward him and motioned for him to eat. When he was chewing, she added, "Millie and I decided a few years ago that the reason we seldom hear from Winston is that he is a spy for the Crown."

Flaherty started coughing. Pippa got up and patted him on the back until he could clear the mouthful of cake from his throat. "Are you all right? I've never seen anyone choke on a bite of cake before."

He sipped his tea and frowned at her. "Do ye have any other questions before I take another bite? This cake is too good to be wasting."

"Just that Millie and I also agreed that the reason she received so little information about Roarke is that he too must be a spy. That being the case, it would be detrimental not only Millie and her babe, but to her father as well. Earl Haybrook has powerful connections within the *ton*—but so does my father. We were hoping our fathers would make the time to go to the War Office while the House of Lords is in session. Neither Millie nor I have heard from our fathers recently. The fear that Roarke was indeed working undercover was the main reason Millie did not confide what was happening to her father."

"And that is why ye neglected to tell *yer* father or the one brother who would be able to assist ye in the threats to Millie and yerself."

"I never said..." She closed her mouth and crossed her arms in front of her, letting her husband see her irritation with his last remark.

Instead of trying to soothe her frustration—and therefore her fears—Flaherty grumbled something that sounded like a curse beneath his breath before he said, "I don't have the time to extract all of the information from ye now. But know this—I expect ye to tell me the whole of it when I come home for supper!"

Pippa did not answer him. She turned her attention to topping off the tea in their cups.

Flaherty grunted. "Finish yer cake, lass, so I can bathe ye and determine whether or not ye'll be sitting on a pillow for the next few days, or if all ye need is me attention and tender care."

Pippa's neck and face flamed. She wished she did not embarrass so easily and hoped she would be able to control that reaction in the not-too-distant future.

A FEW HOURS later, frustration added fuel to the fire of Flaherty's temper. "Are ye telling me not to confide in me wife after she already discerned that two of her brothers are no doubt making their way toward Summerfield Chase even as we speak?"

Tremayne calmly asked, "Would you go against a direct order?"

Flaherty inhaled deeply, ready to blast the lieutenant with his temper, but could not. Tremayne had the right of it. "Ye know I would not. 'Tis just that I've never been in this position before. Though, recently, I've had the suspicion that O'Malley and Garahan have with Caro and Prudence."

Tremayne nodded. "Coventry has with Miranda as well, but there are times when I would think it would be permissible to bend the rules, but only after you ask the person directing the operation—and you know for a fact that that isn't me—for permission."

"Aye." Meeting the lieutenant's direct gaze, Flaherty asked,

"Do ye have a quarter of an hour to spare?"

"Aye."

Flaherty grinned. "Well now, as it happens, so do I—'tis the time allowance between shifts. Care to go a few rounds in the outbuilding?"

Tremayne laughed. "I won't even need half that amount to time to knock you off your feet."

"Care to make that a wager? I'm thinking I may need the extra blunt now that I've a wife—and her best friend and babe to provide for."

As they walked toward the stables, and the outbuilding just beyond, Tremayne asked, "Do you mean to tell me Millie and her babe are going to be living with you?"

"Aye. Until we can find substantial proof of her brother-in-law's threats, I gave me word she'll be under me protection—Garahan and O'Malley have too."

"And you cannot do that unless she is near at hand."

"Aye." Flaherty opened the door and waved his hand for Tremayne to precede him. "'Tisn't much, but it has been home for a couple of years. As well as the safest place to store munitions and extra weapons. Until recently, the three of us bunked here prior to marrying."

The lieutenant scanned the room and nodded. "I see that you've cleared a large portion of the room."

Flaherty slipped out of his coat and tossed it on a bench along the wall. "We rarely require more space to maintain our bare-knuckle skills." He slowly smiled. "How rusty are yers?"

The lieutenant removed his frockcoat and tossed it next to Flaherty's. In a few moments, they had removed their cravats and waistcoats. Rolling up his sleeves, Tremayne asked, "Do we have time for best two out of three rounds?"

Flaherty snorted with laughter. "I'll only need one blow to take the starch out of yer legs."

With that, the men exchanged blows. Tremayne wavered on his feet, but did not go down. Flaherty followed his right cross with two quick jabs to the throat—both of which the lieutenant blocked, before delivering an uppercut that had Flaherty's head ringing.

"Faith, ye're harder to knock out than I thought!" The door burst open and hit the wall twice, but neither Tremayne nor Flaherty turned to see who it was. They were both determined to win the fight decisively with a knockout.

"Why did ye not wait for us?" Garahan demanded.

"Ye know we aren't supposed to be sparring in the middle of the morning," O'Malley barked.

Flaherty gritted his teeth and delivered another right cross, this time putting every ounce of his strength and his anger at the situation his wife, Millie, and her babe were in behind it. Tremayne dropped his hands, rubbed his chin, and blinked. "Hell of a blow," he rasped, reaching for Flaherty's shoulder.

Flaherty coiled, ready to strike another blow, but noticed Tremayne's eyes weren't focused. "Ye'd best sit down, lieutenant. O'Malley, toss that bucket of cold water on him."

"Aye," Garahan agreed, "that should do the trick and fix his vision."

That done, Tremayne cursed, then shook his head, sending droplets of cold water everywhere. "I could have done without the bath, O'Malley."

Flaherty and his cousins snickered. "Let's have a look at yer eyes, boy-o. The dazed look is gone." He grunted. "Works every time." Turning to Garahan, he said, "Toss me that drying cloth for our friend here." He handed it to Tremayne. "Need me help?"

Tremayne chuckled. "You've helped enough, Flaherty. I need a shot of—"

Before he finished speaking, he had his choice of three flasks. He grabbed the one Flaherty offered. "I may need more than a shot."

"Drink as much as ye need. I can refill it, as I keep a supply of the Irish here with our ammunition."

Tremayne emptied half the flask, wiped his mouth with the

back of his hand, and gave it back. "Thanks, Flaherty. I have just one question."

"Oh?" Flaherty said. "What's that?"

"I hit you square in the chin with that uppercut. Is your jaw made of granite?"

O'Malley and Garahan laughed. "We've been building up the callus on his chin," Garahan replied.

"Aye," O'Malley agreed. "A few years ago, 'twould have knocked him flat."

Flaherty chuckled. "I wish I could lie and say it isn't true, but I cannot. Lads, we'd best get back to our duties. I've a wife to check up on—"

"Ye might want to let the ladies have a bit more time," Garahan suggested. "Caro and Prudence were on their way to yer cottage with two baskets loaded with provisions."

"I suppose I could wait," Flaherty said.

"Give them half an hour—I'll have one of the men cover the rest of yer shift," O'Malley said.

"I'll do it," Tremayne said. "After all, it isn't every day a man bests me in a round of bare-knuckle."

"How many hardheaded Irishmen have ye sparred with?" Flaherty asked.

The lieutenant chuckled. "As of today, I'd say six, possibly eight—and all of them related to you, Flaherty."

"I'll be taking that as a compliment—"

Flaherty stopped midsentence as the shrill whistle they'd taught the men who protected the baron and his family sounded in the distance. "Trouble!"

As one, the cousins reached for their rifles, shoved the door open, and ran like hell toward the sound. Two more whistles sounded as one of the men guarding the perimeter shouted to the roof top guard, "How many?"

The guard on the roof lifted his spyglass and called out, "Three—no, wait, four! Riding in formation with two in the front, one injured rider in the middle—his head is bandaged and his arm is in a sling. One man bringing up the rear."

"How far off?" O'Malley called out.

"They just rounded the curve by the copse of trees, should be here—To arms, O'Malley! The brigands are armed to the teeth!"

O'Malley reacted with a calm every man in the guard adopted when faced with the enemy. "Garahan, get the horses. Tremayne, go with him. Flaherty, warn Timmons and his lordship. Move the women, the twins, and Millie's babe to the nursery with two guards posted at the door and one at either end of the hall."

Flaherty thanked the Lord for the foresight to have someone fetch his wife as soon as he arrived for duty. He had a moment of fear wondering if the lass would venture back to their cottage without telling him.

Shaking that thought from his head, he concentrated on the dire situation they were in.

Flaherty knew they had time to ready their defense, given the distance, and that the riders approaching were not galloping. He sprinted toward the rear door of the house, and heard O'Malley give the order for two of their auxiliary guard to man their posts in the treetops on either side of the road leading up to the estate. A warning shot over their heads should be a surprise that the bloody bastards riding up to Summerfield Chase were not expecting!

As he reached the door, he saw Garahan and two men galloping toward O'Malley. He knew O'Malley would mount up and hold one of the horses for him. Flaherty yanked the door open, ready to shout for Timmons, but the butler and Summerfield were waiting for him. The baron had a brace of pistols tucked into his waistband—and the butler had a blunderbuss.

"We heard the signal. The women are in the nursery," the baron said. "*All* of the women, Flaherty, your wife included—along with Percy, Phineas, and Roarke. Two men are stationed outside the nursery, one at the head of the staircase and one guarding the servants' staircase. What is the status?"

Flaherty managed to nod, though his guts were tied in knots.

He had a wife, as well as her best friend and babe, to protect, and it added a new level of responsibility to his critical thinking. "Thank ye, yer lordship. I'll let the men know. They're waiting for me to mount up. We'll be waiting for the brigands to arrive."

"How many?"

"Four."

"Armed?"

"Aye, yer lordship. We've got our sharpshooters in position on either side of the drive, men on the roof, and more in position by the outbuildings. O'Malley, Garahan, Tremayne, and I will be on horseback, on the rise—the first thing the riders can see as they approach."

"What if they shoot first?" one of the younger footman asked.

Without hesitation, Flaherty replied, "I doubt they will. If they are approaching armed, they know me cousins and I are stationed here. They are either working for Millie's brother-in-law and have nefarious plans...or they could be me wife's brothers with plans of their own."

"You aren't afraid," the footman said. "Are you?"

Flaherty grunted. "Nay. 'Tis themselves that should be afraid of us!"

"If the situation changes, give the signal," Summerfield ordered him.

"Aye, yer lordship. Tell the women not to worry, and tell our wives we love them!"

"Done."

Flaherty sprinted outside, confident that Summerfield and Timmons had the matter well in hand. "I passed along yer messages!"

O'Malley and Garahan nodded. Though they had not asked, Flaherty knew from past experience to pass along word from his cousins to their wives that they loved them. It wasn't the first time trouble had come to Summerfield Chase...and it would not be the last.

He swung into the saddle and joined his cousins and

Tremayne as the first line of defense between the unknown and those he'd vowed to protect with his life.

CHAPTER TWENTY

PERCY AND PHINEAS took turns using the spyglass to report on what was happening outside. "It's my turn!" Phineas insisted reaching for the glass in his brother's hands.

Percy blocked him with his elbow. "The man in the middle has a bandage wrapped around his head—there's blood on it. His arm is in a sling. He could be a prisoner."

"Why on earth would they be riding here?" Prudence asked her cousins. "Unless it has something to do with His Grace and his lordship."

Caro added, "A valid point. Did you notice how Ryan and the others give every indication the group is a threat?"

"Do not forget to add that we have been sent to the nursery for our safety," Lady Phoebe grumbled.

Pippa blew out a frustrated breath. "It seems as if you're angry that your husbands and mine are trying to protect us." She glanced at Millie before adding, "They could have been sent here by Trentchester!"

Millie met Pippa's direct look and sighed as she continued to rock her babe. "It could just as likely be your brothers riding to fetch you home."

"I'm a married woman now. I *am* home," Pippa reminded her.

Lady Phoebe smiled. "From your dazed expression when you

arrived here earlier, not one of us have any doubt that you are *well* and truly wed."

Caro and Prudence dissolved into laughter, while once again, Pippa's face flamed. Millie smiled. "I recognized the signs too, Pippa. You might want to think over what you'll be saying to Randolph or Miles or whoever it is that brought reinforcements to take you home. You don't want Flaherty to have to shoot one of your brothers."

"You have a warped sense of humor, Millicent," Pippa grumbled. "I have no intention of going anywhere with my autocratic brothers!" The thought of being parted from her husband turned her stomach. The man had worked his way under her skin from the moment they met. First it was irritation—he was irritatingly handsome. Then annoyance—he managed to get a rise out of her whenever he opened his mouth. When she accepted his proposal of marriage and protection with one condition, he'd agreed without hesitation, firmly embedding him under her skin...and in her heart.

Flaherty had a gruff exterior with an intimidating, formidable temper, but he had a soft spot for widows and babes. How could she hold back her growing feelings and attraction for the man when he had readily accepted her condition, that Millie and her son would live with them?

Millie spoke up, interrupting Pippa's thoughts. "It would have been lovely living with you and Dillon. If you are forced to leave with your brothers, I do not relish explaining everything to my father. He'll want to know why I did not send word to him when Trentchester first started hurling threats."

"We both thought we could handle the braggart," Pippa reminded her. "Everything would have been fine, if your brother-in-law was not a complete reprobate...and if only—" She snapped her mouth shut. Millie's eyes welled with tears. Her friend knew Pippa so well, she knew what Pippa had not said. "Forgive me, Millie. I did not mean to mention—"

Phineas flinched at the sound of shots fired.

"What happened?" Percy demanded, rushing to look out the other window facing the stables.

"The men in the trees fired warning shots—probably Forrester and Mattison," his brother answered.

Lady Phoebe placed a hand on Percy's shoulder. "None of the duke's guard have changed their positions on the rise. We'll have to be patient to see if it is indeed Pippa's brothers who've come to call."

"What about the man riding in the middle?" Phineas asked. "With the bandage on his head and his arm in a sling, he's got to be their prisoner."

The baroness patted Percy's shoulder. "Wait here." She walked over to the other window and held out her hand. "May I borrow the spyglass, Phineas?" The boy did not hesitate to hand it to her.

Pippa moved to stand beside the baroness as the woman lifted the glass to her eye. "What do you see, your ladyship?"

"The injured man is as broad as our husbands—which, of course, is not an indication of guilt or innocence, simply a statement of fact."

Caro and Prudence moved to stand behind Percy, watching the scene unfolding below them. "The two men riding in front appear unruffled by the shots fired," Caro remarked.

"If they were closer, we would be able to see their faces," Prudence said.

Lady Phoebe handed the spyglass to Pippa. "Do you recognize any of the riders?"

Praying she did not, Pippa gazed through the glass and swore. "Botheration! It's Randolph, Miles and…dear Lord…it's Winston riding behind—" She handed the spyglass back to the baroness, grabbed Millie by the arm, and tugged her toward the door.

Millie resisted, refusing to budge. "I'm not leaving Roarke until we know who the men riding with your brothers are."

"But Millie, Roarke—"

"Is finally asleep after being awake for hours. I'm exhausted and not up to listening to you argue with your brothers, Pippa. You Stanhopes are so stubborn!"

"Millie, Roarke is—"

"Still asleep, despite our raised voices," Millie said. She patted Pippa's hand before she shifted out of her friend's grip. "You are the best of friends to think of my son. He will be so lucky to have the sister of my heart watching out for his welfare too!"

A loud, familiar roar had the room falling silent. Shock had Millie grabbing hold of Pippa's hand. "Is that… Did you hear… Pippa, am I dreaming?"

"That's what I've been trying to tell you. It's *Roarke*! Come on."

Pippa pulled Millie toward the door. This time, Millie swatted at her arm. "I am not going outside to meet my husband without our son!" Tears welled up and spilled over. "Oh, Pippa! He's not dead!"

Pippa struggled to hold her tears inside. She could weep later. "Hurry, Roarke's calling you." She tried once more to grab hold of her friend. "Don't make him wait."

Millie wiped her eyes with the backs of her hands and tucked in a loose hairpin. "Not without our son!"

"But you just put him down," Pippa reminded her.

"And he is about to meet his father!"

Prudence solved the argument by scooping up the sleeping babe, blanket and all. "Shall I carry him for you, Millie? That way you can greet your husband with open arms."

Pippa noted that all three women had tears in their eyes. Sisters of the heart, one and all, crying tears of joy for Millie and her babe. "What do you think, Millie?"

Lady Phoebe spoke up. "Before there is a melee down there, I suggest we *all* accompany Millie and her babe."

Prudence handed the sleeping infant over to Millie before motioning for her nephews to accompany her and Caro downstairs.

Pippa was closest to the door and opened it.

The two footmen eyed the group of women. "His lordship told us no one is to leave this room."

Lady Phoebe crossed her arms over her pregnant belly and glared at the men. "You two accompany us. Pippa's brothers are outside, and they've brought Millie's *dead husband* with them."

The men frowned. "Isn't that too gruesome a sight for a new mother to behold?" one footman remarked.

"Do you have to identify the body?" the other asked.

The baroness laughed softly. "Reports of his death were premature—"

"MILLICENT TRENTCHESTER!"

Millie beamed as her babe stirred in her arms. "That would be my husband. I best not keep him waiting."

"One of you lead the way," Lady Phoebe said. "The others may follow us. Once Summerfield sees us all together, he will know that I countermanded his orders."

"Again," the younger footman grumbled.

"Yes," the baroness said with a laugh. "You should be accustomed to that by now."

"Aye, your ladyship," the reprimanded servant replied.

Two guards led the way down the servants' staircase. It was closer to the back door. Two more guards brought up the rear. Pippa noted that all four men braced, as if they knew they were about to get their heads handed to them.

Pippa slipped her arm through Millie's on the way down, and had to hold her back when Millie tried to scoot around their guard to dash outside. "Wait. Please, Millie. Let the men do their job and protect—"

"Bloody hell, Phoebe! Are you mad?" Summerfield strode over to the women, who moved to form a semicircle of staunch support behind the baroness and Millie. "You were told to wait inside."

"You are the one who is mad!" the baroness retorted. "How could I possibly keep Millie from reuniting with her husband, who is very much alive?"

The baron's frown was fierce, but he gentled his touch when he reached for his wife's hand. She resisted at first, then acquiesced, allowing him to tuck her against his side. "We shall discuss this later."

The baroness laughed, and Pippa locked gazes with Flaherty, whose frown was just as fierce as the baron's had been. He, his cousins, and Tremayne moved to form a broad-shouldered wall between the baron and baroness and Pippa's brothers. Safely tucked behind Summerfield and Lady Phoebe, Pippa tugged on Millie's elbow until she moved to stand beside Pippa. Studying the couple, Pippa wondered if she and Flaherty would become as comfortable with one another in time. Would they be able to discern each another's thoughts and actions as easily?

Millie stiffened beside her and rasped, "Roarke, is it really you?"

"Millie!"

The two groups of men shifted—though Flaherty and the others did not relax their guard or human wall. A gaunt man, with his head wrapped in a bandage and his arm in a sling, slid off his mount one-handed. Pippa was smiling as Roarke strode toward Millie, who had slipped around them all to stand in front of Flaherty. As one, the men in the duke's guard shifted and crossed their arms in front of them.

Pippa was so proud of her friend, watching Millie flash a bright smile at Flaherty as she ducked beneath his elbow and slipped between him and Garahan. They'd perfected that tactic and used it more than once over the years when they'd disobeyed their fathers' orders to stay out of the stables.

"Millie?"

The anguished sound of Millie's name had tears welling in Pippa's eyes. She watched her friend close the distance until she stood a step away from the husband. "They told me you were dead," Millie rasped.

Captain Trentchester brushed the tips of his fingers along the curve of her cheek. "I'm not. You promised to write to me,

Millie," he said. "I never received any letters."

"I wrote to you every day," Millie told him. "I was devastated when you did not reply to my news about our babe."

"Colonel Stanhope rescued me from—well, I cannot tell you where…yet…if ever—and he explained that the War Office had reasons for withholding our correspondence. My superiors must have read them and confiscated them," he murmured, "and decided the news would distract me from my assignment. Do we have a daughter?"

Millie's smile was tremulous. "A son… I named him after you."

Captain Trentchester's Adam's apple bobbled, and Pippa's heart went out to the injured soldier as he wrapped his arm around Millie and gazed down in wonder at their babe…his son.

"'Tisn't a lie, then, Millie?" Flaherty asked. "This man is yer dead husband, come back to life?"

Captain Trentchester's head snapped up. "Who are you and what business is it of yours?"

Flaherty waited a beat before answering, "Name's Flaherty, and as it happens, yer wife is going to live with me."

"Over my dead body!" Captain Trentchester growled to the echo of snickers. He glanced over his shoulder at the three men who were laughing. "I'll gut Flaherty where he stands. You won't be laughing then."

"Well now, that depends on yer technique," Garahan said. "Me name's Garahan, cousin and member of the duke's guard along with Flaherty and our cousin O'Malley here. As I was saying, there's some who think they know the proper placement of a blade to the gut…but they don't."

Pippa rolled her eyes at Garahan's claim, wishing the tension would ease. It was making her head ache. She wondered why neither Garahan nor O'Malley introduced their wives, then noticed the baron had not done so either. Mayhap they were waiting until the brewing confrontation had either risen to a head or calmed.

"Aye, messy for certain, but not lethal," Flaherty remarked.

Pippa spoke up. "Husband, do tell Roarke the rest of what I asked of you."

A familiar deep voice called out, and Pippa sighed. Her brother Randolph was always the most outspoken. "So the rumors are true, Pippa? You're married."

"Yes, Randolph," she answered. "Allow me to introduce my husband, Dillon Flaherty, one of the Duke of Wyndmere's private guard."

The men eyed one another like opponents ready to do battle.

She sighed. "I'd like everyone to meet my brothers, Winston is a colonel in the army—though we have never had confirmation of which regiment he is attached to. Millie and I suspected for some time now that he is not at liberty to tell anyone what role he plays. We think he's a sp—"

Winston interrupted, "That's quite enough, troublemaker."

Pippa smiled at him before nodding to the brother on Winston's left. "Randolph is a captain in the navy, and Miles is a lieutenant in the marines. Our eldest brother George is currently working with Father's estate manager, learning all he will need to know to take care of the estate and everything the barony entails."

As no one else seemed ready to do so, Pippa took it upon herself to do the rest of the introductions. "Brothers, meet my husband's cousins, Ryan Garahan and his wife Prudence, and Thomas O'Malley and his wife Caro. Both men are also members of the duke's guard, stationed here at Summerfield Chase protecting the duke's sister, Lady Phoebe, and her husband Baron Summerfield. Lieutenant Tremayne was in the dragoons and currently works for Captain Coventry, the Duke of Wyndmere's London man-of-affairs and very good friend."

Garahan and O'Malley nodded without saying a word, and Tremayne mumbled a barely audible greeting. Her brothers did not acknowledge the introduction—they were too busy trying to stare the Irishmen down.

Pippa threw up her hands. "The polite thing to do would be to offer a hand or nod to my husband and his cousins. But I should have known my family would not care about my happiness."

"We care." Miles looked at his brothers. "I *told* you she would do anything to protect Millie—even marry a man without Father's permission."

"You forgot to mention that he is the man I happen to *love*, Miles," Pippa replied.

"Ye're a lucky bugger, Flaherty," Garahan said.

"We knew it the moment we heard the lass shot ye," O'Malley added.

"I know it, lads." Flaherty turned toward Pippa and slid his arm around her waist. Tucked against his side, he bent and kissed the top of her head. "I'll never be forgetting to tell ye I love ye, lass."

Pippa sighed again, reveling in the emotions swelling inside of her. It was as if her mother in Heaven was giving her approval. Emboldened by the idea, she demanded, "Why are the two of you here?"

"Have you forgotten that I'm here, too?" Winston interrupted. "What of the rest of the rumors?"

Pippa bit the inside of her cheek to keep from shouting at him. "I was not entirely ignoring you. But since you mention it, I wrote letters to the three of you, and not one of you deigned to respond. I can understand why Randolph and Miles didn't—they were on ships at the time. You weren't. Why should I answer you now?"

Flaherty tucked her more firmly against him. "*I'd* have made the time to answer yer letters, lass."

She smiled up at him, but before she could speak, Winston grumbled, "It seems you are still causing trouble for our father, hellion."

Flaherty tugged on Pippa's hand and eased her behind him. Garahan and O'Malley moved to stand in front of their wives, while Tremayne moved to stand behind Flaherty and Pippa, protecting their backs. "Ye'll apologize to me wife for the insult," Flaherty warned. "She's courageous and protected Millie and her babe with her life."

"She *did* shoot you," O'Malley reminded him.

"Though only because she did not know who you were," Garahan added, "even though you offered aid."

Pippa did not know whether to be happy that O'Malley left out the fact that the shooting was an accident, or be irritated that her cousins-in-law were airing her private business in front of her brothers. She decided to ask what she needed to know: "Why are you here armed to the teeth?"

Flaherty grumbled, "Yer brothers and I are going to settle this, Pippa-lass. Ye can ask yer questions later."

Pippa noted her brothers were staring at Flaherty, and for once, she was relieved not to have to butt heads with her siblings.

"Wonderful idea, Flaherty," Millie said. "My husband looks exhausted and has yet to be properly introduced to his son."

Ignoring her brothers, Pippa turned to Millie and Roarke and asked, "Is he not the most beautiful babe you have ever seen?"

"He's got a voracious appetite, just like his father," Millie said.

"I want to know what in the world you were thinking moving in with a married man," Captain Trentchester said.

"I thought you were dead…and then when Grant—"

His face lost all expression. "Then that part of what we've heard is true, too?" Millie and Pippa nodded simultaneously. "I should have known my brother was involved in this."

"He's involved in far more than you know," Tremayne said.

"Why do you say that?" Captain Trentchester demanded.

"Working undercover for Captain Coventry, your brother hired me to find your wife and son and deliver the babe to him," Tremayne replied.

"You blackguard!" Trentchester lunged toward Tremayne and was immediately restrained from behind. He looked over his shoulder. "Let go, Winston."

"Let's hear what Tremayne has to say first," Winston replied.

"Enough!" Baron Summerfield barked at the group, calling their attention to him. "You have arrived at my home, presenting arms that you obviously have every intention of using. I have a problem with that. Most are welcome at Summerfield Chase. In fact, when Flaherty brought Pippa, Millie, and her babe here for their safety, I did not question it. I accepted the responsibility of housing them under my roof. In addition to a mother and her newborn son, I have the responsibility of three"—he glanced at Pippa, tilted his head to one side—"possibly *four* pregnant women under the protection of the duke's guard, myself, and my staff. If anyone is going to be answering questions, the four of you shall be answering *mine!*"

The baron didn't wait for anyone to reply—he started walking back to the house. "We shall take this discussion inside, where our wives will be comfortable, and can see to Captain Trentchester's injuries. They appear to be recent." Summerfield nodded to two of the footmen who'd accompanied the women outside. "Tell Mrs. Green to expect a large party for tea—with all the trimmings. Our guests look hungry."

"At once, your lordship."

"Now then, Colonel Stanhope, your horses look as if they could use a good rub-down before they are cooled, watered, and fed."

The tenor of the volatile discussion having been shifted to one of practicality, as far as the baron and baroness were concerned, the colonel replied, "Thank you for the offer, your lordship—"

"Summerfield," the baron said.

"Thank you, Summerfield. Our horses have been ridden hard...but we can discuss that over the tea you graciously ordered on our behalf. Captain Trentchester and I were hailed by my brothers a few hours ago when by happenstance, we arrived at the same inn, with the same goal, while en route to find and rescue Pippa and Millie."

"We do not need rescuing!" Pippa insisted.

Flaherty pinched her waist. She gasped and glared up at him. Pity he was ignoring her in favor of staring at her brothers. She would talk to him about his outrageous behavior later.

"We did not expect to run into you, Winston—or Captain Trentchester, for that matter," Randolph muttered. "The both of you look like hell—though Roarke looks worse, as if he'd been a prisoner."

Neither Winston nor Roarke answered the unasked question—what happened, and how did they end up at the same inn as Randolph and Miles?

Miles spoke up as he led his horse to the stables. "There is a decade between myself and Pippa. She has always been headstrong. These two were hoydens growing up. As far as I can tell, they are—"

"Rare and beautiful women," Flaherty interrupted. "Would ye not agree, Captain Trentchester?" The captain inclined his head, and Flaherty continued, "Me wife has the courage of two men. She protected yer son from kidnapping—there was a traitor in our midst—and took a blade to the back for her trouble. Yer wife's courage was evident from the first, when we learned Millie made the journey here just days after giving birth."

"Stabbed!" Captain Trentchester roared. "Where were you when she was stabbed, Flaherty?"

"Searching the estate for your son, who had been kidnapped when Millie fell asleep."

Pippa's brothers rounded on the baron, who held up his hand. "We will continue this discussion at a lower volume in the comfort of the sitting room," Summerfield stated. "If you choose to keep shouting, you can remain in the stables with your horses."

Relief speared through Pippa. She was grateful that the baron had taken charge of the conversation.

"Our stable master will take good care of your mounts."

Lady Phoebe finally spoke. "If you gentlemen would please

join us, there is a washstand in the room right inside the back door with plenty of hot water, and another just off the kitchen. I shall ask Mrs. Green to come and take a look at your head, Captain Trentchester. Has a physician seen to it?"

"Aye, your ladyship," the captain replied.

"She has experience with the men protecting us and will let us know if we need to summon Dr. Higgins."

"Thank you, though I am certain there will be no need to summon another physician."

Millie smiled as she leaned against her husband. "Roarke does not like to be poked and prodded."

The baroness smiled. "What man does? Now then, gentlemen, there is always hot water on the boil for tea, and scones and iced teacakes always ready for unexpected guests. Though from the pinched expressions on your faces, I shall see what Mrs. Green has prepared for our midday meal. She normally keeps a supply of meat pies on hand for my brother's guard, who at times eat while changing shifts."

Pippa noticed the hesitation on her brothers' part and almost took pity on them. They were accustomed to having the upper hand, just like Father, but that was no excuse. They had offended the baron—not to mention Flaherty and their cousins—by arriving with their weapons displayed. "Of course you will have to remember to use your inside voices and mind your manners, my dear brothers."

Flaherty's snort of laughter was echoed by O'Malley and Garahan. "Faith, I love it when ye're feisty, lass."

Pippa smiled, rose on her toes, and kissed his cheek. "I know."

The women entered the building first and walked toward the kitchen. Pippa paused when she noticed the men were filing into the room with the healing supplies. "Dillon, are you joining us?"

"Shortly, love." When Garahan called his name, her husband said, "Save me a scone or two," and followed Garahan into the room.

She dragged her feet, wanting to stay with Flaherty. It had happened rather quickly, this need to be with him. Pippa had never felt anything like this around any of the men her father had considered as prospects for her hand. She lingered in the hallway, but ducked into the pantry when she heard an ear-splitting whistle. Careful not to be seen, she peeked out of the doorway and heard O'Malley give the order to wait here, while he led Garahan, her husband, and Tremayne outside.

Indistinct shouts told her nothing. She waited another moment, then a few more, relieved when Tremayne came back inside. Her relief was short-lived when she heard his rumbling voice say, "Six men on horseback are approaching. We could use your expertise, men—not you, Captain Trentchester. Stay here and let Mrs. Green finish cleansing that wound before she bandages it. O'Malley wants you to check on your wife and babe, but asks that you not let her ladyship or the others know there is a situation brewing outside."

"Aye, Tremayne. I'll do my best to keep the women calm and distracted."

"They're a crafty bunch."

"Thank you for the warning," Captain Trentchester replied. "So are my wife and Pippa."

"I'll send word if the situation becomes volatile," Pippa heard Tremayne say.

Her heart sank as she watched her brothers rush outside. They were honorable men—just like Flaherty and the others—rushing to defend the innocent. She was torn... Should she alert Millie and the others, or wait until one of the men returned to advise the situation had been handled?

Her mind raced as she vacillated between wanting to warn the women and sneaking outside to find out who the new threat was. Millie would be feeding her babe soon, and Pippa did not want her friend worrying needlessly. She had been through enough. Decision made, Pippa checked that the hall was empty and slipped out of the pantry. Praying neither Roarke or the cook would see her, she quietly opened the rear door and stealthily made her way outside.

She heard voices and slunk around the side of the building toward the sound. She spied the two groups of men lined up facing one another as if ready to do battle. O'Malley, Garahan, her husband, Tremayne, and her brothers faced six armed men who were hurling threats against them if they did not turn Millie and her babe over to them. She craned her neck to get a better look, but did not see Millie's brother-in-law among the men making their demands. Grant must have hired the disreputable bunch to help him capture Millie and her babe, but where was he?

From the sound of the angry voices, Flaherty and the others would comply when hell froze over. She smiled, remembering just how fierce the duke's men were. Watching them handle the situation and the group of men, horror filled her as a shout went up and a lone rider galloped up the drive toward the two groups of men. Instead of joining them, he veered to the right, vaulted over a low stone wall, and cut through the baroness's rose gardens—trampling them. She heard Winston, shout, "Grant! Stop!" as the man rode hell for leather toward the manor house.

Dear Lord, Grant is here! Fear had her spinning around and running toward the rear entrance. In that moment, Pippa knew that she and Millie had misjudged her brother-in-law. She had to get to Millie and warn the others! There was no doubt in Pippa's mind that Grant would keep trying until he achieved his goal of abducting Millie and her babe. He would never give up!

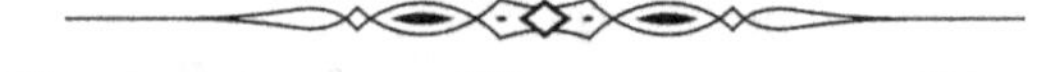

CHAPTER TWENTY-ONE

Captain Trentchester was already on his feet, heading for the back door to follow Pippa.

"Flaherty is going to need to know what his wife is up to," Mrs. Green warned.

"Warn the baron!" Roarke slipped the sling over his head, shoved it in his frockcoat pocket, and grabbed the brace of pistols from the sideboard where he'd placed them. He stuck them in his waistband. "I'm going after her."

"But you're injured," the cook protested.

"Thank you for tending to my wound, Mrs. Green—I'm grateful—but if anything happens to Pippa, my wife will have my head on a platter."

"Be careful."

Captain Trentchester nodded and slipped out the door. A muffled shriek had him bracing in time to catch Pippa in his arms. "It's Grant," she gasped. "He's—"

"Get inside. Now!" As his brother rode toward them, Roarke had the satisfaction of watching Grant pull back on the reins and slow to a stop. He drew his weapons, pointed them at his brother, and shouted, "Looking for someone?"

"You're supposed to be dead!"

"Ah, then the ploy worked. My superiors knew someone has been feeding our enemies information from the War Office." He cocked his pistols and aimed them at Grant. "I had no idea the extent you would go to, coveting Millie—but to be a traitor, too? You're despicable!"

The sound of a horse fast approaching had Roarke calling, "Dismount slowly. I'll make certain that you answer for your crimes against the Crown, threatening my wife while she was pregnant, and attempts to kidnap Millie, our son, and Pippa!"

"But Roarke," Grant rasped, "I'm your brother."

"Don't move!" Flaherty yelled, riding toward them.

The split-second distraction had Grant digging his heels into his horse's sides and bending low in the saddle.

Flaherty's shot went wide. Roarke's grazed his brother's arm, but it didn't slow Grant down. He gained momentum as his mount galloped along the back of the house, turning at the corner.

"I'll go after him," Flaherty shouted. "Warn the baron! Protect the women!"

Roarke ran inside to deliver the message, then turned back around to follow after Flaherty and was nearly trampled by Pippa's brother. Winston leaned to the side, held out a hand, and yanked Roarke up onto the back of his horse.

"Are my sister and your wife and son safe?"

"Aye. What of the six armed men?"

"Minor skirmish. Nothing to worry about. My brothers, O'Malley, Garahan, and Tremayne have things well in hand. Is that Flaherty up there, headed north through the woods?"

"Aye. Follow him!" Roarke urged. "Flaherty was right behind my brother when I went inside to warn the baron."

As they rode past the rear of the house, Summerfield waved at them, shouting, "Grant has Pippa!"

Winston slowed long enough to hear the baron add, "Pippa slipped outside before anyone realized she was gone. Millie said Pippa insisted she would create a diversion to keep Grant away from the women and save Millie and your son."

Roarke shouted, "After them!"

CHAPTER TWENTY-TWO

PIPPA'S HEART WAS in her throat, a dangerous place to be, as the blade in Grant Trentchester's hand was pressed against it.

"You have caused enough trouble for me! Millie is like a meek and mild lamb, following you and listening to everything you tell her to do. This stops *now!*"

Spittle from Trentchester's impassioned speech splattered on her forearm. But she refused to let go of his wrist to wipe it off. If she loosened her hold, she would feel the knife thrust deep, and the icy-cold blade would instantly be coated with her blood. Drop by drop, her life would ebb, and with it her chance at happiness with Flaherty.

Dillon. His name was a prayer whispered in her heart. She dared not say it aloud for fear that Trentchester would go after Flaherty and take his life as well. Though Pippa did not want to spend eternity without him, she did not want Flaherty to die because of her foolishness.

Dear Father in Heaven, she should have listened and stayed put with the other women. Why did she always have to hurtle headlong into trouble? She'd been in more scrapes over the years than her older brother Miles—and he was the mischief maker.

The tip of the knife against her throat reminded her not to make any sudden moves. She wondered how long her strength would hold out. The only thing keeping the knife from plunging into her throat was the hold she had on her captor's wrist.

"Don't move, Pippa-lass. Drop the knife, Grant, or I'll gut ye from neck to navel!"

Pippa gasped. Flaherty was here? How did he find her?

"Don't move, lass."

Fearing that she'd be the one gutted, she froze, while her mind reeled.

Her questions would have to wait. The knife lowered as Grant's grip on her loosened. She heard Winston shout a warning as she was flung toward the massive oak tree in front of them. She had seconds to act, and used her forearms to guard her face before she felt the impact as she crashed into the tree.

Her arms ached and her forehead burned. The last thing she saw was blood dripping onto her arms. Her tortured mind heard Flaherty shouting her name a heartbeat before darkness claimed her.

⫸⫷

"I'VE GOT GRANT, Flaherty. Pippa needs help!" Roarke shouted. He disarmed his brother, sweeping his feet out from under him, then put his knee in the middle of his back. "You will pay for all you have done to Millie and Pippa."

"You don't have the resources I have—"

Roarke growled, "You have *nothing*! There are witnesses who will testify to your cruelty and attempts to steal my wife—my Millie! Damn you to hell!"

"It will be your word against mine. You're just a lowly army captain, while I have connections within the military,"

"Viscount Palmerston of the War Office has a warrant out for your arrest, Grant," Winston told him, as he helped Roarke restrain Trentchester.

"But I am a wealthy man of business," Trentchester shouted,

"My wife is an heiress who—"

"Your wife has sought sanctuary with her aunt and will be filing for divorce," Roarke told his brother. "You have not been especially clever, covering up your misdeeds, Grant, nor the extravagant baubles and houses let for your three mistresses. Those expenses, added to your attempts to steal my son the moment he was delivered, will keep you locked up for years."

When his brother stopped struggling and lay still, Roarke called over his shoulder. "How is Pippa, Flaherty?"

"She's unconscious. Her arms are scraped raw and bruised. The left one badly—and the angle's all wrong. It may be broken." Flaherty felt as if every ounce of air had left his lungs. *God, why could I not have arrived a few moments sooner? Me wife has suffered enough, please let her regain consciousness so that I may tell her how much I love her?*

"She must have struck her head when my brother flung her out of his way."

Flaherty ripped off his cravat and dabbed at the steady trickle of blood from the cut high on her forehead. With pressure, he was able to control the bleeding. "'Tisn't as deep as I feared. I'll need to wrap it so I can carry her home. We need to get her back to Summerfield Chase as quickly as possible. Tie up the bloody bugger!"

"No rope," Roarke replied, pressing his knee harder against his brother's back.

"Ye have a cravat," Flaherty reminded him. "Use it!"

Roarke removed his cravat and tied Grant's hands behind his back—as of this moment, he no longer had a brother. "Done!"

"I have a spare cravat in me pocket, but me hands are full. Winston, can ye retrieve it for me? I need to put Pippa's arm in a sling before I lift her."

"Go ahead," Roarke told his friend. "I'll lend a hand after I flip the prisoner onto his back."

"Let him eat dirt!" Flaherty growled.

"Dear God, Pippa!" Winston rasped, "What happened?"

"Grant had a hold of her from behind, with his knife to her throat," Flaherty explained. "I convinced him to drop his weapon, but didn't anticipate that he'd fling me wife against a tree! He'll pay for that." Winston stalked over to where Flaherty cradled his wife to his chest. "The spare cravat's in me left pocket."

Pippa's brother retrieved the cravat from Flaherty's pocket and said, "You love my sister."

"With all me heart. We need to get her back as quickly as possible. Dr. Higgins will need to set her arm as quickly as possible. It'll swell soon."

Her brother winced. "We rode double to get here as fast as we could. Thank you for saving my sister's life, Flaherty."

"She's the other half of me heart. I'd lay down me life for her." When his wife stirred in his arms, he rasped, "Why did ye not stay put, lass?"

"I could not take the chance that he'd try to take Millie and Roarke's babe." Pippa slowly opened her eyes and grimaced. "Everything hurts."

Flaherty brushed a kiss to her cheek and shifted the cravat around her head until he was satisfied it would stanch the blood. "Aye, lass, not that ye deserve to feel pain, but mayhap it'll keep ye from running off, when ye should be telling yer husband there's trouble and leave it to him to deal with."

Pippa struggled to lift her one arm and realized it was being held immobile. She looked up and gasped. "Winston? Why are you here, and what are you doing with that cravat?"

Her brother quickly fashioned a triangle out of the cloth and handed it to Flaherty.

"Obliged, colonel. Hold still, lass, and while ye are, answer me question. Why did ye not stay put?"

Flaherty felt the cool touch of her small hand on his jaw and glanced down into tired blue-gray eyes shadowed with pain. "I did it for Millie. She's the sister I never had. Not that I do not love my brothers, but a sister is different."

"I know it, lass, as I've had occasion to watch more than one of me cousin's wives form an attachment to their sisters-in-law. I've yet to meet me brother's wives, but I'm certain they'll be like sisters to us in no time, like Caro and Prudence have become. None of them have been close friends as long as yerself and Millie."

Winston nodded. "You're right, Flaherty. They are sisters in all but blood." He held out his hands. "Here, I'll hold my sister while you mount."

"No need—I can do both." Before Winston or Roarke could stop him, Flaherty slung a leg over his horse and settled on its back with Pippa safely tucked against his heart. Once she was securely on his lap, he nodded to her brother. "If ye could cart the refuse back to Summerfield Chase, I'd be obliged. Ye can use this." He reached into the leather sack slung over his horse in front of the saddle and pulled out a length of rope. "I keep varying lengths of rope handy, as well as cravats, which are more useful to manacle hands. Ye never know when ye'll need a good, sturdy length of rope. Tie it to the bugger's hands and make him walk back alongside yer horse."

Winston did as Flaherty suggested.

Glancing down at his wife, Flaherty whispered, "Close yer eyes, lass, and rest yer head on me. I've got ye, and I'm never letting ye out of me sight again!"

Winston was tying the rope around Trentchester and paused. "That sounded like a threat, Flaherty."

"And so 'tis, but I'd never raise a hand to me wife."

Roarke shoved Winston out of his way. "Let me tie it."

Winston stalked over to Flaherty. "Just what did you mean by not letting her out of yer sight?"

"If ye've been promoted to the level of colonel without knowing what that means, I'll lose all faith in the army."

Roarke laughed. "You're an Irishman."

"That I am," Flaherty said, with an upward tilt of his chin. "And yer point would be?"

Roarke snickered. "You probably do not have any faith in the royal army to begin with."

Flaherty nearly choked on his laughter. "Well now, I knew ye had a good brain inside that thick head of yers. Faith, but I like ye, Roarke."

The small hand cupping his cheek had Flaherty looking down into his wife's bruised face. "Are ye all right, lass?"

"Just what *did* you mean by that comment, husband?"

"I'm thinking the knock to yer head rattled yer brains if ye're asking me that."

She poked him in the cheek. "Well?"

He chuckled as he captured her finger and brought it to his lips to kiss the tip. In a low voice that only she could hear, he whispered, "After ye heal, I intend to keep ye tucked away in our cottage wearing only a smile."

Her gasp was a mixture of shock and curiosity. "And my chemise."

He shook his head. "Ye won't be needing one, as I'll be keeping ye in me bed until I'm certain me seed has taken hold. It's going to be a joy to watch ye grow round with our babe, lass."

Pippa licked her lips, and Flaherty gave in to the overwhelming need to kiss her. Gently. Reverently. "Promise me ye'll not run off again without telling me, or one of me cousins, where ye're headed?"

"I promise."

"And that ye'll give meself and me cousins the opportunity to do what we pledged."

"To protect Millie and her babe with your lives?"

"Aye, that, of course, but the other half of that vow…to protect ye with our lives, *mo chroí, mo ghrá*. Never forget that ye're me heart and me love, lass."

But Pippa didn't not answer right away. Flaherty glanced down and noticed the soft smile tilting her lips upward as she drifted off to sleep. His wife was brave, loyal, and courageous. She'd make a fine addition to the growing ranks of strong women who had been beaten down by life, but not conquered by it. The women who'd married his brothers and cousins.

Aye, his wife would give him strong, sturdy sons who would learn to fight alongside himself and his cousins, continuing their legacy, serving the next Duke of Wyndmere.

He was smiling as he rode toward Summerfield Chase. Home to the cottage they would now have all to themselves—Millie would no doubt be leaving with her husband, who was on leave until further notice. But he would wait to share that news with Pippa until after she had rested.

As they rode toward home, Flaherty sent up a prayer of thanks to God for the courageous and beautiful woman who soon would be the mother of his sons.

CHAPTER TWENTY-THREE

A FORTNIGHT LATER, Flaherty braced for his first meeting with Pippa's da. Summerfield had extended an invitation to Baron Stanhope and Earl Haybrook to visit with their daughters, both of whom were on extended visits until Dr. Higgins proclaimed either woman fit to travel.

Flaherty would rather have waited another month or so for the impending visit. Though, truthfully, if he had been in his father-in-law's place, he wouldn't have waited for an invitation to see his daughter and the man who'd dared to marry her without his permission.

The need to pace, while going over what he would say to Pippa's da when he arrived, would have to wait. Flaherty had the rooftop shift, and had to be vigilant scanning the perimeter, ready to protect and defend. "He'd be within his rights to blame me for not protecting his daughter when she'd been stabbed—and held at knifepoint before getting tossed into a hundred-year-old oak tree!"

Scanning the perimeter to the south, he frowned, recalling the baron's ready agreement and reasoning as to why waiting a few weeks more would be wise: it would give Pippa's bruises time to heal. Would it ever not gut him, replaying that moment in his mind when Trentchester thought to save himself by flinging Pippa away from him and into that oak tree?

He shoved those thoughts deep to pull out another time. Following the movement at the base of the tree line, he was relieved to note it was a doe moving into the open—not a sharpshooter. Watching the movement to the west, he sighed, remembering how vehemently the baroness had insisted that she and the baron extend an immediate invitation not only to Pippa's father, but Millie's as well. Flaherty could still hear the emotion in Lady Phoebe's voice, and see tears well in her eyes, when she reminded him that if *her* father was still alive, she would want him to meet Marcus so they could share the good news that he was going to be a grandfather.

In the next breath, Lady Phoebe had reminded Flaherty that he should be grateful that at least one of their unborn babe's grandparents was in England. His parents were still living on the farm in Ireland that had been in their family for generations, while Pippa's ma had died years ago.

He heard the rumble of carriage wheels in the distance, and gave a short, sharp whistle. He waited for his cousins to answer his alert. A few moments later, Garahan ran toward the building his cousin was guarding on the perimeter from the ground. "Well now, shall I relieve ye, so ye can climb down and meet yer father-in-law?"

"Where the bloody hell is O'Malley?"

In answer, they heard the rear door of the manor house open.

"How many carriages?" O'Malley asked as he rushed over to stand next to Garahan at the foot of the ladder to the roof.

Flaherty sighed. "Two, and damned if they aren't huge. Bloody hell—he's arriving in a coach fit for royalty."

"State coaches," O'Malley reminded his cousin.

Flaherty shrugged. "Thought they were town coaches, though why do they need them when they aren't calling on royalty?"

"Ye're just nervous," Garahan said. "I would be too, if me wife was as battered looking as yers, I hadn't asked the man's permission to marry his daughter, and was meeting him for the first time."

"Aren't ye a fecking ray of sunshine, Garahan."

Flaherty's cousin grinned. "Ah, 'tis what me darling wife calls me."

Flaherty grunted. "She's blind to yer faults, Ryan." He watched the two sleek coaches with coats of arms emblazoned on the doors slowly make their way up the long drive. "Twelve horses in all. Are the first six Cleveland bays or chestnuts?"

"With their dark manes and tails, Cleveland bays," O'Malley replied. "The second coach has six beauties, black as night." He motioned to one of the stable lads. "Tell the stable master 'tis twelve horses that will need to be cooled down, then watered and fed." The young man sprinted back to the stables, returning with half a dozen men to handle the horses.

Summerfield greeted the men. "Ah, I see our guests will arrive momentarily, and the stable master has been alerted. Excellent. The stables will be full for the next few days."

By the time the coaches rolled to a stop in front of the manor house, O'Malley, Garahan, and Flaherty stood off to one side of Baron Summerfield, while the servants lined up on the other, ready to greet the newcomers, welcoming them to Summerfield Chase.

For the life of him, Flaherty had no idea why the servants had to be trotted out and then back inside to be ready to fetch and serve. He preferred the cottage where he and Pippa lived. It was warm and cozy, and the little touches his wife added brightened their home. He wished he could be inside when she greeted her father, but instead he was outside neglecting his normal post in order to be on hand to take the measure of the servants that accompanied their esteemed visitors.

"Stanhope," Summerfield said, beaming. "Welcome to our home. My wife is waiting inside to greet you—she tires easily."

"Thank you, Summerfield," Stanhope replied. "I remember those days well. I hope Lady Phoebe is following your physician's advice. I have enjoyed her correspondence, and updates on my daughter's health." The silver-haired baron scanned the line of servants, inclined his head, and unerringly pinned Flaherty with his gaze. "Ah, the man who married my daughter." Stanhope did not have to add *without asking permission*—his expression indicated his displeasure.

Bloody hell!

"And saved your daughter's reputation and her life," Summerfield reminded Pippa's father.

Before Stanhope could say another word, Flaherty watched the man's irritated expression relax into one of concern, and knew without turning around that his wife, the light and love of his life, had come outside to greet her father. He wished she had stayed inside until he and his cousins had been able to perform a cursory evaluation of the servants: two coachmen, four footmen, and two valets in all.

"Father, it's wonderful to see you."

There was a telltale hesitation in the lass's voice. Was she still worried that her father would censure her for marrying without his consent?

Before Flaherty left his position standing beside his cousins, she walked over to stand next to him, linking her arm with his. "I'd like you to meet my husband, the love of my life, and father of your first grandchild—Dillon James Flaherty."

His feisty wife was a delight. He watched the baron's face, waiting to see his reaction, and nearly snorted with laughter when her da asked, "Did you say *grandchild*?"

"I did, Father."

Summerfield spoke up. "Speculation was rife and spread quickly through Summerfield-on-Eden as to why your lovely daughter arrived with an exhausted mother and her newborn babe—without an escort. 'Twas their arrival, lack of escort, and broken carriage wheel that started the rumors," the baron told him. "Not what you're thinking."

Pippa's father shifted his gaze to Flaherty once more before he turned back to the baron. The man's demeanor softened, though Flaherty detected a flinch the man was not quick enough to hide when his eyes took in his daughter's fading bruises and the sling protecting her broken arm. "You're looking surprisingly well, Phillipa—all things considered."

"I feel wonderful, Father."

"Aren't ye supposed to be inside, resting with Millie and the others, lass?" Flaherty interjected.

Her father's eyes narrowed, but before he could comment, a jovial voice called out, "Pippa, you look wonderful, despite your broken arm."

She laughed. "So do you, Uncle Haybrook."

Flaherty leaned close and whispered, "I didn't realize he was yer uncle."

Pippa smiled up at him. "He isn't—it's an endearment. Our families have always been close."

Earl Haybrook quickly took Flaherty's measure and nodded. "Introduce me to your husband."

"I'd be delighted to. Uncle, meet Dillon James Flaherty, of the Dublin Flahertys, members of the Duke of Wyndmere's private guard stationed here at Summerfield Chase."

Millie's father extended his hand to Flaherty. "Thank you for protecting my daughter and grandson, and dear Pippa, Millie's sister of the heart."

Flaherty smiled. Millie and Pippa were indeed sisters: bosom friends one moment…arguing the next. "It has been me pleasure. The duty has been shared between me cousins, Thomas O'Malley and Ryan Garahan. As members of the Duke of Wyndmere's private guard, we have the honor of being assigned to Summerfield Chase, protecting the duke's sister, Lady Phoebe, and her husband Baron Summerfield."

Haybrook nodded. "That's quite a lot of people under your protection."

Summerfield smiled. "O'Malley's wife and Garahan's wife and twin cousins are also under their protection." With a nod to Flaherty, he suggested, "After you speak with Stanhope's and

Haybrook's servants, join us in the sitting room. I'm certain our guests would like to speak to you in a more comfortable setting."

I just bet they would. "Aye, yer lordship."

Lord Haybrook nodded to Flaherty, O'Malley, and Garahan before asking, "Is Roarke here?"

Pippa smiled. "Both your son-in-law and grandson were in the sitting room with Millie a few moments ago, awaiting your arrival."

Haybrook smiled and glanced over his shoulder, "Are you coming, Stanhope?"

Pippa's father hesitated, then offered his arm to his daughter. "Mind your step, Phillipa."

There wasn't any time for Flaherty to do more than smile and nod at his wife, before he turned back to his cousins. "Who do ye want me to interview first?"

O'Malley waited a beat then replied, "Footmen, coachmen, valets. Garahan, you begin questioning the coachmen, while I speak to the valets. We ask the usual: length of service, prior employment, family, and working conditions."

"'Twill be a good start," Garahan remarked.

"Unless there are any concerns, we'll reconvene after Flaherty returns from the lion's den."

Flaherty nudged O'Malley aside with his shoulder and walked over to the footmen gathered by the carriages. "After I finish me interviews, send for me, if I don't resurface after half an hour."

"Done," O'Malley agreed. "I'll send Garahan."

Their cousin snickered. "And I know just what to say—"

Flaherty grunted. "Save it for later."

FLAHERTY WAS SURPRISED to have an instant connection with two of the footmen—lads from Cork, who were acquainted with the Cork branch of the O'Malley family. The other two men were from London. Any of the four would have made a fine addition to the baron's household.

The coachmen were a grizzled pair: one from Dorset, the

other from the Lowlands, and both had served king and Crown as foot soldiers a decade earlier. It was the valets that had Flaherty's interest. Stanhope's had shifty eyes—though that was not a crime. Haybrook's valet's eyes were soulless.

Flaherty decided not to wait to share his worry about the valets with his cousins. He hailed O'Malley, who was speaking to the butler. When O'Malley ended the conversation, Flaherty walked over and asked, "Have ye asked Timmons to have two of the lads assigned to the valets?"

"I have. Did ye note Haybrook's valet's eyes?"

Flaherty watched the man in question bristle when Timmons spoke to him. "Dead eyes, they were," Garahan said, joining his cousins.

"Stanhope's valet has shifty eyes," O'Malley said. "Either 'tis his nature, or we'll have to keep an eye on the silver."

Flaherty snorted. "I wouldn't mind adding the two Cork footmen to our numbers, but 'tisn't up me. I'd best see if me wife needs rescuing—she was more than a bit worried about her father's impending visit."

"Ye don't have to worry about her," Garahan said, "as long as Millie and the baroness are in the same room."

O'Malley agreed. "Lady Phoebe has a talent for redirecting difficult conversations without those involved being the wiser."

Flaherty rolled his shoulders and winced, wishing the weather wasn't threatening rain—his numerous injuries liked to make themselves known whenever it was damp. "Don't forget, O'Malley—half an hour."

O'Malley grumbled, "I won't."

Flaherty squared his shoulders and strode toward the rear entrance. It was quiet when he entered…too quiet. He quickly made his way along the hall, through the kitchen to the door to the main part of the house. A sense of foreboding filled him as he stalked toward the closed door to the sitting room. He knocked and was immediately bidden to enter.

Instead of finding his wife browbeaten, as he'd anticipated, given her description of her da, he found Millie quietly crying in her husband's arms while Pippa held their babe. Flaherty nodded to Summerfield and the baroness first, then Stanhope and Haybrook. "Millie-lass, whatever is wrong, count on meself, Garahan, and O'Malley to set it to rights."

Roarke lifted his head and met Flaherty's gaze. "Millie and I will always be grateful that you were the man to find them, offer your assistance, and bring them to the safety of Summerfield Chase." Millie's husband turned to Summerfield. "Your hospitality-laced safety saved Millie and our babe. Whatever you need, however I can be of assistance, you have but to ask."

"Have you cashed out of the army?" Summerfield asked.

"Due to my son-in-law's injuries sustained in service to the Crown," Haybrook said, "Roarke has been retired with honors—"

"And," Stanhope interrupted, "according to Palmerston in the War Office, their grateful thanks."

Lady Phoebe's tremulous smile had Flaherty moving to stand between where his wife sat beside her father on the settee, and the baroness on the velvet lady's chair that matched her eyes. If need be, he could reach either woman in seconds.

"The War Office should be offering their abject apologies to Millie and Roarke," the baroness said. "Was it an oversight and error that Millie received that missive with but one line stating her husband was dead? No explanation, no 'we regret to inform you,' nor 'we're thankful for his ultimate sacrifice'!"

The baron rose from the chair across from his wife's and walked to her side. Placing a hand on her shoulder, he said quietly, "There are times when speed is of the utmost importance. We are not privy to information essential to the military branches that protect our king and country, Phoebe. Therefore, we do not—and should not—have the authority to judge the deeds and actions of others."

Haybrook inclined his head. "Well said, Summerfield, though in this instance, because it is Roarke we are speaking of, I lean more toward your wife's way of thinking."

Stanhope harumphed. "Having three of my sons in the military, I can say—"

"That you are immensely grateful Winston was assigned to find and retrieve Roarke," Haybrook said.

Stanhope patted the back of Pippa's hand and smiled at Millie. "I am. Though we are not among those who know where Winston is stationed, or what his duties are, if I did know, I would venture to say that I would be concerned *and* proud. As it is, I have to be contented with only the facts that are deemed what I need to know."

Flaherty wondered at the change in his wife's father—he seemed to have dropped his baronial persona and was nearly human. The man's next words had Flaherty thinking he just might like the man.

"Millie, you and Roarke have been blessed with a son—you'll not have the worry that your daughter will run wild with the sister of her heart, haunting your stables, riding bareback through the meadow, jumping obstacles while she should be plying needle and thread or painting landscapes to add to her portfolio."

Flaherty knelt beside his wife's chair and took her hand. "If Pippa and I are blessed with a daughter, I'll be teaching her how to shoot her great-grandfather's blunderbuss."

Pippa's gasp hung in the silent room for a heartbeat, before Stanhope started to chuckle and Haybrook joined in. Flaherty lifted Pippa's hand to his lips and met her eyes, before kissing her hand. "What do you say, lass?"

Pippa smiled. "I agree that you should teach her to shoot, I'll teach her to ride, and we'll hire a fencing master."

The pained expression on Stanhope's face had Flaherty holding in his laughter. "I'll agree to fencing lessons, lass, if ye agree to allow her to spend time in the stables. 'Tisn't enough to learn to ride. Me brothers, cousins, and I know that a horse is a true and trusted friend. Never will he—or she—spread rumors, or speak ill of ye."

"Hear, hear," Haybrook said, raising his teacup and toasting

Flaherty and Pippa. "Now then, when can we expect *your* babe to arrive?"

"Papa!" Millie gasped.

Stanhope stared at his daughter and Flaherty. "Well?"

Pippa sighed. "You won't be the first to know, but we will certainly share our good news when the time comes."

Summerfield answered the knock on the sitting room door. "Enter."

Garahan crossed the threshold and scanned the room. Raising one eyebrow at Flaherty, who had yet to stand, he announced, "There is a matter that requires Flaherty's immediate attention."

Flaherty rose to his feet. "I'd best answer the summons. Be sure and rest now, lass. Ye're healing, but still have a ways to go."

"I will."

He bent and brushed a kiss to the top of her head. "I have spies that will tell me if ye're resting or off exploring the secret passageways with Percy and Phineas."

The sound of her musical laughter curled around Flaherty's heart. He carried it with him as he returned to his duties. Patrolling the perimeter on horseback, he admitted to himself he'd love to have daughters—and sons.

Nine months later...

"CONGRATULATIONS, FLAHERTY!" THE midwife smiled. "You have a beautiful daughter."

He thanked the woman while he counted fingers and toes, as he'd been instructed to by his wife. Looking down into the radiant, but exhausted, face of the woman who held his heart, he smiled, confident that their next babe would be a son.

Kneeling beside the bed, he pressed his lips to Pippa's forehead. "Ye're a warrior lass. Stout, brave, resilient to pain."

"Just because I didn't shout our roof down, doesn't mean I wasn't in pain."

He kissed her on one cheek, then the other, then her nose,

and finally her mouth. When she sighed into his mouth, he murmured, "Rest now, *mo ghrá*."

Her eyes slowly closed, and his heart felt full, content. "Thank ye, Lord, for me wife and daughter. We've the beginnings of a fine family."

Pippa opened one eye and glared at him. A fine feat, that. He opened his mouth to speak, and she held up a hand. "If you are going to tell me you want a son before I have even recovered from giving birth to our daughter, leave now!"

Flabbergasted, Flaherty sputtered, but no words emerged. Finally, he managed two: "Leave? Now?"

"And don't come back until you promise to stop telling me about O'Malley's and Garahan's sons. What is wrong with a daughter?"

"Not a thing, lass."

He watched, horrified, as his wife's eyes welled with unshed tears. "Even if I could," she rasped, "I would not send her back."

"*Mo chroí*…I would never think that. Hush now—ye need to rest and not get riled up. Remember what the midwife warned; ye need calm surroundings so ye can feed our babe."

"How can we have calm, when I'm married to you?" she cried, tears streaming down her cheeks.

How in the hell had their conversation gotten turned around and upside down? It shredded his heart, but his wife's happiness was worth the dent to his pride. He cleared his throat to ask, "Do ye want me leave?"

Her bottom lip trembled as she reached for him with one arm—the other had their daughter tucked against her breast. "No. Forgive me, Dillon. Please don't leave me. I didn't mean to insult you, it's just that I—"

"Just gave birth to the most beautiful babe in the world." Enfolding her in his arms, he murmured against the top of her head, "She has the softest auburn curls on top of her head and blue eyes. Fear not, lass, I won't be leaving ye until the Lord calls me home, *mo ghrá*."

As Pippa's tears dried, their babe started to fuss.

"Feed me daughter, lass, and tell me, have ye decided on her name yet?"

Flaherty shifted so his wife could settle their babe to her breast. The sight filled him with an abundance of love. Love for his wife, love for their babe, and hope for the sons that had yet to be born.

"I'd like to name her Anna Maeve. Anna after my mother—she'll be a powerful guardian angel for our babe."

"That she will, lass. And Maeve after—" Flaherty swallowed against the lump in his throat. "After me ma's ma. Mave O'Malley."

Pippa laughed softly. "I had thought to name her Anna Connor, after your mum's father, but..."

Flaherty was laughing when he kissed the keeper of his heart. "A fine ma ye'll be to our brood, lass. Our daughter will keep her younger brothers in line."

Pippa stared at him without speaking until he had to ask, "Why are ye thinking?"

"Have you ever heard the saying, be careful what you wish for?"

"That I have, but I've got ye and Anna Maeve, and for now, I could not ask for more. I love ye, lass." Silently, he prayed for sons.

"I love you enough to forgive you, Flaherty."

Exhaustion from staying up during the long hours his wife labored to birth their daughter, he shook his head. "For what?"

"Praying for sons."

"I... That is to say, how..."

She grabbed the front of his cambric shirt, tugged him close, and kissed him until his eyes crossed. "I know how your mind works, Dillon, but love you anyway."

"Faith, I'm a lucky man."

"You'd best remember that."

"I'll not likely forget. Now then, let me take Anna Maeve and hold her while ye close yer faery eyes to rest, lass."

As his wife relaxed, he crooned to their babe, "Ye'll love yer little brothers. I'm thinking four or five ought to round out our family nicely, but we'd best not mention that to yer ma until she's back on her feet."

Little did Flaherty know, his wife fell asleep praying for daughters.

※ ❖ ※

EPILOGUE

Six years later...

"S ORCHA, DIDN'T YER ma tell ye on her way out of the door to stop deviling Grace?" The squabbling was not as loud as it had been before he'd separated the twins, Eileen and Emily. Flaherty shook his head and asked, "Can't a man have peace in his household?"

"Of course he can, Da," Anna replied. "Ma said she'd only be gone for an hour or two."

"Two?" Flaherty raked his hands through his hair and silently wondered why the Lord had blessed him with daughters instead of sons. Then, as if by magic, the room quieted as Anna Maeve wove her calm around her younger sisters. Though but six summers, their eldest daughter was able to soothe hurt feelings and solve disagreements between her siblings.

"I'm proud of ye, Anna Maeve."

"Are you proud of me too, Da?" Sorcha asked.

Grace pouted. "Me too, Da?"

"Us too!" Emily and Eileen said, patting him on the knee.

He picked up the two-year-old-twins and set one on each knee. "Faith, the Lord blessed yer ma and me with five of the finest daughters in the whole of England!"

"We're hungry!" the twins said.

"I want tea!" Grace grumbled.

"Da, can we eat the scones yet?" Sorcha asked.

He kissed the twins and set them on their feet, and bent to brush a kiss to the top of Grace's head, then Sorcha's. Anna was already setting the table for tea and reaching for the plate of scones. Flaherty kissed his eldest daughter's cheek. "I'll heat the water and pour it into the teapot to steep, if ye'll start yer sisters washing their hands. What were they playing in to get so grubby?"

Sorcha wiped her dirty hands on her gown. "We were helping the Garahan boys."

"Oh?" Flaherty asked as he checked the water level in the kettle. "And what were they doing?"

Grace bounced on her toes and threw her hands out to the sides in sheer delight. "Chasing chickens!"

Flaherty poured water over the tea leaves and waited for it to steep while the girls slowly made their way over to the table. He helped each of them onto their seats while Anna poured cream into a pitcher.

"Chickens!" Flaherty groaned. "Why can't ye play with O'Malley's girls?"

Sorcha and Grace exchanged a frown. "They don't like to play outside in the dirt or chase chickens," Sorcha answered.

"They're learning to sew and spend all day inside. Why would we want to do that, Da?" Grace asked as Flaherty finished pouring their tea.

He slumped onto his chair and bowed his head. "I'm only yer da. Sure and I have no idea what goes on inside a woman's mind. 'Tis a mystery to me."

Anna patted his hand as she placed another scone on Sorcha's plate. "That's all right, Da. We love you anyway."

Flaherty set his teacup down and looked at the tableau of beauty surrounding him. Five healthy, beautiful daughters with hoydenish tendencies, who, with their ma, were the loves of his life.

While the little ones chatted and sipped, he silently prayed, *Thank ye, Lord, for the gift of me daughters. I'll not be asking ye for sons. I'm hoping the babe due in a few months will be another daughter.*

Six months later…

PIPPA GAVE BIRTH to twins—two lusty-lunged boys who were the image of their da.

As Flaherty stared down in wonder at the sons he had prayed for since he learned Pippa was expecting the first time, he thanked the Lord for blessing he and Pippa with five healthy daughters and two healthy sons. What more could a man ask for?

Ten months later…

PIPPA GAVE BIRTH to another son. This time, Flaherty sat down on the bed and lifted his wife's hand to his lips. "Ye've given me another beautiful babe to love—another son."

"You've always wanted sons, Dillon."

He pressed his lips to hers. "We've a fine and beautiful family, lass. I'm thinking ye'll have to stop seducing me into lying with ye, lass, when we both know—"

"That you love it when I do," she interrupted him. "So shut yer gob and kiss me, Flaherty!"

He was laughing when their lips met, and she kissed him senseless.

Author's Note

Researching one of my books for a minute detail that I need to understand in order to keep writing (because it would drive me crazy otherwise) has at times led me down more than one rabbit hole, which inevitably had me going off on any number of tangents that piqued my interest. For this book, I needed to know if the head of the British War Office was a gentleman with a title, or a former general/military man, etc. Discovering that there were in fact two people involved in running the War Office—one who was the figurehead, overseeing things, and the other an individual who handled the actual duties—was a surprise, but should not have been.

Here's what I discovered while writing this book: the head of the British War Office from 1812 to 1827 was Henry Bathurst, 3rd Earl Bathurst. His actual title was the *Secretary of State for War and the Colonies*. In that capacity, he handled military policy and oversaw military and colonial affairs.

en.wikipedia.org/wiki/Henry_Bathurst,_3rd_Earl_Bathurst
britannica.com/biography/Henry-Bathurst-3rd-Earl-Bathurst
recherche-collection-search.bac-lac.gc.ca/eng/home/record?
app=fonandcol&IdNumber=98615&ecopy=e010790221

His subordinate was Henry John Temple, Viscount Palmerston, whose title was *Secretary at War*. He served from 1809 to 1828 and handled the administrative and organizational duties for the army and ran the War Office. I should not have been surprised that their titles within the British peerage were reflected in who was the top man at the War Office.

en.wikipedia.org/wiki/Secretary_at_War
britannica.com/biography/Henry-John-Temple-3rd-Viscount-Palmerston
historyofparliamentonline.org/volume/1820-1832/member/temple-henry-1784-1865

Author's Note: I was born in South Carolina and lived most of my life in New Jersey. Our familial hierarchy was more along the lines of the Morgan family from Llewellyn's classic tale *How Green Was My Valley*. I can still hear the narrator saying, "For if my father was the head of the family, my mother was its heart."

About the Author

If we have not met yet, I'm delighted to meet you. Here's a little bit about me...

I have been writing romance novels for almost half my life—well, at least for the last thirty years. I'm a die-hard romantic and have to confess the broad shoulders and wicked glint in the brilliant green eyes of a stranger had my breath snagging in my breast, my heart beating madly, and my future flashing before my eyes. At the age of seventeen, I'd met the man I knew I was going to spend the rest of my life with.

I write Historical & Contemporary Romance featuring characters that I know so well: hardheaded heroes and feisty heroines! They rarely listen to me and in fact, I think they enjoy messing with my plans for them. Over the years I have learned to listen to them. I have always used family names in my books and love adding bits and pieces of my ancestors and ancestry in them, too! Visit my website to learn more about my books.